Gold Coast Detective
Scotty Stephens

Book 5

GOOD RIDDANCE

ANDREW McDERMOTT

Good Riddance by ANDREW McDERMOTT
www.andrewmcdermott.com.au

First published in Australia by X Press Publishing 2026
P.O. Box 395 Coolangatta
Queensland 4225 Australia
mail@andrewmcdermott.com.au

A catalogue record for this
book is available from the
National Library of Australia

ISBN: 978-1-7638597-9-1 (pbk)
ISBN: 978-1-7640630-0-5 (ebk)

Cover design by X Press Publishing © 2026

Typesetting and design by X Press Publishing © 2026

For the Blower boys...

BOOKS BY
ANDREW MᶜDERMOTT
(see samples and more details at back of this book)

Gold Coast Detective Scotty Stephens series:
X'posé (X prequel)
Book 1 – X
Book 2 – Mary's Mansion
Book 3 – Tarnished
Book 4 - INSEXT
Book 5 - Good Riddance

Detective Joe Dean series:
Hidden Moon (Flirting with The Moon prequel)
Flirting with The Moon

The Tiger Chase

Speculative fiction:
Quest of The New Templars series:
Birthright (prequel)
Book 1 – RESURRECTION

Children's books:
The Last Tiger

1

No one crossed the notorious Declan O'Donnell. No one except, it seems, his mistress, Anita Madison. And although she feared for her life, all Anita had to do now was hide until the morning. Then she would be free.

Hardly inconspicuous, Anita left her flat on Castle Boulevard for the last time and made her way onto the tree-lined streets of The Park Estate. Although she may have looked a little out of place in this affluent suburb, a tall young woman with exotic long, black hair, Anita never dressed tackily. She was a true professional—a hard-working woman, smart, confident, and ruthless.

It was 9.00 pm on the summer solstice. Darkness would have been an advantage, but night wouldn't fall for at least another hour. And this year, Britain's longest day was the warmest on record, with clear blue skies and a hint of a summer that no one believed would really come. It had certainly been Anita's longest day; even the beautiful outro of a blackbird from the branches of a sycamore tree, did little to calm her nerves.

The client she'd serviced earlier at the Hilton would be her last. The money she'd saved over the last couple of years, without Declan's knowledge, while also skimming off a percentage of his fortune, and more recently claiming what was rightfully hers from her brother, Javed, meant she could live a comfortable life, far away from Nottingham.

***

'Just get it done no matter what,' Bill Patterson had demanded on the phone. 'The stonemason's coming in the morning. That fireplace needs to be sealed and ready for him. Got it?'

'Yep, got it.' Colin Webster (Col) was not happy about having to work on a Friday night. And the fact that it was his wife's birthday didn't help. Carol wasn't impressed! But the money was too good to turn down; even Carol couldn't argue with that. Actually, that wasn't true. The couple seemed to argue about anything lately. Not that the job was difficult—a simple wall partition to hide the old fireplace and recent plumbing from the floor above. No, it was just a pain in the arse. Saturday morning was all about football for Col and his lad, and even though the season was long finished, the Bobbersmill Bombers under 14s had done so well that season, they had earned a place in an unofficial summer league of the surrounding districts. And this meant they'd often have to travel out of town. Tomorrow was a 9.00 am kick off in Chesterfield, a good hour's drive, so Col and Shaun, his thirteen-year-old son, would need to be up and out early.

The partition would be lined with steel sheeting, then fortified the next morning by a wall of hand-placed stone. Col had purposely done all the cutting earlier to limit the noise going into the night. While working outside in the driveway, he'd noticed a neighbour across the street trying to catch his eye. Prolonging the inevitable complaint, he continued his work without making eye contact. On the very last cut, his fears were confirmed when he noticed the man standing at the gate.

'Excuse me, do you know what time it is?' the man asked when Col turned off the grinder.

'Sure,' Col said, glancing at his watch. 'It's nine o'clock, me owd.'

'Exactly,' the man said, 'a little late to be operating power tools, don't you think?'

'You're absolutely right, and I'm sorry. Good news, though. I've finished cutting now, so I shunt be ere too much longer.'

'I'll be complaining to the owner when next I see him. My mother is very sick, and we can't be doing with all this noise.' His ex-boarding school accent was a far cry from Col's Nottingham slang.

'Ah, mek sure ya do. Ta rah then.' Col lifted the last sheet of 6 mm-thick steel and carefully guided it through the front door.

***

Like many buildings in The Park, the Chambers Hine Coach House was a remnant of the Industrial Revolution that swept through the Midlands and the North of England in the 18th century. Surprisingly, the building was spared when the main house, built by Thomas Hine Chambers in 1830, was demolished in 1936 and redeveloped.

But none of this was on Anita's mind as she approached the skip outside the property. The gate to the courtyard was open. A white van stood in the driveway. There was radio music coming from inside the house. This was confirmed when Anita heard the familiar jingle of Radio Trent.

***

Col was placing one of the sheets of steel on the timber frame when he heard the front door open. Expecting to see the neighbour once more, probably here to complain about the radio, he was surprised to find a beautiful young woman, a bloody model perhaps, standing in the doorway.

'Can I help ya, duck?'

'Who the hell are you?' Her accent wasn't as posh as His Lordship across the street, but it was refined. She certainly wasn't a Hyson Green girl.

'I'm Col. Are you the owner?'

The young woman nodded. 'What are you doing here?'

'I'm almost done.' Col stepped back and waved his hand like a magician revealing his handy work. 'I've just got these last pieces to put on, then I'm out of here.'

'Can you go now, please?'

Col shook his head. 'I've got strict orders to make sure this is finished before I leave. You've got Les Lane coming in the morning to do the stonework.'

An impatient sigh suggested she didn't know who the famous stonemason was. 'Just finish up, then get out, okay?' She turned away and headed for the stairs.

'Alright, duck. And I'll lock the door behind me. Good night,' Col called after her.

True to his word, Col finished the work quickly and packed his tools into the van. Checking his watch, it was 10.30 pm—too late for him and Carol to go out now; in fact, she'd probably be in bed. Should he go home or have a quick pint in The Old General before last orders? First, he needed to lock the front door, so he dropped the latch and was about to close it when he paused and glanced at the staircase leading up to the master bedroom.

***

Lying in the king-sized bed, listening, Anita hoped the builder had packed up and gone. She wasn't too concerned about Declan. He wouldn't even suspect anything. Would he? She'd been smart, only taking small amounts. The way she'd executed her plan meant she'd be long gone before he realised things weren't right. No, her biggest worry was her brother, Javed. She'd pretty much cleaned him out, and it was likely that, Javed being Javed, the family son and heir, had already noticed his zero bank balance. At least though, unlike Declan, he had no knowledge of her hiding place. Tomorrow morning this would all be behind her. The first-class flight enroute to Bali would be the beginning of her new life.

A creak in the floorboards just outside the bedroom door startled her. It was a familiar sound because she had initiated the same reaction from the ancient timber when she'd crossed the landing earlier. Loosened from years of use, the tarnished brass doorknob rattled slightly as someone grasped it from the other side. Turning, it grated, and the door creaked with a little more protest than the floorboard.

Realising it was impossible to hide, Anita attempted to sit up, but before she could, her attacker was on top of her. Strong hands grasped her neck, squeezing hard. She tried to fight back, but her assailant was too heavy and too strong.

The assault was quick, thorough, silent, and final. When the hands slowly released, Anita's staring eyes remained fixed on her killer.

2

Thirty years later

'Bloody 'ell.'

'What?'

'It looks like a ...' Mick Smith squinted into the darkness. 'Like an Egyptian mummy.'

Christopher Collins patiently nudged the smaller man to one side so he could look. Adopting the same squint, he peered into the thickly insulated cavity of lagged pipes. Gradually, the shape that Mick had described revealed itself through the darkness. It was standing wedged between a series of pipes of varying thicknesses. Mick was right; it *did* look like an Egyptian mummy. Human shape, average height. Only it was wrapped in the same dusty pink fibreglass insulation that covered the inside of the sealed space.

'What do you reckon it is, Mister Collins?'

Christopher reached in and prodded the thing with an outstretched finger. The air inside was warm and dry. The thing was hard to the touch. 'A mannequin perhaps ... put there as a joke.'

'Some joke. It's thirty years since anyone's been inside here,' Mick said, vying over Christopher's shoulder.

Christopher stepped back and rubbed his hands on his corduroy trousers. 'Get the rest of this down so we can get it out.'

'Okay,' Mick said, replacing his goggles and lifting the sledgehammer.

Christopher watched as the builder demolished the rest of the stone, the same stone that Ellie liked and wanted to keep, but council rules were council rules. Since the last renovation in the mid-nineties, the Chambers Hine Coach House on Cavendish Crescent had become a Grade II-listed building. It had taken Christopher eighteen months to convince the Nottinghamshire County Council that his vision to restore the building to its former glory, while installing the modern luxuries, was the right thing to do. Even for a partner of one of Nottingham's most prestigious law firms, Christopher had found it tedious dealing with the bureaucracy of the local council.

When the final plans were at last approved, they weren't exactly the vision the young solicitor had originally hoped for—but close enough. Unfortunately for Ellie, this meant removing the stone wall and the utility cavity that it enshrined, which would not only reclaim about three feet of the room, but also reveal the original fireplace.

Christopher stepped outside for a smoke and listened as Mick went about his business. *Bang, bang, bang!*

It was mid-November, and the winter bully was slowly taking hold. Christopher and Ellie had hoped to be in their new home by Christmas, but because of the council's lack of haste, this was looking very unlikely now.

Ellie would be furious if she knew Christopher was smoking. But it wasn't a habit; it's not like he was a full-time smoker—more of an opportunist. The cigarette was cadged from Mick. As he drew heavily on the unfiltered roll-up, he noticed the strange man across the street watching him from over his fence. Christopher waved, but the man frowned and ducked out of sight.

Funny old sod, Christopher thought.

The banging and the sound of stone crumbling to the floor continued for a little while longer. By the time Christopher had finished his smoke, Mick appeared carrying a sheet of thin steel with a layer of thick insulation on one side.

'Where's the lad, Mick?' Christopher asked. 'Should you be doing this on your own?'

'Ahh,' Mick grunted as he threw the sheet into a freshly emptied skip. 'He an't turned up agen. Lazy little shit. That's it now; he's done.'

'Oh dear.'

'Ya just can't get good help nowadays, Mister Collins.'

'Must be hard. How long do you think before you'll have the rest of the wall down?'

'I'll just need to move all the rubble first. Here, do you know that wall was built by Les Lane? *The* Les Lane?'

'I do. But unfortunately, it had to go.'

Mick retrieved a wheelbarrow that was leaning against the outside wall and he disappeared with it back into the house.

Christopher climbed into his Range Rover and checked the messages on his phone. He should really have been at work. There was no real reason he had to be at The Coach House, but he'd taken a few weeks off to oversee the renovation. His brothers weren't too happy, but he was sure Collins, Collins and Collins would survive without their youngest partner for a little longer.

Moments later, Mick was back pushing the barrow fully laden with stone pieces. Christopher marvelled as he watched the strong little man negotiate a plank that led into the open-ended skip, dump the stone and then return to the house.

This routine lasted for about an hour. Then the banging started again, only this time it was different—more of a metallic sound. Once again, Mick appeared, this time carrying another sheet of steel. After another hour, the skip was laden with what were the remains of the cavity wall.

'Do ya want to come an av a look, Mister Collins?' Mick asked, tapping on the Rover's window.

Christopher climbed eagerly out of the car and followed Mick back into the house.

'Wow!' It wasn't the extra space that caused this response, or the Victorian stone fireplace that was now visible. It was the mummy. Still suspended between the pipes that hung from the bedroom suite above, down to the cellar below, the entombed figure stood upright and proud.

'Can we get it out?' Christopher asked.

'Yeah, should be easy enough.' Mick put on his gloves, took hold of the object by the shoulders and carefully prized it out from between the pipes. As he did so, a sheet of dust fell from the ceiling above it. 'I think you might be right,' Mick said. 'It feels hard, rigid. A dummy, I reckon. Tint evy or owt.'

'But what on earth would it be doing in there all this time?'

'Buggered if I know,' Mick said, lifting out the object and placing it on the floor.

The two men stood silently for a few moments, peering down at the figure, until Mick said, 'Should I unwrap it?'

Christopher was having second thoughts. What if this wasn't a dummy? What if it were a dead body? His mind raced at the implications of finding a body behind the wall of his new house, and the more he thought about it, the more questions arose. If this was just a dummy, why was it hidden behind the wall for over thirty years? Fortunately, his legal mind took precedence over his common sense. 'I think we need to call the police.'

'The police? What for?' Mick asked in surprise.

'This could be a crime scene.'

'Eh?'

Christopher retrieved his mobile from his pocket and dialled 999.

PC Kahn and WPC Childers arrived twenty minutes later. From the body language and tone of her voice, it wasn't apparent whether WPC Childers had more authority than the younger male PC, or just more confidence.

'I'll get you both to step back, please, Sir,' Childers said after Christopher had explained the situation. She knelt and prodded the object. 'It's hard … and it's been in there for about thirty years, you reckon?' Her question was directed at Mick.

'That's when the wall was built.'

'Could anyone have been inside since it was built—maintenance, repair?'

'I doubt it,' Mick said. 'It wa' covered in stone.'

PC Kahn squatted by his partner's side. 'What do you reckon? Shall we call it in?'

'What, and tell them we've found the Marks and Spencer mannequin that mysteriously disappeared in 1996?' Childers looked up at Mick and said, 'Do you have a knife?'

Mick nodded and, with his usual industrious flair, he produced a Stanley knife from his tool belt, handing it to the WPC.

Childers extended the sharp blade, glanced at her partner, then carefully inserted the knife into the dusty fibreglass towards the top of the head. The soft material was easy to cut. Childers put down the knife and gently peeled back an itchy layer.

The two constables suddenly jumped to their feet. Mick drew away in shock, while Christopher stood in silence, already mentally battling the bureaucratic shit fight that would follow.

With a piece of the two-inch-thick insulation peeled back, revealed inside the cocoon was a face. And although the skin was a dark brown leather texture, the eye sockets sunken and the cheek bones taught and drawn, it was obvious that the face once belonged to a beautiful young woman with long black hair.

3

Even though I am tall for a fourteen year old, I am still too short to reach the accelerator. The enormous truck is hurtling along a dimly lit highway. The huge steering wheel turns easily in my hands, but the vehicle remains straight as if locked on its path of destiny. It is the same dream I've been having since I was a teenager, but it is the first time I am reliving that terrible night from the truck driver's perspective. Suddenly, a loud explosion causes the cab of the semi-trailer to jolt violently to one side and skid across the tarmac. The accident report will state that the front passenger-side tyre blew out, causing the truck to jackknife. Within seconds, I am almost thrown out of the driver's seat as the cab crashes across the central reservation. The headlights of the oncoming traffic are almost blinding, but thankfully, most of the cars veer right, all except, that is, for one. The 1990 Toyota Camry slows almost to a stop but remains in the centre lane.

And then it's gone.

As usual, I awake with a jolt, but this time darkness remains, and I sit there for a moment, my mind racing in time with my elevated heart rate. Even though I was five miles away when the accident happened, I'd witnessed it now from every angle in my recurring dreams. If Mum were still alive, she would have assured me it wasn't my fault.

But of course, *it was!*

It was me who was the arrogant, selfish teenager, who had just scored the winning goal of the under-15s AFL Grand Final. It was

15

me who had missed the team bus back while losing my virginity to a cheerleader in the ladies' toilets, and it was me who had laid the guilt on knowing that Mum was petrified of driving at night.

Slowly, realising I was sitting upright, strapped to a chair, the constant drone brought my mind back to the present. I was wearing an eyepatch and earplugs. When I removed them, the cabin was dull except for the screen in the back of the seat in front of me, where an icon of an aeroplane hovered over the Middle East.

It's not that I'm tight, although some of my friends would disagree. It's just that I've never been used to having money, so I've always been careful. 'If not business class, at least fly premium economy,' Jenny, my fiancée, had said when I was booking my flight to the UK. Now sitting in economy, with a bloke in the next seat snoring and taking advantage of the limited space between us, I was kind of regretting my stubbornness. Don't get me wrong, there was nothing wrong with Qantas economy on a long-haul flight—the seats weren't too bad, food and service okay, and lots of movies to watch. It's just that I got a glimpse of business class while boarding, and then of premium economy while making my way to steerage towards the back of the plane.

It's not like I couldn't afford it now. My situation had improved considerably since being promoted to detective inspector and placed in charge of the *X* murders. Scotty Stephens, the saviour of the Gold Coast (the media's words, not mine), cracking the case and bringing down a ring of corruption. Then later, after quitting the Queensland Police, becoming a private detective and being involved in a few high-profile cases, my bank account was looking pretty good lately. Even the prospect of getting married and building a new house did little to dent the bank balance too much.

The guy next to me suddenly gave out an enormous snort and spasmed at the same time. That was it. I'd had enough. An elbow to the ribs was warranted.

'What the fuck!' he yelled, rising in his seat, eyepatch still in place.

'Mate, you're snoring.'

'No, I wasn't!' He lifted the patch from his eyes and stared at me through tired, angry eyes.

'Elvis … you were bloody snoring, trust me.'

Elvis exhaled loudly, pulled the patch back down over his eyes, and attempted to turn away from me with a fastened seat belt.

I had to smile. Elvis' snoring had been a big part of my life over the last twenty years. Best mates since pre-school, long-time housemates, surfers, footy fanatics (AFL), and drinking partners, we were living the dream.

All that had changed, though, during a series of events over the last eighteen months. Elvis, Tetley (our little pommy mate) and I were the 'Three Amigos' of Kirra Beach, on the southern end of the Gold Coast, Australia. But over time, I'd gradually rejected the bachelor lifestyle, wanting more perhaps. 'Be careful what you wish for, Scotty,' my mother always used to say. Well, I've never been much of a believer in positive thinking, but things changed, and not necessarily for the better. Tetley and his family left for a prolonged trip back to the UK (more on that later), while Elvis, God bless him, went through some difficult times. He owned his own accountancy firm. Apparently, there was a discrepancy with his largest account (some mining corporation), and he was sued. Financially, he almost lost everything, but what was more distressing was his mental health. Depression saw him return to Melbourne to his parents and put up the house for sale that we had shared for the last twenty years. Things could have gone completely belly up after I purchased the house from him and then lost it to fire the very same day I'd signed the contract.

But they didn't.

Thankfully, everything turned out alright. Elvis finally got his act together, fought the lawsuit, and won, returned to Queensland, and fell in love with the architect, Cassie, who had designed the new house. You couldn't write this stuff.

For me, life was going well. With the insurance pay out, I decided to build a new house on the old site. My on-off girlfriend, Detective Inspector Jenny Radford, was buying the house next to mine (I was building a duplex) until out of the blue she proposed to me. After years of not knowing where my life was going, I accepted her proposal, which meant we would move into the new house together. And to top it all off, Elvis and Cassie purchased the house next door. Told you, you couldn't write it.

So, it was all happy days ... until I get a call from Tetley in the UK, telling me his dad, Col, had been arrested for murder. WTF!

So, there I was on a plane, forty-thousand feet somewhere between Australia and England. Elvis had insisted on joining me, which I had no problem with at all. The 'Three Amigos' reunited; I just wish the occasion was under better circumstances.

Tetley had arranged to meet us at Heathrow Airport. Then he would drive us the two and a half hours north from London to his hometown of Nottingham.

Although I was yet to see the official police report, Tetley had filled me in on the basic details of the arrest via email earlier in the week and I'd learned as much as I could from the media reports. Colin Anthony Webster (aka Col ... Tetley's dad) was arrested a week ago and charged with the murder of Janita Sharma in 1996. So, the arrest was the product of a cold case—a killing that took place thirty years ago. The discovery of a young woman's mummified body prompted the investigation during a recent house renovation. Apparently, Col was working at the house the night the young woman went missing. A witness claims to have seen the victim enter the house, and then Col leaving the property alone later that evening. And that was pretty much all I had to go on. Of course, I had lots of questions, and I was hoping I'd be able to get my hands on the official police report once I arrived in Nottingham. There was apprehension on my part, though. I wasn't a copper anymore, and even if I was, I had no jurisdiction in a foreign land. I was a licensed private detective, of course, but my licence was issued in Australia. How would the poms react to an Aussie detective poking his nose into their business? Time would tell.

A twenty-five-hour flight, broken only by a two-hour stop in Dubai Airport, is a bloody long time. I spent it watching a couple of Marvel movies, surprising myself with a much-needed nap, playing a few rounds of solitaire on my phone, and staring out of the window. Elvis seemed to sleep most of the way. When breakfast had been served and the captain finally announced our descent into Heathrow Airport, I felt somewhat excited. As we were crossing the English Channel, I'd noticed a gradual buildup of cloud. By the time we reached the South Coast of England, all I could see beneath us was a thick blanket of dishwater grey.

4

I have to say, I wasn't as impressed with Heathrow Airport as I thought I would be. Underwhelming to say the least. Apparently, there was no gate allocation, so we had to sit on the plane for forty-five minutes, then disembark on the tarmac and ride a bus to the terminal. It was early spring but as cold as any Melbourne winter day. I was grateful for Tetley's advice to bring a coat, but now, wearing my only puffer, I was wondering if it was enough as we made our way to the bus through wind-swept rain. A firsthand view behind the scenes followed this at one of the world's busiest airports. The bus took us to the back door, or should I say, where the bins were kept. Welcome to England! Once we were inside, things didn't get much better. The terminal was undergoing renovation. Brisbane Airport this was not. Then, something dawned on me. *Bloody hell!* I'd been in the UK for less than an hour and I was already acting like a whinging pom. *Bloody hell!*

It took another hour to pass through customs. I wasn't sure if it was the inquisitive mind of a novice traveller or my detective awareness, but although my body was feeling a little tired after the long trip, my brain was switched on. I was watching everything, noticing, observing. After the initial shock of the weather, followed by the underwhelming entry through the backdoor, my next observation was the people who worked there, and I realised how multicultural England had become.

'You alright, bud?' Elvis asked after we'd collected our cases from the carousel and were heading for the final queue.

'Yeah, you?'

'I will be once we get out of here.'

'Me too.'

After one last scan of our passports and being regarded by the final gatekeeper, we trundled along a dim corridor and through to a typical airport arrivals terminal.

We both spotted him right away. How could we have missed him? He was literally standing at the top of the ramp, blocking the way for the other weary passengers.

When he saw us, Tetley dashed forward and threw his arms around us. 'I can't believe you two are here!' he cried. 'Thanks so much for coming.'

We hugged like reunited brothers. And that's exactly what we were. I know Elvis and I were experiencing the same feelings; we were both so happy to see our little mate for the first time in two years.

'Bloody hell,' I said, stepping back to inspect him. 'You've put on some weight, youth.' My early launch into the English banter and my attempt at the Nottingham accent that I'd picked up from him over the years, wasn't missed. The inadvertent cringe on my part was in anticipation of the barrage of return fire, but it never came, and I realised straight away that Tetley had changed.

'Come on, let's get you out of here,' he said, helping us with the cases.

A mid-sized hire car was parked in a multi-storey car park not too far away.

Tetley said very little as he negotiated the drive out of the airport complex.

Elvis, on the other hand, was in overdrive. 'So how have you been, mate?' Not waiting for a reply. 'Sorry to hear about, Col, but this is all one big mistake. Scotty'll sort it out. How's your mum? Have we got far to go? How long will it take to get to Nottingham?'

'Elvis … for fuck's sake,' I said. 'Calm down, mate. Give the lad a chance to answer.'

Tetley smiled, but I could tell he was hurting. The reason I could tell was because I'd witnessed no other emotions from him other than joy, playfulness and confidence. The dark rings under his eyes, in place of the usual laugh lines, and the disengaging eyes told me he was scared.

From the passenger seat, I placed a reassuring hand on his shoulder as he drove. 'It's going to be alright, mate. Col's going to be fine, and before you know it, we'll all be back in Kirra living it up.'

Tetley nodded and offered that same brave smile.

'Seriously, mate …' I squeezed his shoulder. '… I'll do everything in my power to help.'

'Cheers, lad.'

'Yeah, so now cheer up, you miserable little bastard!' Elvis said. 'The 'Three Amigos' are back together and in fucking England, can you believe?'

The banter was sometimes harsh, but it was exactly what Tetley needed. I mean, he *was* the king of the art as far as we were concerned. This time the smile spread into a familiar, cheeky grin. 'You're right. Everything's going to be just fine.' He was putting on a brave face, and I loved him for it. 'So, you've lost a bit of weight, Elv. Orders of the new girlfriend?'

'I've lost it. Looks like you found it, podgy!'

'And what about you, Scotty?' Tetley said, turning his attention to me. 'Getting married?'

'Yeah.'

'Finally sold out. We always knew he'd be the first to go, didn't we, Elv?'

'Yep. Ken-keen Scotty.'

'What do you mean, sold out?' I said, turning in my seat, knowing exactly what they meant. It had been an ongoing joke for years. Who would be the first to split up the group?

'You owe us both fifty bucks,' Elvis said.

'Seriously?' There was a vague recollection of us all sitting in the man shed one night, drinking heavily after agreeing that whoever was to get engaged first would pay the other two fifty dollars each.

We fell into silence as three brains suddenly shared the same emotion as the vision of our beloved man shed entered our minds. Not just a part of the house that was destroyed in the fire, it was a massive part of our lives. A part that was gone forever.

'So, I bet Kirra's changed since I've been away,' Tetley said, breaking the silence.

'My bloody oath,' Elvis said. I was happy for him to do the talking. 'Building's going up everywhere.'

'And the house has gone,' Tetley said, bringing us all back down.

I noticed signs of panic in his eyes. There was one thing that I hadn't found the courage to tell him yet, and that was that his beloved classic Vespa was no more. It was destroyed by the Wasps bikey gang during the *Tarnished* case, when I'd ridden it down to their clubhouse for a service, while secretly nosing around looking for their leader, Mick Brennan. I'd need to find the right time to tell him.

The silence returned as we followed the signs to the M1 North.

5

Eager to reach our destination, we resisted the temptation of stopping at one of the large motorway service stations for a break, and drove straight through. During the two-and-a-half-hour trip, and after some light banter, Tetley filled us in on the latest news about the case. Col was being held at Lincoln Prison on remand. He'd been charged with the unlawful killing of twenty-three-year-old Janita Sharma in June 1996. After a brief hearing, he was detained without bail and awaited trial.

'This is complete bollocks,' Elvis said. 'Anyone who knows Col would know he wouldn't harm a fly.'

'I know,' Tetley said. The sadness returned to his eyes.

'What does the brief say?' I asked.

Tetley sighed and remained focused on the road ahead. 'He reckons it's not looking good. The witness has testified that he saw Dad leave the building an hour or so after the victim arrived. He was the only other person on the premises. The builder—Dad's boss at the time—testified that it was Dad who sealed the wall, and the stonemason and his apprentice agree that it was completely sealed by the time they arrived early the next morning.'

'So basically, all we have is the word of the witness. What do we know about him?'

'Not a lot. Middle-aged. He's lived in the house across the street all his life.'

'I'm gonna need to get a list of names: the witness, the builder, stonemason, and anyone else involved with the build or who may have had access to the property, the owner, the victim's family and friends. Will that be possible?'

A remnant of the mischievous grin I knew and loved appeared across Tetley's face. 'Shouldn't be a problem.'

'What?'

'What?'

'I know that look.'

'What look?'

'That bloody look. What's going on?' From experience, I associated that smirk with the many past, *I know something you don't know*, situations.

'You'll see.'

Another silent interlude followed. The first sign for Nottingham appeared up ahead—forty miles. Surprisingly, to us green Aussies at least, the M1 was the same as the M1 between Brisbane and the Gold Coast. I'd somehow expected it to be much bigger, much busier, and although there was plenty of traffic, it wasn't that much different from home.

'How's your mum holding up?' I asked, breaking another silence.

'As well as can be expected. As you know she's been sick, and this obviously hasn't helped.'

The family trip was only supposed to last a month, but soon after they arrived in the UK, Tetley's mum, Carol, fell ill and was diagnosed with bowel cancer. Medical advice had warned against travelling back to Australia at that time and suggested undergoing immediate surgery to remove the tumour, followed by a course of chemotherapy. Being with her sister, Jen, was also a factor in her decision to stay on in the UK and have the treatment there. That was two years ago. The good news is that since the treatment, Carol is in remission. The bad news is that Colin's arrest has affected her recovery.

We exited the motorway at Junction 25 towards a place called Sandiacre. The scenery immediately changed from grey concrete to a typical English village.

'Not be long now,' Tetley said.

Checking my Apple watch, which had automatically adjusted to the local time, it was 12.15 pm.

The drive to Bobbersmill took another twenty minutes, during which we got our first view of the surrounding Nottingham suburbs. Although it was spring, people still seemed to be dressed for winter. The sky was still overcast and grey, and short drifts of fine rain caused the car's windscreen wipers to remain on intermittent.

Finally, we pulled onto a street where the houses were all the same. Mostly in rows of four, two storeys, they were white rendered with black slate roofs. Each had a small garden out front, wooden waist-high gates, and privet hedges, but the thing I noticed the most was the number of cars parked either side of the narrow road. Tetley had to drive in a snake fashion to avoid them.

'Here we are. Home sweet home,' Tetley said, pulling up at the kerb.

The houses were in blocks of two, with only a narrow passage between each block.

'This is Aunty Jen and Uncle John's place. They've been kind enough to let us stay with them since Mum got sick,' Tetley said.

As we climbed out of the car, a familiar face greeted us. 'Scotty, Elvis!' Carol came rushing out of the front gate and threw her arms around us. 'It's so good to see you both.'

A familiar face, yes, but different in many ways. Carol had lost an awful lot of weight, and the crew cut hairstyle did little to enhance her appearance. She looked older, thinner and more fragile, but her warmth was still apparent.

'Ay up, duck!' Elvis exclaimed, initiating his first attempt at the Nottingham greeting.

'G'day, Carol.' I couldn't help myself.

'I can't believe you guys are here. Thank you so much for coming,' Carol said. 'Come on in, come on in.' She shepherded us up the pathway and into the house, leaving Tetley to retrieve the cases from the car.

We entered a small hallway with stairs directly in front of us. To our right was a closed door and a short passage. There was a radiator along one wall with a push bike leaning up against it. At the end of the passage, there was an open door to the kitchen. Beyond that was another open door to the garden out the back.

Carol's sister, Jen, and her husband, John, were avid travellers and had set off for a three-month cruise of the Caribbean.

'It's obviously not like what we're used to on the Gold Coast but there's plenty of room,' Carol said, showing us through the closed door that led into a small room crammed with oversized furniture—an enormous floral, three-piece suite; a glass coffee table; and a flat screen TV standing in one corner on top of a wooden chest.

'I suppose you want a cup of tea,' Carol said. 'And I've got biscuits.'

'My bloody oath,' Elvis said.

Since meeting Tetley on our very first day at Palm Beach Currumbin High School and becoming firm friends, the Websters had instilled in Elvis and myself an appreciation of the finer things in the English culture: black tea (PG Tips) with milk and sugar, digestive biscuits (for dunking in our tea), Yorkshire puddings, bangers and mash, and fish and chips with mushy peas and vinegar.

Tetley came bounding into the house. 'Are you gonna help me wi' these cases or what?' His face flushed from exertion.

'You boys get settled in your room while I put the kettle on, eh?'

'Thanks, Carol,' I said, giving her one more hug. We didn't mention the reason we were there, and I was glad of that. There would be plenty of time for talk later, no doubt.

It was a bit of a struggle to get the cases up the narrow stairway, but we soon found ourselves standing in a small bedroom at the back of the house. The disappointment on my face must have been apparent.

'Sorry, lads, you'll have to share,' Tetley said, reading my expression.

Two single beds side by side with a small bedside table in between them, an old hand-painted sky-blue gloss wardrobe and what looked like an IKEA chest of drawers left little else room in the small space.

'But …' I was struggling to find the words. 'You know as much as anyone how much he snores.'

Tetley grinned, and in his best Aussie accent, he said, 'Bugger!'

6

A dinner plate stacked high with chocolate digestives was the centrepiece of the circular dining table, around which four of us sat, each with a mug of tea in hand. On the bench was a dozen packets of Tim Tams and a couple of jars of Vegemite, that Elvis and I had brought from Australia as gifts. The Tim Tams would be saved for a special occasion.

Tetley reached over and took a biscuit.

'Hey, I wanted that one,' Elvis complained.

'They're all the same, ya knob!' was Tetley's reply.

'But I wanted *that* one.'

Tetley crammed the whole biscuit into his mouth, chewed it and then opened his mouth so that Elvis could see the churning chocolate inside. 'Still want it now?'

To an outsider, my mates' interaction may have appeared as childish or nonsensical, but at that moment it was much more than just playful banter; it was proof that the Tetley we knew and loved was still in there. Even though he was hurting, he was still there, and it was our job to nurture and protect him, to nurse him back to normal. Elvis had skilfully initiated the therapy that our old mate needed, and I was glad to be witness to the beginning of his revival.

While the banter continued, I glanced over at Carol and realised that she was staring at me, solemn faced and oblivious to anything else.

'He didn't do it, you know, Scotty?' she said when our eyes met.

As if realising their behaviour was out of line and suddenly remembering why we were there, Tetley and Elvis fell into silence.

'I know he didn't, Carol,' I said, placing my hand over hers.

'He'd never hurt anyone. Not my Col.'

'I know.' It's all I could think of to say.

'I dread to think of him sitting in that prison cell.' She lowered her eyes to the table. 'He should be here with me. We've never once been apart in over forty years.'

I wanted to reassure her, tell her that everything was going to be alright, but I couldn't find the words, so I squeezed her hand.

'You will help us, won't you, Scotty?'

'Of course I will. That's why I'm here.'

Like a dam bursting its wall, tears suddenly rolled down her face, and she sobbed. 'Thank you.' Producing a scrunched-up tissue from the cuff of her cardigan, she blew her nose. 'Thank you so much for coming. We really appreciate it.'

'That we do,' piped in Tetley. 'Dad was ecstatic when I told him you were coming.'

All eyes were on me now, as if I were about to deliver the opening statement for the defence, something I'd prepared after my initial findings. But the truth was, there *were* no initial findings yet. The only thing I knew about the case was the information I'd found online, and what Tetley had told me earlier on the phone and had updated during the drive up from London, which wasn't much.

'We can't get in to see Dad until Monday,' Tetley said. Today was Thursday.

'Did you get everything I asked for?' I asked Tetley.

'Yep.' He jumped up from the table, disappeared into the hallway, then came back momentarily carrying a large, thin rectangle box. After placing it on the floor, he tore it open to reveal a whiteboard inside.

Elvis and I munched on the biscuits, dunking them in our tea, as we watched Tetley assemble the board on its stand.

Then, from his pockets he produced a strip of Blu Tack and half a dozen whiteboard markers, the chunky kind—four black, one red and one blue.

'What's that for, Scotty?' Asked Carol, nursing her tea in both hands.

'I want to set up an incident room.' It was old school, I know, but it was how I worked. Adding the details of the case in a visual form helped me keep tabs of what was happening, and then adding information to the board as it came to light helped me reassess, to ruminate and to move forward. 'Is there anywhere private that we can put it? Somewhere quiet and out of the way?' I asked.

'You can have this room,' Carol said. The dining room was at the back of the house. It was similar in size to the front room but less cluttered.

'Perfect, thank you!'

While Tetley and Elvis moved the table and chairs back towards the wall, I placed the whiteboard by the window and put the pens and the Blu Tack on the little ledge at the bottom of the board. From there, I got my first view of the back garden. It was terraced with a patio and steps leading down to a narrow strip of lawn the same width as the house. The three sides were bordered by a tall privet hedge. There was still no sign of the sun, or even the sky, but at least the rain had stopped.

Next, I set up my laptop on the dining room table and was thankful to Elvis for remembering we needed an adapter for the cumbersome UK power points. Once everything was set up, I asked everyone to take a seat.

'Okay.' I needed to choose my next words carefully. 'So, I think it'll be best if we can keep people out of this room while I'm here.'

There were nods of agreement.

'And I think that should include you, Carol.'

'Me …? Whatever for?'

'Well, there might be information displayed on the board that could be upsetting, or a bit sensitive.'

'Oh, I see.'

'This goes for you guys, too, if you don't mind,' I said, directing my attention to Tetley and Elvis.

In unison, they shrugged and said, 'Sure.'

'Carol, could I borrow a photograph of Col?'

'Yes, love, of course.' She backed out of the room, and I heard her ascend the stairs.

'Have you got a printer, mate?' I asked Tetley.

'Yeah, follow me.'

We moved out into the hallway. Tetley opened one of the two doors under the stairs. The one on the left was a closet; the one on the right, we later learned, was the toilet. Inside the closet was a shelf with a large Wi-Fi router and a printer.

'You should be able to hook up your laptop via Bluetooth,' Tetley said.

'Perfect!'

Carol reappeared carrying a small box of photographs, so we returned to the dining room/incident room.

'How's this one?' Carol asked, holding out a photograph.

'That will be great,' I said, taking it from her hand. The picture was a head and shoulders shot of Colin standing in front of the Christmas tree. Taking it over to the board, I tore off a small strip of Blu Tack, rolled it between my fingers for a moment, then used it to stick the photograph top centre of the board.

Carol wiped away another flood of tears, then disappeared into the kitchen.

I'd already downloaded as much information as I could find onto my laptop; now, I needed to print out photographs of the victim and anyone else I thought was important to the case. There would be a lot to do over the next coming days—visit the crime scene, if possible, speak with the detectives in charge of the case, the witnesses and anyone else involved, but to be honest I was starting to feel a bit knackered. Remembering that we'd just flown in from Australia, it wasn't surprising. Sleep seemed like a good proposition for now.

Elvis, on the other hand, was totally pumped. 'Let's go to the pub!'

7

With his head down and his hands in his pockets, Tetley set a pace that was hard for me and Elvis to follow.

'Bloody hell. Slow down, mate,' Elvis said.

'Sorry,' Tetley said, pulling back. 'I've got so used to rushing around.'

'You're a long way from the Gold Coast, lad,' I said.

'I know. I can't wait to get back.'

We were heading up Bobbersmill Road, following Tetley to the nearest pub. Once again, I was amazed at the number of cars randomly parked in either direction along each side of the road. Outside every house there were two wheelie bins, and in some places, there were bags of rubbish piled up ready for collection. Squinting, I got a glimpse of how I imagined this area would have once looked. Manicured privet hedges, instead of overgrown, undernourished perimeters. Wide, clean, uncluttered kerbs, with children playing hopscotch, and little girls with skipping ropes. A handful of cars parked at the side of the road. The sound of an ice-cream van approaching on the next street on a warm summer's day. These were the recollections of Tetley's childhood that he had often spoken of during our evenings in the man shed. This was what Elvis and I had been expecting. Oh dear. I was assuming the transformation had happened over the last thirty years since Tetley had moved to Australia, so I was guessing the appearance of his beloved hometown was more of a shock to him.

At a vandalised telephone box, we crossed the road and entered a housing estate with different architecture, obviously built in more recent times. The houses there were plain brick and box-like. I couldn't help but notice the litter on the ground and more dog shit than I'd seen in my life.

'I can remember what was here before all this was built,' Tetley said. 'Rows and rows of terraced houses on cobblestone streets. People seemed to have more pride in the way they lived back then. They might have been living in slums, but at least they were clean.'

Like a Victorian oasis and a monument to better times, the Avenue Hotel stood tall among the 1970s suburban estate.

'The Clock!' Tetley exclaimed. 'This wa' me dad's local when he wa' a youth.'

The three-storey whitewashed building took up an entire corner block. Above what was once an entrance was a large clock embedded in the wall. A red neon sign on the wall said, Shipstones Ales.

The entrance was an inset double doorway along the side of the building. Taking the lead, Tetley stepped into the doorway and pushed his way through the door. Elvis and I followed.

We entered a dim bar where a pool table dominated the room. There were a couple of pokies on one wall and two dartboards side by side on another. There were only a few other patrons present, either seated at the sprinkle of bar tables or standing at the bar. An old boy slapped one of the pokies while feeding it an endless supply of coins. Over the bar was a TV screen, showing a game of football. The 'proper' football apparently—or as Tetley would have us believe—not that word Tetley had warned us never to use while we were over there if we feared for our lives—soccer.

The barman was a tall black guy. His wide smile when he noticed Tetley approaching the bar was infectious.

'Ay up youth, y'alright?'

I wasn't expecting that. A more exotic Caribbean accent perhaps, not the same twang as Tetley.'

'I'm good, mate, yourself?'

'Not so bad.'

'Henry, these are my mates from Australia—Scotty and Elvis.'

Henry reached over the bar and shook our hands. 'Ah, the detective, eh?'

'That's me,' I replied sheepishly.

'Come to save old Col from the gallows.'

'Something like that.'

'What can I get ya, Sean?' Henry asked, directing his attention back to Tetley.

It was strange to hear our little pommy mate being addressed by his proper name. From the moment he first opened his mouth on his first day at high school all those years ago, he was christened 'Tetley' because his accent sounded to us like the Tetley Tea TV commercial that was playing at the time.

'Three pints of bitter, tah.'

By the time we'd approached the bar, my detective eyes had already scanned the room—number of exits, windows, potential escape routes, that kind of thing, and the finer details like the variety of beers available. I was surprised to see Fosters on tap, something we never saw nowadays on the Gold Coast. Oh well, it wasn't XXXX (Castlemaine Four Ex), but at least it was Aussie.

But when Henry grabbed three pint glasses from beneath the bar and filled them from the large Shipstones tap, Tetley grinned at our worried expressions as we watched the darkish brown, frothy liquid being poured.

'Bitter?' Elvis said.

'Shurrup. Don't start already,' Tetley said with one hand on the bar. 'I thought you might like to try the local brew.'

Elvis and I shared an anxious glance. 'Is it … is it cold?' Elvis asked.

'Course it's bloody cold.' Tetley chuckled as he passed the first pint to me.

My first touch of the glass told me it wasn't as cold as I would have liked. Elvis, reading my expression, started to nervously step from one foot to the other.

When Henry had poured all three beers, he watched us eagerly as Tetley held up his pint.

'Cheers!' Tetley took in a mouthful and seemed to savour the taste.

Elvis and I, not so adventurous, each took a tentative sip.

Trying desperately not to offend the barman by screwing up my face when the thick, hoppy substance came into contact with my tastebuds, I swilled the coolish liquid around my mouth a few times before swallowing.

Elvis, not so conservative, cried, 'Uhh, that's fucking horrible!'

Tetley and Henry burst into laughter.

'It's an acquired taste, man,' Henry yelled playfully.

'Drink it up and you'll have no problem shitting in the morning,' Tetley exclaimed.

Henry's laugh was high-pitched and caused the rest of the patrons to turn their heads in our direction.

'Ger' um two pints of Fosters, Henry. Soft cocks!' Tetley said.

To our relief, the replacement Fosters served in tall, cold glasses were closer to the temperature we were used to. It tasted bloody good too. A silent nod between Elvis and I cemented a pact—never again would we wander from our beloved Australian beer.

We took a seat in the corner so that Tetley had a view of the TV. But after a mere glance at the screen, he turned his back on it and faced us instead. Notts bloody County. We'd heard this name before—a term used sparingly by our friend referring to the other Nottingham football team. However, as a lifelong devoted Nottingham Forest fan, there was only one thing Tetley hated more than Notts County, and that was Derby County.

We didn't have a big night; in fact, one beer was enough. Elvis and I were both starting to feel the effects of jet lag. To put it in more layman terms, we were knackered. Me more so and more apparent from the fact that I was falling asleep at the table. Tetley had hoped we might have met up with a couple of his mates, but we were glad when they didn't show up. It was a typical quiet midweek night in a local pub, albeit halfway across the world, but something Elvis and I were thankful for nonetheless.

The old boy, who had been playing the pokie machine, approached us. 'Ay up, youth, y'alright?' he said, directing a slurred greeting in Tetley's direction.

From the gnarled ruddy complexion, the barnacled swollen nose, and the phlegmy tone of his voice, I deduced he was a regular patron of The Clock.

'I'm alright, Don, ya'sen?'

'Fair to middlin, lad. Ya know how it is.'

'Ah.'

'So, who's this then?' He asked, directing his attention to Elvis and me.

'Oh, these are me mates from Australia—Scotty and Elvis.'

I thought Don was about to keel over as he leaned forward and shook my hand. When he grasped Elvis' hand, he said, 'You must be that bloody detective Sean's been telling us about. You're a big lad, aren't ya?'

'No, not me,' Elvis said. 'That's Scotty. He's the detective.'

'Really?' Don's eyes widened and then narrowed as he tried to focus on me. 'Ya dun't look much like a detective, youth … more like one of them poofy surfers.'

'Thanks.' I lowered my voice and leaned a little closer. 'I'm undercover.'

'Ah …' With a wink, the old boy tapped the side of his nose with an index finger. 'So, you've come all this way to 'elp young Col, ave ya?'

'That's right.'

'Good. He needs it, cause them bloody coppers don't care. Col's a good lad, always 'as been. I've known him since he were a nipper, standing outside this place waiting for his dad all night.' He leaned in and lowered his voice once more. 'I used to take him out a bag a crisps and a bottle 'o pop, I did. Poor little sod. Stood out there in all weathers.'

'So, he's a good bloke then?' I asked.

'The best.' He let his eyes drift between us, and I sensed the consciousness drifting away. 'Right,' he staggered backwards. 'I'm goin' for a slash. Nice to meet ya, lads.' Then he snaked away towards the toilets.

The conversation from then on was as flat as Tetley's beer. After we finished our drinks, we bid goodnight to Henry, the barman, and headed back home. The walk back was a quiet affair. When we reached home, Elvis and I turned down the offer of a cup of tea and retired to bed. But before we climbed the stairs, Tetley said, 'Big day tomorrow, Scotty. I've got someone coming to see you in the morning.'

'Who?' I asked, hardly able to keep my eyes open.

'Only the DI in charge of the case.'

'Really? Why?' I'd familiarised myself with the English detective ranks, which were slightly different to the Australian system. 'The detective inspector in charge of the case is coming here to talk to me?' This seemed highly unusual. There must have been another reason for his visit—to speak with Carol perhaps. I'd hardly expect him or her to have any interest in me. If anything, I was bracing myself for a little resentment at me coming over here and poking my nose in police business.

'You'll see,' Tetley said, grinning. 'Night night!'

<h1 style="text-align:center">8</h1>

We'd done it. By taking everyone's advice and following the most important tip for surviving the day following a long-haul flight, we'd remained awake for the whole of the first day. This was crucial, apparently, to avoid jet lag. And the pint at the end of the evening even assisted with the deep sleep Elvis and I both achieved. I woke up first the next morning. Of course, I did. Early morning surfer, around 7.00 am. My movement gently lifted Elvis from his slumber.

'Hey mate. How are you feeling?' I asked with a groggy, dry mouth.

'Not too bad,' Elvis replied with a similar croaky voice.

The only bathroom was on the first floor, and comprised of a toilet, a sink and a bath. Thankfully, a shower had been installed at some point over the bath.

Like the true gentleman I was, I allowed Elvis to go first, while reminding him of Carol's warning about the limited hot water.

To my surprise, Elvis was back only a few moments later with a towel wrapped around his waist.

'Bloody hell, that was quick,' I said.

Elvis nodded, and I couldn't work out if the smirk was the humorous kind or the product of his anxiety.

'What?'

'You'll see.'

Likewise, with a towel wrapped around my waist and my little toiletry bag in hand. I made my way across the landing and into the bathroom. Locking the door behind me. I leaned over the bath and turned on the tap. The water from the showerhead was little more than a trickle. Climbing into the bath, my attempt at adjusting the head to increase the flow proved useless, so I directed my attention to adjusting the temperature. With a super-sensitive tap, it soon became apparent that the choice was boiling hot or freezing cold. 'Bugger!' I opted for the latter and cleansed myself with cold water. At least it was invigorating, I guess. Now I understood why Elvis had returned so quickly. His laughter was no tonic when I returned to the bedroom just a few minutes later.

'How will we cope?' Elvis asked with sincerity.

'Adaptation, remember? We need to adapt to our surroundings.' This was something we had discussed prior to the trip. We weren't going to become known as the whinging Aussies!

After unpacking our suitcases and placing our clothes in the drawers and wardrobe, we ventured downstairs. Carol and Tetley were already awake, sitting at a small rectangle table against one wall of the kitchen.

'Good morning,' Carol cried, jumping to her feet.

'Good morning,' Elvis and I replied in unison.

'Did you sleep well?'

'We did, thank you,' I said.

'That's great. Well done,' Carol said excitedly. 'That means you've cracked it. You've adjusted to the time zone. No jet lag for you, lads.'

We nodded wearily.

'It's not so bad coming this way,' Carol said. 'Something to do with flying back in time. It always hits me flying back to Australia.'

We took the two empty seats at the tiny table. All this time Tetley had remained quiet, but I knew that mischievous grin.

'How were your showers?' He asked before taking a swig of his tea.

Carol stopped what she was doing and stood silently, like a statue. The only movement was her eyes flicking back and forth between me and Elvis.

'Uhm … yeah … it was alright,' Elvis said.

Tetley burst into laughter.

'Oh, it's terrible, in't it?' Carol said. 'Not like what we're used to on the Gold Coast.'

'No, I spose.'

'Will it be okay?' Carol was genuinely concerned.

Tetley, on the other hand, was enjoying the moment. That bloody patronising chuckle meant he was warming up for a bout of banter.

'Yeah, it's fine,' I said, trying not to look at Elvis.

'We can have a swim later in the River Lean,' Tetley said.

'Oh, is there a river close by?' I asked innocently. The image of Constable's 'Haywain' coming to mind.

This time, Tetley's laughter caused him to spill his tea.

'Don't listen to him,' Carol said. 'He's pulling your leg.'

'That's not like Tetley,' I said sarcastically.

'There's a nice little inlet just past the soap works,' Tetley said. 'We all used to swim there when we were kids.'

'Oh, you *did* not,' Carol said playfully, slapping her son on the shoulder. 'There is a nice swimming baths not too far from here though if you wanted a swim. Are you ready for some breakfast?'

'Yes please,' Elvis piped up.

After a full English made with tinned tomatoes, streaky bacon and fried eggs, the 'Three Amigos' retired to the incident room, aka the dining room.

'Did I hear right last night when you said the DI in charge was coming to see us this morning?' I asked Tetley after he'd closed the door behind us.

'Yep.' Tetley checked his watch. 'He should be here any minute now.'

'But how? Why?' As an ex-detective inspector myself with the Queensland Police, I knew only too well the time constraints that such a position held, and how I would have reacted if an unknown private investigator was snooping around the case I was working on. My instinct told me that the only reason for the DI's visit was to warn me off. But why go to such an extreme? Or perhaps he had some news to share with Carol and Tetley? Yes, that must be it. There's no way an official of this rank would waste his time coming out here just to dress me down.

On cue, we heard a knock at the front door.

'I'll get it,' Carol called out.

Tetley opened the door to the incident room and stood just inside the hallway, a big smile across his face. 'G'day mate!' he called out towards the front door.

Elvis and I looked at each other, confused.

A tall man wearing an ill-fitting suit followed Carol down the hallway and shook hands with Tetley.

'Lads, this is Detective Inspector Stewart Weston,' Tetley said, showing the guest into the incident room. 'Stewie, this is Scotty—'

'Mate, you don't have to tell me who this is,' the detective said with a broad smile and an Australian accent. 'It's only Scotty Bloody Stephens.' He grabbed my hand and shook it wildly.

'Do I know you?' I asked.

'No, but I know you,' the tall young man said, still shaking my hand. 'The saviour of the Gold Coast. Ex-footy player. Overall bloody legend.' He let go of my hand and directed his attention to Elvis. 'And Elvis. I remember you too.'

Elvis glanced towards me and frowned. 'How on earth would you know me?' he asked while his hand was being shaken as wildly as mine was.

'Ah, you two blokes were my heroes. You wouldn't remember me. I was at Essendon Keilor Collage.'

'You went to the same high school as us in Melbourne?' I asked.

'Yep, but I was a couple of years younger, so only a little kid when you were there, but I was a keen footy fan. I watched all your games.'

'You've got to be kidding,' Elvis said.

Until I was fourteen, I went to school in Melbourne. Both Elvis and I were budding Australian Football players (AFL), me more so with a strong chance of turning professional after leaving school. That was before my mum died, though, and before my dad moved us up to Queensland.

'Small world, in't it?' Carol said, standing in the doorway. 'I'll put the kettle on.' She disappeared into the kitchen.

'I used to play myself,' the detective said. 'Turned pro and signed with The Bombers.'

'Fair dinkum?' Elvis said.

'Yeah, but got injured before I even started. Bloody knee. That was the end of my football career.'

'And now you're a copper in Nottingham,' I said.

'That's right. Funny how life works out, isn't it?'

9

Over tea, we sat at the formal dining table chatting. DCI Stewart Weston, or Stewie, filled us in on how he came to be living and working in the UK.

Originally from Melbourne, Victoria, he'd been on holiday in Far North Queensland after recently graduating from the Victorian Police Academy. While out on a snorkelling trip at the Great Barrier Reef, he met a backpacker from Nottingham called Sarah Jones, who was travelling around Australia on a three-month visa. The pair hit it off, and Stewie extended his leave so they could be together. When it came time for Sarah to return to the UK, Stewie couldn't bear to be apart from his new love, so ended up following her a few weeks later.

That was fifteen years ago. The pair ended up marrying. Stewie became a UK citizen and joined the Nottinghamshire Constabulary. The couple live in Long Eaton, a town on the Nottinghamshire-Derbyshire border, and they have a six-year-old son called Toby.

'I bloody miss Australia, though, boys.' He stared down into his mug. 'Never thought in a million years I'd be living overseas. The plan was always to move up to the Gold Coast once I became an established copper.'

'Have you been back?' I asked.

'Nope, but we're planning on moving back as soon as possible. Sarah was an only child, and very close to her mum. Poor old girl's on her last legs. Once she pops it, we're out of here.'

'To the Gold Coast?' Elvis asked.

'My bloody oath. Coolangatta, here we come!' He finished his tea. 'Anyway. That's not why we are here, is it?' His demeanour changed to that of a serious senior detective. 'I'm here to tell you to back off.'

'I knew it.'

'Big mister detective coming over here. What, you think you're just gonna waltz in and solve the case, do you, Scott? Find the clues that we missed?'

'Well …' That was kind of the plan, but the last thing I wanted to do was upset the local police.

'Prove Col's innocence, expose the real killer, and become the big hero again? Just like when you solved the *X* case?' His jaw was set, and his intimidating stare gave us a glimpse as to why he was a good detective.

'No, not at all. I'm just here to help a mate …' I glanced at Tetley for support.

Thankfully, Tetley was impossible at keeping a straight face, always had been. He suddenly burst into laughter.

Stewie and Carol joined him.

'Just kidding, mate!' Stewie boomed, playfully slapping me on the shoulder. 'I had you, didn't I?'

'You did, mate,' I said through an embarrassed grin.

Elvis looked as relieved as I felt when he joined in on the laughter.

Stewie reached down into his briefcase, pulled out a Manila folder, and slapped it on the table in front of me. 'There you go. Everything we have so far.'

'You're kidding me.'

'Nope.'

It was a copy of the official police report. This was a great start. I couldn't have imagined in a million years that I'd have access to this vital, unbiased information on day one.

'It's not all good news though,' Stewie said. 'It wasn't me who gave you this, Scotty, and this needs to remain between the five of us.' He shifted his eyes to each of us as if securing our support.

'There will be hell to pay if my superiors find out I've shared this information. Do you understand?'

I did understand—probably more than Elvis, Tetley and Carol—but I could see by the determination on their faces that they understood the importance of keeping this quiet too.

'Unfortunately, not everyone on the local police force will be so welcoming. In fact, I'm sure, as you would expect, they're not going to be too happy having a Steve Irwin lookalike snooping around.'

This was the kind of response I'd expected before coming here. Stewie would be an unexpected, but very welcome, lifeline. 'Mate, I can't thank you enough for this,' I said, lifting the file.

'That's okay, just don't let me down, eh?'

'No worries … so … what's your take on all of this? Is it an open and shut case as the media would have us believe?'

'Well, I have to be honest,' Stewie said, shooting an apologetic glance towards Carol. 'The evidence is pretty damning.'

'And this witness, uhm …' I sifted through the file looking for the witness' name.

'William Henley,' Stewie said.

'Yeah. Credible?'

'On paper, yes, but … a bit strange. A middle-aged bachelor, lived at home with his mum all his life until she died.'

'Is that strange?' I asked.

'You'll see what I mean when you meet him. I think that's probably a good place to start.' Stewie jumped to his feet. 'Well, I've got to go. Lots to see and people to do.' He handed me his card. 'It really is great to meet you, Scotty,' he said, shaking my hand. 'And anything you need, just let me know, yeah?'

'Great to meet you too, Stewie. And thanks for this; I really appreciate it.'

'No worries.' He shook Elvis' hand. 'What happened to the quiff, mate?' He was referring to the Elvis Presley hairstyle—and the reason for his nickname—that Elvis sported as a teenager.

Elvis sighed. 'Long gone, buddy.'

'But not forgotten.' Stewie shook Tetley's hand and shared a mischievous grin. Then he hugged Carol. 'It's going to be alright, Carol. You've only got Detective Scotty Bloody Stephens on the case!'

'I know, I know,' Carol said, a reluctant doubt tinging her enthusiasm.

With the gait of an Aussie Rules forward, Stewie bounded towards the front door, turned before leaving and said, 'Hooroo.' Then he was gone.

'What do you reckon, Scotty?' Tetley asked as we returned to the dining room.

'Mate. This is awesome. How did you get to know Stewie? You both seem pretty tight.'

'Just met him after Dad was arrested. He was the detective in charge of the case, but being an Aussie, we hit it off, especially when he found out I was mates with you.'

'If you blokes don't mind, I'd like a bit of time to read through the report and get the whiteboard sorted,' I said, flicking through the file. From a cursory glance, I could see it held everything I needed to get started: photographs of the victim (both pre-mortem and post-mortem) and of the crime scene, and profiles and records of witnesses and anyone who was interviewed in relation to the case. This would give me a tremendous boost.

'Right-o,' Carol said. 'I'll put the kettle on.'

10

Before setting up the whiteboard, I spent some time seated at the dining room table, going through the file. Most of the content was an expanded version of what I already knew, except, that is, for one important fact about the victim that hadn't been reported by the press. She was around eight weeks pregnant. Was this important? Time would tell.

The possible cause of death was determined as asphyxiation. The victim was survived only by an older brother called Javed Sharma.

The most important thing the report gave me was the contact details of everyone involved—the witness, the two owners of the property (current and at the time of the murder), the builder who Col worked for, the stonemason, the victim's brother, and even the peripheral players like the stonemason's apprentice who was the first person on the scene after Col. It was a stroke of luck to have this information; thanks to Stewie, my leg work would be cut down no end.

The pictures of the crime scene and the victim were pretty gruesome and, mindful of Carol and Tetley and the fact that the room wasn't secure, I decided not to place any of them on the board, choosing to keep them out of sight instead. There was a nice head and shoulders shot of the victim though, taken prior to her death. This replaced Col's picture at the top of the board, relegating him down to the next branch. Beneath the victim's picture, I wrote 'Anita Madison–real name Janita Sharma'. Pondering for a moment, I analysed the information I had about her.

Of Indian descent, twenty-seven-year-old Janita was originally from Aspley, a place not too far from where I now stood. She worked as a high-end escort for five years prior to her death but apparently gave this up when she got involved with the leading Nottingham crime boss Declan O'Donnell. The official report states that, on the night of her death, she arrived at the house—which was purchased some months earlier by O'Donnell—around 9.30 pm and wasn't too happy at finding building work taking place. The witness claims to have heard shouting prior to a deadly silence before the accused left the building around an hour later. Janita is survived by an older brother, Javed Sharma, who owns a news agency on Alfreton Road, also close to where we were based.

There was no need for me to write anything below Col's picture, but I did anyway. I simply wrote his name, Colin Webster. Col had been like a second dad when I moved to the Gold Coast with my father and my older brother, Todd. My real dad was more interested in my elder sibling, or so it seemed to me at that time, so I'd found solace in the Webster family. Col used to take me and Tetley fishing and camping. He'd watch from the beach as we learned to surf off Kirra Point. He was a mentor and an inspiration. There was no way he had committed this crime. Not in a million years.

Leaving room for more pictures, which I would inevitably collect as the case progressed, I began my list of the players, the suspects and witnesses. Although at this time there was only one suspect, and one witness, from experience I knew there'd be more to learn from speaking to everyone involved, more witnesses and hopefully more suspects.

Under Col's name I wrote William Henley (witness). Basically, that was all the information I had on him at that time.

Third on the list was the owner of the property at that time, and Janita's sugar daddy, Declan O'Donnell. From all accounts, O'Donnell was Nottingham's leading crime figure in the 1990s.

The owner of two nightclubs in the city, one upmarket, one not so. He also owned the security firm that supplied the bouncers to pretty much all the pubs and clubs in the area. He owned a tow truck company as well as a string of tattoo parlours in the surrounding suburbs. Money laundering and prostitution were a big part of the ex-pat Irishman's empire, but there had been no convictions or proof of his involvement with these activities. Unfortunately, Declan O'Donnell died in 2019 from a drive-by shooting outside his home in a place called Broxtowe. His widow, Sheila O'Donnell, who on all accounts is as tough as her husband, survived him, and now runs the firm at the age of 77. The couple had one son, Rodney O'Donnell, who moved down to London after his father's death. I added these two names to the list beneath Declan.

Next there was the builder, Bill Patterson, who contracted Col to do the job. The report states that there was a need for speed in finishing the job because Les Lane, the stonemason, was booked to finish it off the next morning. In a recent statement by Bob's son and then apprentice, Tony Patterson, it was impossible to hire the prominent stonemason back then; he was fully booked for at least five years. I wondered if the influence of O'Donnell had anything to do with him taking on the job. Unfortunately, Bob died of prostate cancer in 2013, but like O'Donnell, his name still went on the board. Below him, I wrote his son's name, Tony Patterson. His statement had been short; he'd left just as Col was arriving, but I'd need to talk to him nonetheless.

Next, the obvious choice was Les Lane, the stonemason, a flamboyant artist type who grew up in Nottingham. Apart from the high demand for his work, there was a dark side that few people knew about. He was charged with raping a young woman in the 1970s but was acquitted on a technicality, *Interesting. As the ever perfectionist, would he have arrived at the job early the next morning to find Anita in the house?* Although he'd be ninety years old now, he was still alive, so I would be paying him a visit at the Mapperley Top Nursing Home.

Beneath Les's name, I wrote Dave Anderson. Dave was Les's labourer. He'd had orders from his boss to arrive earlier to check the work was done correctly, which he did, and reported nothing out of the ordinary. I was surprised to learn from the report that he now owned a barbershop on Parliament Street in the city. At that moment, I had no idea of the location of these addresses, but I was looking forward to getting out and finding them.

There was only one more name, for now, to add to the list, and that was Donna Simpson, Janita's friend and co-worker at the escort agency. In her statement, Donna claimed Anita was planning to get away from Nottingham for good. Now married and a mother of two, she lived in a suburb called Wollaton.

So that was it for now. The whiteboard was officially activated. Over the next few days, weeks or however long it took, I'd be adding names and scenarios to the list no doubt, but mostly I'd be standing in front of it ruminating, going over the evidence in my mind. I couldn't help but wonder how long I'd be away from home … away from … Jen—'OH SHIT!' I suddenly yelled out loud as a realisation hit me like a brick to the back of the head. I'd forgotten to call Jenny. 'Call me as soon as you get there!' she'd demanded just before we parted at Brisbane Airport. Through all the excitement of arriving in the UK, meeting up with Tetley and Carol again after all this time, and fighting the onslaught of jetlag, I'd completely forgotten to call my fiancée to tell her we'd arrived safely. I was about to grab my phone when the door opened and in walked Elvis. He was talking on *my* phone, so I must have left it in the bedroom. His face was tinged with faux sympathy as he handed me the phone.

'It's Jenny!'

11

'Hi Jen, how's it goin'?'

'Don't you bloody *hi Jen* me, how's it goin'!'

'I'm so, so sorry, I just—'

'You just what?'

'I completely forgot.'

'You said you were going to ring me as soon as you got there.'

'I know, I know. I'm sorry. What with one thing and another and the jetlag and—'

'*Phhh…*'

She was pissed. And rightly so. It was so unlike me to forget something so important.

'I truly am sorry, babe. I've got no excuse.'

Silence.

'We arrived safely. The weather's been crap so far, but it was great to meet up with Tetley and Carol.'

'How are they holding up?' she said, her delivery more with detective curiosity than interest.

'Ah, you know. They're as good as can be expected.'

'When will you get to see Colin?'

'Not until Monday.'

'I don't suppose you've made a start on the case yet.'

'I have actually. I've got the whiteboard, and you won't believe it, the DI in charge is only an Aussie.'

'What?'

'And he went to the same school as Elvis and me.'

'No.'

'And that's not all; he's agreed to help as much as he can.'

'You're bloody kidding, aren't you? Could you imagine a pommy PI coming over here and asking for help from the Queensland Police?'

My chuckle reflected my thoughts exactly. 'I know. What a stroke of luck, eh?'

'So, what's first up?'

'I want to visit the crime scene today, if possible, then talk to some folk.'

'Are there many witnesses?'

'Only one who claims to have seen Col and the victim together the night of the murder.'

'Credible?'

'Not sure yet. Hoping to speak to him today.'

There was an awkward pause in the conversation.

'So, how are things in Kirra?'

'Pretty much the same as they were when you left two days ago.'

'How are you?'

'I'm good.'

I could tell by her voice that she was tired, then I realised it was just after midnight on the Gold Coast. 'I'll let you get to bed, eh?'

'Yeah, no worries.'

'I'll call you tomorrow.'

'Okay. See ya.' She hung up.

Oh dear. I was in the doghouse. All too aware of the pressure that Detective Inspector Jenny Radford was under, I needed to remind myself of the stress involved in holding that rank after my short stint in the role. Unlike my promotion that had been a complete farce to enable the ex-Gold Coast mayor and the Queensland Police Commissioner to control the outcome of the X murder case, Jenny had earned her promotion purely because she was a damn good copper.

'How'd it go?' Elvis asked when I entered the kitchen.

'As well as expected. Have you rung Cassie yet?'

'Yeah. Rang her as soon as we got here yesterday.'

'Why didn't you remind me to ring Jen?'

Elvis' shrug was the nonchalant kind. 'I don't know. I thought you'd rung her.'

'Did she give you a bollockin'?' Tetley, asked struggling to suppress a smirk.

'No. Well … kind of.'

'E' are love,' Carol said, handing me a cup of tea.

More bloody tea? Tetley certainly wasn't exaggerating when he often told us over the years how anything can be achieved, fixed, negotiated or sealed over a cup of tea.

'So, what have you got planned for today, Scotty?' Carol asked.

'I was hoping to get out to The Park Estate, have a look around, maybe speak with the witness.'

Tetley nodded. 'I'll take you out there.'

'Thanks, but, uhm … I was thinking maybe I should hire a car.'

'What for?' Tetley's question mirrored Elvis' expression.

'Well, think about it. I'm going to be investigating. I can't be turning up with Laurel and Hardy.'

Carol laughed out loud, and it was good to see the laugh lines on her face getting some use.

'What do you mean Laurel and bloody Hardy?' Tetley said.

'I'll be approaching people who probably won't want to speak with me. It's gonna be a bit intimidating for them if three of us rock up, isn't it?'

Tetley and Elvis shared a glance and a shrug that said, 'Suppose so.'

'You don't have to hire a car; you can use John's,' Carol said.

'Mum?' Tetley said. 'Remember what Uncle John said before he left.'

'I know, but this is different. This is Scotty.'

'He distinctly said that his car is to remain in the garage at all times and no one must touch it.'

'Well, I won't tell him if you don't!'

Mother and son shared the same mischievous smirk, and it wasn't hard to see where Tetley got his sense of humour from.

'Cool, let me know when you're ready to go, Scotty, and I'll take you up to the garage.' Tetley said.

'Best finish me tea first, eh?' I said, lifting the mug to my mouth.

The three of us walked at a steady pace with our hands in our pockets. Elvis and I were glad for the loan of coats that belonged to Tetley's Uncle John. I wore a grey, felt, knee-length jacket. Elvis' was similar but blue and with narrower collars. Tetley informed us that this type of coat was called a Crombie. It was still quite cold … well, cold for three lads from the Gold Coast, but at least the rain had stopped. We continued up the street. I say 'up' because there was a slight incline. When we reached the telephone box on the corner, we turned left and found ourselves at the top of a reasonably steep hill. The street sign read, 'Darley Avenue'. On the opposite side of the road, I noticed a row of garages running at a right angle with the street. Ten units in all that resembled the sheds like the storage companies in Australia.

'These are owned by the council,' Tetley said. 'If you're lucky enough, or if you've had your name on the waiting list for donkey's years, you can rent one.'

'So, your uncle keeps his car in one of these?' Elvis asked.

'Yep.'

'Away from the house?'

'Yep. The only other option is to park it on the street. And you can imagine what a shit fight that is.'

We strolled along the row of garages, each with identical roller doors and chipped paint, until we reached number 9.

'This is it,' Tetley said, producing a bunch of keys from his pocket. After finding the right key from the bunch, bending down and placing it in the lock, he lifted the garage roller door with all his might and let it fly to the top of its rails. 'Ta dah!' he cried, turning towards us with his arms out wide.

'Bloody hell!' Elvis and I said in unison.

Inside the garage was a gleaming classic. 'A Jag?' I wasn't sure if I was asking a question or exclaiming the point.

'Yep, 1982 Jaguar XJ6.'

'Wow!' Once again, Elvis and I were in sync. Then we waited patiently as Tetley squeezed into the narrow space down the driver's side of the car, carefully opened the car door and struggled to get inside. Once he was in, he turned the ignition, and the engine purred to life. Being the owner of a classic car myself—first the VW Beetle (the Dub) that I'd owned since leaving school, and tragically lost when my house burnt down, and more recently a 1969 Porsche 911 that was gifted to me by Australian rock star Phil Sexton after I'd solved the case of his brother's murder—meant I understood why Tetley was sitting in the car allowing the engine to warm up. After a few minutes, he gingerly drove it out of the garage.

<h1 style="text-align:center">12</h1>

The car … no … the *limousine,* was immaculate. Subtle metallic flake in a highly polished burgundy paint. Chrome grill, bumpers, trim, and wheels that glistened even though there was no sun. The interior was just as impressive. Chocolate brown leather seats as big as armchairs. An enormous teak dashboard, and thick, beige carpets that made you want to take off your shoes. *Wow!* I'd be riding the streets of Nottingham in style. The only fly in the ointment was that I'd need to take out insurance. In the UK, unlike Australia, it is the driver that is insured and not the vehicle, which meant you needed more than just a driver's licence to drive. You needed comprehensive insurance. And it wasn't bloody cheap. We were able to take out a policy online. Carol had insisted on paying for it, but I was having none of that. Elvis and I agreed to go halves. Incidentally, we probably could have hired a car for around the same price, but a Kia ain't no Jaguar.

The engine was smooth, but I could feel the weight of the vehicle as I slowly pulled out onto the street. The car, although immaculate inside, obviously wasn't equipped with all the mod cons. The original FM radio and cassette player were the only tech. Thankfully, Tetley's uncle had installed a phone holder that hung from one of the aircon vents, so before heading off, I'd entered 'Cavendish Road, Park Estate' into my phone's sat nav. Doris (or Dorey, the fond name I used for my sat nav girl) gave me a sense of welcomed familiarity as she told me, in an Australian accent, to proceed to the end of the street and turn right onto Bobbersmill Road.

Elvis and Tetley waved, and I gave a gentle tap on the horn as I pulled away.

I'd heard from a few people who travelled to the UK how bad the traffic was, and if you'd asked me five or ten years ago, I would have agreed. There were cars everywhere. But to be honest, it's not much better on the Gold Coast nowadays. Having lived there for over twenty years, I'd witnessed a lot of change. The growth of the population, sparking an immediate need for development and infrastructure, has proved quite drastic over a relatively short period. But I couldn't complain. I still lived in the best place in the world, and you couldn't blame other people for wanting to do the same.

One thing I did notice was the courtesy of the other drivers. They seemed happy to give way on the narrow streets. I was grateful for this while driving a car that felt as wide as a house, weaving through the parked cars on either side. A mutual wave as you passed seemed to be the correct etiquette, something I would adopt as well as learning to give way.

Alfreton Road at the bottom of Bobbersmill was a main road, and heavily congested. Edging out into the traffic, I wondered if borrowing Uncle John's car was the right choice. A small rental would have been more practical.

By cutting across Alfreton Road and heading up Churchfield Lane, I was hoping Doris had found a shortcut and wasn't sending me on one of those fruitless errands that happened now and again. Ten minutes later, I turned off Derby Road and into The Park Estate. Well done, Dorey.

Wow, what a difference compared to Bobbersmill. Wide, tree-lined streets and large detached houses, mostly old, greeted me. As you entered the estate, some buildings appeared to have been converted into flats, probably student accommodation. From my research, I'd learned that Nottingham was a university city, so I guessed that this area, being central to the two main campuses, was a temporary home for the students from wealthy families. But as I drove deeper into the estate, the area became more exclusive, with red brick Victorian mansions. Most of these houses were on large plots with driveways and garages. Doctors, lawyers, high-profile businesspeople and footballers, I surmised, were the occupants of these beautiful homes.

From the overhead view on the sat nav, I could see that the estate was circular, its streets surrounding what looked like a village green in the middle. There were two of these areas called circuses. Cavendish Road was the second street from the centre.

'You have arrived at your destination.'

'Thanks, Dorey.'

There were a couple of police cars parked outside The Coach House. A line of vehicles: a van, a late-model Mercedes and what looked like some kind of old Austin, meant I had to park a little farther down the street.

When I climbed out of the car, a sense of calm struck me as a gentle breeze rustled through ancient chestnut trees, stimulating the *coo coo* of a distant wood pigeon.

There was no need to check which house the witness, William Henley, lived in. I was pretty sure he was the old guy watching me from over his fence across the street.

'G'day!' I called across with a friendly wave.

As if being sprung for doing something he shouldn't have, he immediately ducked behind the fence.

I wasn't about to let that go. 'Hi. William, isn't it?' I asked after crossing the street.

'I've got nothing else to say.' The voice came through the fence.

'My name's Scotty, I—'

'I know who you are. Another one of those reporters.'

'No, I'm not a reporter.' For some reason I thought twice about telling him I was a detective. 'Mr Henley, if I could have a minute.'

Still silence. The fence, a weaved timber that smelled of creosote, was only about 1.2 metres high, but was set on four courses of brick, which made it higher. Behind it was a manicured privet hedge that gave it another foot.

'Are you still there, Mister Henley?'

I couldn't be sure if he'd ducked back into the house or was hiding behind the fence. The latter proved to be the case when I stepped up onto the course of bricks and peered over.

When he saw me, he froze with fright.

'It's okay, Mister Henley. I'm not here to harm you. I just wanted to—'

'I've told the police everything I know. I just want to be left alone now.'

'I appreciate that, Sir.' And I did. I'd read his statement, so I was up to speed with his account of what happened on the evening of Janita's death.

'Go away. Now please.'

I was getting nowhere. A glance around what looked like a stolen corner of a botanical garden told me that the man was an avid gardener. Knowledge I could use later perhaps.

'Scotty, what the hell are you doing?'

Stepping down from the fence, I turned to find DI Weston (Stewie) marching across the street towards me.

13

The Coach House was hidden behind a large arched gateway, and a six-foot wall. Both were built from stone blocks, giving them an older appearance than the surrounding houses. The gate was dark hardwood, probably English oak, and if it were closed, you'd have no way of knowing what was behind it. Today it was open, with crime scene tape hung across it, and a uniformed officer standing on guard.

Lifting the tape, allowing me to enter, Stewie showed me into a cobblestoned courtyard. The house was surprisingly small, but then I remembered it was a coach house, and the only survivor of an enormous estate that once stood in the surrounding area. An arched doorway of about the same size as the gate was obviously once the entrance for the Squire's stagecoach. The steel and glass door was in two halves. The windows were quite small, and the wall was hidden behind a blanket of ivy. Squinting, it wasn't difficult to imagine how the place would have looked 150 years ago. Apart from the double glazing and the satellite dish below the guttering, I guessed it had changed very little.

'Your timing's good,' Stewie said. 'Today's the last day we have it. We hand it back to the owner tomorrow.'

One side of the door was open. Stewie led the way into what was now an open space. After a quick scan of the room, which had basically been stripped during the renovation, the floor was flagstone paving, which I assumed was original. The kitchen had been ripped out, leaving bare crumbling plaster and exposed pipes. But what caught my eye was the artificial wall that spanned the opposite end of the room. About a metre and a half deep, and made of timber framing, the stonework and sheeting that once covered it had been removed, revealing a coppice of pipes and wires. On closer inspection, I also noticed it had been hiding a lovely Victorian fireplace.

'You see, there was no plumbing when this place was built,' Stewie said. 'Not even electricity. Before O'Donnell acquired it, it had been standing empty for years. Still had the original gas lights, apparently.'

'So, this is where the body was found?' I already knew the answer but felt the need to ask anyway.

'Yes, she was propped up between those two pipes there.' Stewie pointed to the two largest pipes that were sheathed in dusty pink insulation. 'Go in and have a good look if you like. We've been over it, so you won't be disturbing anything.'

Carefully stepping between the framework, there wasn't much to see. The area was well preserved. The old fireplace had been bricked up and there was a small ventilation block in the centre. But apart from that, the space would have been airtight, dry and very warm because of the hot water and the central heating pipes running from the floor to the ceiling. The perfect conditions for mummification. *Would the killer have known this?* Doubtful. The opinion was that this was a random killing, not one that had been planned out. I tended to agree, and a couple of scenarios were appearing on the secondary whiteboard that was stored inside my head.

Declan O'Donnell, by all accounts, was a powerful underworld figure with a history of violence. What if Janita had crossed him? Perhaps she was seeing someone else behind his back and he found out? Would this be enough to write her death warrant? O'Donnell had purchased the property without the knowledge of his wife and was setting it up as a love nest for himself and Janita. I guess he'd be pretty pissed off if he found out his cosy little arrangement wasn't going to be as perfect as he'd hoped. *Would he have killed her though?* Although he was never convicted of any killings in the past, it was widely believed that he was the orchestrator of many hits. I knew the type. A gangster running his patch with a heavy hand. Every town had at least one. The Gold Coast was no exception.

'Not much to see, eh?' Stewie said. 'The pipes, although insulated, were hot, and what with the lack of air and moisture, the body was preserved.'

'No fingerprints in here?'

'No, too old. Nothing we could lift anyway.'

After climbing back through the frame, Stewie gave me a quick tour of the rest of the house, which was basically a suite that took up the whole of the second floor. The walls had recently been stripped back to brick, with small chunks of plaster still hanging in places. The room was the same footprint as below but divided into three parts—a large bedroom at one end, a void in the middle (which I assumed would become the walk-in robe), leading into the bathroom at the farthest end, which would have been directly over the cavity below.

'This would have been the groomsman's quarters back in the day,' Stewie said. 'Kitchen, living and bedroom all on this floor. No bathroom. The old toilet's still out the back.'

'So, when O'Donnell bought it, it was still in its original state?'

'Yeah, derelict, had been empty for almost fifty years, but he didn't buy it …' he paused as if about to reveal something juicy. 'It was gifted to him!'

'Gifted? By whom?'

'The previous owner was Taffy Williams. Taffy ran Nottingham prior to O'Donnell; in fact, it was him who employed Declan as a teenager not long after he got off the boat from Ireland. Of Welsh decent, the patriarch of the Nottingham Posse, and an all-round nasty character, took a shine to the young Irish lad and took him under his wing, mentoring him towards bigger things.'

'And O'Donnell turned on him?'

'Of course, as is the law of the jungle. The young buck eventually overthrowing the alpha male.'

'What happened? Was there a showdown or—?'

'No. After a few years, O'Donnell became the powerful number two. Then one day the big boss was no longer around. Vanished into thin air.'

'So, O'Donnell took over. Did he kill him?'

'Of course he did! But there was no proof. Legend has it that the body is entombed in concrete under the Victoria Shopping Centre.'

'Hmm … so O'Donnell was definitely capable of murder.'

'Yep, or to arrange a killing. He had a lot of bad men working for him. The only problem is, we'll never know because he's long dead and buried.'

'Was there anyone else who would have had anything against Janita?'

Stewie exhaled loudly and shook his head. 'Not that we've come across so far.'

'What about the brother?'

'Seems like a nice enough bloke, runs his own business. The pair became estranged when he found out about his sister's profession. They're Sikhs, quite religious. She'd also borrowed money from him and never paid it back.'

'Do you know when he last spoke to her?'

'About a week before her death. They'd had an argument. She'd stormed out, never to return.'

'Do you know what the argument was about?'

'No, he reckons he can't remember, but I'm guessing she came to him for more money.'

'Hmm, I wonder if there is more to it?' I said more to myself.

'Well, that's why Carol and Sean brought you over,' Stewie said, patting me on the back. 'I wish I had more time to look deeper into it myself, but we're just about done now until the trial. Moved on, but I do envy you.'

'Eh?'

'A private detective living and working on the Gold Coast. Your own hours, your own timelines. Must be bloody awesome.'

I felt the need to play it down, but I couldn't argue. My life was great. 'Ah … it's not all that it's made out to be.'

'Bullshit! You're loving it, I can tell … eh … I've just thought of something …' He turned to face me. 'Perhaps we could go into partnership.'

'What?' I was trying to focus on the case, so I was hoping my lack of enthusiasm for Stewie's life-changing aspiration didn't appear blasé. It wasn't meant to be. 'Sounds great,' I added with a simple smile.

14

When we strolled out of the gateway and back onto the street, Stewie gave the constable on guard a nod and he began to remove the crime scene tape.

'That's it. We're done here,' Stewie said.

At that moment, a black, late-model Range Rover turned into the driveway.

'Great,' Stewie said under his breath. 'The owner. Christopher Collins. A bloody pain in the arse.'

A tall, athletic young man climbed from the car and approached us. He wore faded jeans, white scuffed sports shoes, and an old rugby shirt. 'Is that it? You're all done?' Apart from the old boy across the road, his accent was more refined than most of the people I'd met in Nottingham so far.

'That's it, Sir. We're all done. Please accept our apologies for the inconvenience.' A true professional. Dealing with difficult people while remaining polite was something we all learned in the academy, but few of us maintained.

'About bloody time. Have you got any idea how far back this has put us with this renovation?'

'I can only imagine, Sir. But I think you'll agree the circumstances dictated the course of action.'

'But why did it have to take so damn long? The forensics were here the first day. That was three weeks ago.'

'As I said, we apologise for the inconvenience. Can I introduce you to my associate? Mister Collins, this is Scotty Stephens. He's a—'

'A DI from Australia.' He pulled the same face we all adopt when we're confronted with something that isn't quite right. 'Why on earth would *you* be here?'

'You know me, Sir?' I asked, holding out my hand.

'I wasn't sure at first but then recognised you from a news report last year. You solved one of Australia's biggest murder cases.'

'I did, Sir.' My hand was still out and hanging.

Reluctantly, he shook it. 'Ah, that's right. The killer is from Australia. Now I understand. Has he committed previous killings over there? Is that why you're here?'

'No, on the contrary. I'm here to prove his innocence.'

'What? He's obviously guilty. The man killed a woman and hid her body in that house. Excuse the cliché, but it's an open and shut case.'

'Are you familiar with the facts, Sir?'

'Well, I should be. I'll be the leading prosecutor when the case comes to trial.'

'I see.' I looked at Stewie and could tell by his expression that he was as surprised to learn this news as I was.

'So, what's this? Like a working holiday for you, is it? Or did the Queensland Police send you over here in an official capacity?'

'I'm no longer with the Queensland Police.'

'Really?' His eyebrows almost touched as he frowned in my direction.

'I'm a private detective.'

A smirk expanded into a patronising laugh. 'They kicked you out?'

'No. I left of my own accord.'

'But why, man? You had a dazzling career ahead of you, surely.'

My nonchalant shrug was exactly what Tetley had warned me about. 'Whatever you do, don't do that. It'll come across as arrogant,' he said. Unfortunately, it was a natural response to certain questions that I didn't want to answer.

'So, I hope you aren't planning on snooping around here,' Christopher said, his expression suddenly turning serious. 'We've had enough of that, what with the police and the media.'

'No.' I looked to Stewie for support. 'I've seen everything I need to see.'

'Good.'

'We're done here, Sir,' Stewie said, holding out his hand. 'Thank you for your cooperation.'

The young man reluctantly shook his hand but didn't offer me the same gesture. Instead, he turned away and breezed into the courtyard.

Sitting at the kerb of this tree-lined street, the Jag did not look out of place at all. In fact, it looked right at home. Climbing into the comfortable driver's seat, I waved as Stewie passed and gave a gentle toot on his horn.

I'd made a list in my phone of the people I wanted to speak with. The names and addresses were in no particular order. One by one, I placed the suburbs in my phone sat nav. The obvious place to start was with the witness across the street, but feeling the need to tread carefully, I decided to give him a little space after our brief meeting earlier, before approaching him again. The next closest address to The Park was in Wollaton and belonged to Donna Simpson, Janita's friend and ex co-worker. The address was ten minutes away, so I turned on the ignition and activated the sat nav.

It was still mid-morning as I negotiated the way out of the exclusive Park Estate. Traffic was heavy when I turned onto Derby Road. However, a little over ten minutes, I found myself cruising along another tree-lined street. I have to say, there are some beautiful areas in Nottingham, and Wollaton was one of them. Not quite as exclusive as The Park, perhaps, but the houses were all decent-sized Victorian, detached two-storeys, with well-kept front gardens. When I was about halfway down the road, Doris announced my arrival at the destination. 'Thanks, Dorey.' Be kind to the AI. You never know; they might be our superiors one day. It was a joke Elvis and I shared, but, like hedging your bets on the existence of God, it had a ring of truth to it.

Once again, there were cars parked along both sides of the street. The only gaps were the driveways to the homes. Unlike in Australia, English drivers didn't all park their cars in the same direction; nose to nose and bum to bum didn't seem to be an issue, even though they were parked opposite to the flow of the traffic.

Number 59 was a smart 'arts and crafts' style detached building, with a single garage at the side of the house and a driveway long enough to park a second car. After noticing the waist-high wrought-iron gates were open, and a glance down the street confirming there were few options for parking, I turned into the driveway.

A glass porch and a timber French door with swirly glass inserts concealed the front entrance. There was a doorbell at the side of the door. *Ding Dong. Very quaint, very English*, I thought as I listened to the tone ring through the house. This was followed by the deep bark of a dog.

Through the opaque glass, I could make out another door. The front door proper. It was wooden, with a stained-glass panel at the top.

It swung open, and I saw a distorted figure approach. When the outer door opened, I was confronted by an attractive, fifty-something-year-old woman who, I guessed by her tatty jeans, oversized man's shirt, and her dishevelled hair, was in the middle of some kind of cleaning project. Leaning over awkwardly to one side, she struggled to hold a chocolate-coloured Labrador at bay by the collar.

'Yes? Can I help you?' she asked rather impatiently.

The dog continued to bark.

'Hi, my name's Scotty Stephens. I'm a private detective acting on behalf of the Webster family.'

'Australian?' she asked with a wry smile.

'Yep.'

She herded the dog back into the house and then closed the main door behind her.

'Where are you from then?' Her accent wasn't local. London perhaps.

'The Gold Coast.'

'Ah, the Gold Coast. I know it well. I was out there on a visa when I was younger. Worked as a barmaid in Surfers Paradise. Where abouts on the coast are you from?'

'Kirra.'

'Kirra?' She used the same scrunched-up expression Christopher Collins had used earlier. 'Isn't that the shitty little place near the airport?'

I had to smile. Kirra had a bit of a bad rap back in the day. 'You wouldn't know the place now. It's the most talked about suburb in Queensland.'

'Really …? Wow, I guess the developers cleaned up. What can I do for you?'

'I wanted to ask you a few questions if that's alright. I hear you were friends with Janita Sharma?'

She looked around cautiously as if to make sure none of the neighbours were watching. 'That's right, but I've told the police everything I know.'

I'd read her statement, all very formal. As usual, though, there appeared to be a few gaps that only a casual face-to-face chat could fill.

'May I come in?' I asked, nodding my head towards the front door.

She thought about it for a moment, then sighed and said, 'Only because you're cute. Wait here. I'll just put the dog out the back.' She disappeared back into the house.

15

I was beginning to wonder if she wasn't coming back. It had only been a few minutes since she'd returned to the house, but it seemed like forever. *Had she blown me off?* My concerns were dismissed, however, when she finally returned and showed me into the hallway.

A smaller version of a grand stairway greeted us in the reasonably sized space. There was no pushbike leaning up against the radiator like at Bobbersmill, and instead of the utilitarian tiled floor, a thick expensive carpet felt soft underfoot.

A doorway to the right led, or so I assumed, to the coveted and little-used front room. This was something that Carol had explained to me over breakfast earlier that morning. In the older houses, regardless of class, the front rooms were kept immaculate and never used.

Donna led me down the hallway and past the stairs. Through an open doorway I got my first view of an expansive kitchen.

'Would you like a cuppa?' Donna asked.

'Sure. Thanks.'

'Tea or coffee?'

'Tea, please.'

'When in Rome, eh?'

'Something like that. I don't mind a cup of tea, though.'

'Take a seat. I'll put the kettle on.'

The house had obviously been extended at the back. The state-of-the-art kitchen took up the left-hand side of an

L-shaped room. On the right was a large dining table. Around the corner was a tasteful, modern decorated lounge. The whole of the back wall was glass bifold doors, above which the ceiling sloped and had three skylights. The garden out back was quite large—a lawn and flower beds surrounded by privet, which must have been eight feet tall. There was a shed in one of the back corners. Next to that was a child's swing set. At the door, the Labrador barked and nudged against the glass as if trying to break his way in.

I took a seat on one of the barstools that were lined up at the expansive island.

'I say, "Put the kettle on" purely as habit,' Donna said matter-of-factly. 'No need for kettles nowadays, eh?' she said, filling two mugs from one of those dual taps that dispensed boiling and chilled water.

'Milk? Sugar?'

'Just milk, thanks.'

'Romeo, be quiet!' she yelled towards the dog.

'Your dog's called Romeo?' I asked, and the sudden memory of my little dog with the same name, who was no longer with me, brought a solemn wave to my demeanour.

'Yeah, Nigel's choice. He pretty much gets to choose everything around here,' she said as she stirred in the milk.

'Nigel? Is that your husband?'

'Yes. He's in insurance.'

Sliding one of the mugs over to me, she remained standing on the other side of the island. 'The Gold Coast, eh?' she said fondly, holding the mug between both hands. 'Gosh, I miss the weather. And the beaches?'

'Best in the world, I reckon.'

She nodded in agreement and took a sip of her tea. 'Do you surf, Scotty?'

'My bloody oath.'

The old Aussie phrase brought a smile to her face as if it had touched a fond memory. 'I used to go out with a surfer. Billy Willson. Do you know him?'

'Can't say I do.'

'No. It was a long time ago.' Her eyes were looking past me at the vision of a sun-filled life, long ago.

'So, you were friends with Janita?' I asked, breaking a brief silence.

She wobbled her head slightly as if appraising the question. 'Not friends like we would go out and do things together, more like associates really.' She blushed, and I sensed we were heading into sensitive territory.

'How well did you know her?'

'Quite well, or so I thought.'

'What do you mean?' I asked, seizing the opportunity to delve into details that may not have been in the police report. I needed to be careful, though, and ease slowly into the more delicate questions.

'Well, I didn't know her real name was Janita. I always knew her as Anita.'

'And was she friendly?'

'Yeah … well, most of the time. She could be a bit moody. She confided in me quite a bit, though. I got the impression she had no one else to talk to.'

'So, she told you all about her relationship with Declan O'Donnell?'

'Oh yes, but we all knew about that. It was common knowledge, especially when she stopped …' she lowered her voice, '… escorting.'

'But she didn't stop, did she?'

Donna lifted her chin and eyed me warily. 'Who have you been talking to?'

'No one yet. I'm just a brilliant detective.'

My humour seemed to put her back at ease, and she took another sip of her tea. 'She was earning too much money to stop.'

'But surely being O'Donnell's mistress came with a few perks.'

'Oh yeah. He looked after her. Bought her nice clothes, expensive jewellery. Put her up in a flat in town and was renovating the old place in The Park for her.'

'So, what was the problem?'

'He was trying to control her. She may have had all those nice things, but she had no money. Whenever she needed anything, she had to ask for it. I remember lending her some money not long before …' she abruptly stopped what she was saying.

'Not long before …?' My voice was soothing in an attempt to coax out information she may have held back from the police.

'Before she … disappeared.' She took a mouthful of tea and glanced towards the dog, who had now got fed up with barking and was rolling playfully on the grass. This brought back her smile. 'Did you know she was pregnant?' she suddenly asked.

I nodded. 'What was O'Donnell like?'

'A pig. Not that we got to know him or anything. We worked for him but would only see him when he breezed into the club, which wasn't that often. He was your stereotypical successful hardman. A nasty piece of work.'

'So, you used to frequent one of his clubs?'

'Yes,' she lowered her head, and the blush returned. 'That's where we'd meet the marks. It always had to be at the club so that they could lavish us with dinner and drinks with O'Donnell's outrageous prices before we …' She finished her tea and rinsed the mug under the tap.

In the interest of remaining sensitive to a delicate situation, I didn't push her to continue. She was an ex-call girl, an escort, a high-end prostitute. Obviously not the kind of profession that would be welcomed in this affluent neighbourhood. I wondered whether her husband knew about her past.

As if sensing my thoughts, she said, 'I know it all sounds terrible. Me being a ... an escort, but that was a long time ago, thirty years. Not long after Anita got out, I got out too. Went to university, got my degree and became a nurse.'

'Good for you.'

'Would you like more tea?'

'No, I'm good, thanks,' I said, looking down into my half-empty mug. 'When you say she got out ...?'

Donna suddenly appeared shocked. 'Oh gosh, yes. I never thought of that ...' Her gaze returned to the back of the room. 'She didn't get out, did she? She was ...' Lifting a hand to her mouth, she attempted to suppress a sob. 'She was here all the time. Killed and put behind a wall.'

I gave her a moment and then asked, 'But when she went missing, wasn't anyone suspicious?'

'No, we thought she'd just done what she'd planned, saved enough money and gone to start a new life somewhere overseas.'

'Is that what she was planning?'

'Yes, and she told me it was imminent the last time I saw her, so ... I just assumed ...'

'Do you know if O'Donnell was the father of her child?'

She shook her head and raised her shoulders and arms. 'Once again, we all assumed he was.'

'But she was on the game again, without his knowledge.'

'That's irrelevant. Our work would never result in a pregnancy. We took too many precautions.'

'What if it wasn't his, and he found out?'

'I got the impression that he didn't even know she was pregnant. She wasn't that far gone. But ... I have to admit there wasn't much in this town that Declan didn't know about.'

'And if he found out?'

The submissive shrug again.

'Did you ever meet Janita's brother?'

'No, they were estranged. As far as I know, they hadn't spoken for years.' She checked her watch. 'Listen. I've got a Pilates class at one, so I need to get moving.'

A glance at my watch confirmed it was 12.20 pm.

'No worries,' I said, rising from the stool. Before leaving the house that morning, I'd made some crude business cards out of strips of paper with my name and phone number on them with the Australian code. Calls would then come to me via my Australian network at my expense. 'Here are my details in case you need to get in touch. And thanks for talking with me.'

She took the card. 'That's okay, but I'd prefer it if you didn't come here again.'

My inquisitive frown was a mask. I was well aware of what was coming next.

'Nigel, my husband. He's a good man. He knew nothing about my past until all this came out, but he's in the process of accepting it. Hopefully.'

'I understand.'

We returned to the hallway. Donna opened the front door, turned and held out her hand. 'It was great to meet you, Scotty. You never know, one day I might talk Nigel into a holiday on the Gold Coast.'

'That would be great. You'll have to look me up.'

We shook hands, but after stepping through the doorway, I turned back towards her and said, 'Just one more question. Who do *you* think killed Janita?'

She inhaled and immediately exhaled as if she'd been asked the million-dollar question on *Who Wants to be a Millionaire?*. 'It sounds like all the evidence points to the builder chap who they've got in custody, but I wouldn't be at all surprised if Declan O'Donnell was behind it.'

16

Before backing out of Donna Simpson's driveway, I checked the list of names I still needed to speak with and the distances of their addresses in relation to where I was at that moment. Les Lane, the stonemason, lived in a nursing home in Forest Fields that wasn't too far from where we were staying in Bobbersmill. His former apprentice, Dave Anderson, lived in a place called Bilborough, which wasn't far from my current location, but interestingly, he no longer worked in the building trade. He was a barber and had his own shop in the city centre, so I guessed he'd be working at that time of day. Not being game to drive the Jag into the city just yet, I decided it could wait a couple of days. *Perhaps I was due for a haircut?* Tony Patterson was the son of Bill Patterson, the builder, who took over the family business after his father's passing. He lived in a place called Gedling, but if he was also working, he could've been anywhere in the city, so I decided to pay him a visit after hours. This left Sheila O'Donnell (Declan's widow), and her son, Rodney. Sheila lived in Bestwood Park and was probably retired, so paying her a visit during the daytime was on the cards. Rodney lived in London. *Hmm,* I wasn't sure how I'd speak with him. Perhaps a phone call. That left Javed Sharma, Janita's brother. His address was a newsagency on Alfreton Road. I was just about to check the location on my sat nav when my phone rang. It was Tetley.

'Hey, dick splash. Where are ya?'

'I'm in a place called Wollaton.'

'Uhh, posh. What you doin' now?'

'Just deciding where to go next.'

'Well, Elvis and I are heading out for some lunch. Do you want to join us?'

I suddenly realised I was hungry. 'Sure, where are you goin'?'

'Just around the corner, so if you want to come back here, we'll walk around together.'

'Cool, I'm on my way.'

I needed the help of Doris to find my way back to Bobbersmill. It was a fifteen-minute journey. When I drove up Bobbersmill Road, I couldn't believe my luck as I swung into a vacant parking spot close to our house.

'Here he is, Deputy Dog,' Tetley exclaimed when I walked through the door.

When we'd first arrived yesterday, I was worried that we'd lost our old mate. He was more serious than I'd ever seen him, and sad. But now it appeared he was back, and I realised that just Elvis and me being there had worked as a much-needed tonic for him. The by-product of this though was the banter. But I didn't mind that. I'd learned to give as good as I got.

'So, what have you been doing? Cruising around in the Jag all morning?'

'Something like that.'

'Tell us all about it over a pub lunch, eh?' Elvis chipped in.

This time we walked the opposite way, heading down Bobbersmill Road. After a short stroll, we turned left into a side street that had a row of brick terraced houses on either side with no front gardens, and side-by-side front doors opening straight onto the pavement.

Once again, we fell in with Tetley's brisk pace as if we were in a desperate hurry to reach our destination. At the end of the road, we turned right onto Berridge Road and stopped.

'And there she is!' Tetley exclaimed, pointing to an enormous redbrick building across the street. 'Berridge Junior and Infants, my first school.'

There was no need to tell us it was a school. It was lunchtime. Behind a six-foot wrought-iron fence was a playground full of children running, jumping, skipping, and screaming.

'I hope the place has improved since you were there,' I said, continuing the banter.

'What do you mean?'

'Well, they didn't do a very good job with you, did they?' I'd taken charge, and although I knew I'd be paying for it later, I couldn't help myself. 'Thick as pig shit yo' are.' It seemed right to add a bit of Nottingham twang.

'Listen to the teapot.'

We continued down Berridge Road. The imposing school building took up almost the rest of the street on the left. To our right were more terraced houses; these, however, were three storeys. Halfway down was a break between the houses, which opened out onto a paved square. On one corner was a house that was obviously once a shop. Lighter bricks around a small modern window clearly defined the outline of a once bigger, shopfront-sized window.

Two doors down, we stopped outside a house. Basically, it was a front door with a single window to its right. I noticed there was also an iron grill beneath the window, and I wondered if it led to a cellar.

'So, this is where it all began,' Tetley said, grinning from ear to ear. 'In the front room of this house is where my mum was born!'

'No kidding,' Elvis said.

'Yep … me Gromar lived here for over fifty years. I never got to meet my granddad; he died before I was born.' His eyes glazed as he spoke. 'We lived here for the first six years of my life. I remember Gromar scrubbing that front step and swilling the pavement out the front here every week.' He pointed to the grill. The coalman used to come and tip a bag of coal down there into the cellar. The milkman would leave two bottles of milk on the step every other morning. The rag and bone man used to trundle down here on his horse and cart yelling, 'Rag and Bone'. And I remember the chimney sweep coming to clean out the chimney before it got clogged up with soot. Ah, them were the days.' Still glazed, his eyes were seeing the house as it had been in his childhood.

'Are you crying?' Elvis said.

Tetley shook back to the present. 'No.'

'You are! Look, Scotty. He's bloody crying.'

'Soft twat. Come on, let's go. I'm starving,' I said.

The Lilly Grand was a large pub that stood on the corner at the bottom of the street. When we turned right onto Alfreton Road, like flicking through a mental Refidex, the address of Janita's brother appeared in my mind's eye: Sharma Newsagency, Alfreton Road, Radford. And I could see the property, not just in my mind but in person. I was standing directly across the road from it. What a stroke of luck! My next port of call was only a few metres away, and I could go there on foot.

The smell of beer and food met us when we entered the pub.

'Three pints of Shippos?' Tetley asked as we made our way to the bar.

Elvis and I shared a worried glance. Quickly scanning the beer taps, Elvis opted for a Fosters.

'I'll get a Fosters Shandy,' I said. 'I've still got work to do this afternoon,' I added in answer to my companions' expressions.

'Now who's soft?' Tetley said before ordering the drinks.

When the drinks were poured, we sat down on low stools at one of the small circular tables.

'So, how'd you go this morning?' Elvis asked.

'Pretty good, actually. Stewie gave me a tour of the crime scene. I briefly got to meet the witness, and then I went out to Wollaton to speak with a friend of the victim.'

'Sounds like you're making headway,' Tetley said in a rare serious moment.

'I am, mate. It's still early days, but I'm beginning to put together a picture of what happened that night.'

'Cool.' Tetley took a swig of his beer. 'I knew you'd be able to help us. Listen … I uhm … I haven't had the chance to thank you both yet for coming out here.'

'That's alright, mate,' I said, feeling a little uncomfortable. This truly was a rare moment.

'You've not only lifted our confidence but just having you here has lifted our spirits. Mum's hardly said a word over the last couple of weeks; it warms my heart to see her smile again.' He placed a hand on my shoulder. 'You've given us hope, mate.'

'It's the least I can do. Your mum and dad mean everything to me.' And they did.

'Thanks, mate. I appreciate it.' He squeezed my shoulder hard, then added, 'But you're still a knob!'

17

After a pint of shandy and a cheese and onion roll, or cob, as Tetley insisted on calling it, I bid the boys farewell and left them in the pub. Of course, there were complaints about my premature departure until I reminded them why I was there.

'No … you're right, mate. Sorry,' Tetley said. 'I appreciate the effort. Another pint then, Elv?'

You didn't need to be a detective to recognise the beginning of an afternoon session.

The pedestrian crossing at the bottom of Berridge Road literally led you straight to Javed Sharma's newsagency. A typical paper shop from the outside, a sign in the window read, 'Nottingham Evening Post'. And a handwritten sign on the door read, 'No credit given'.

After entering the shop, the inside was just as typical as the outside—rows of magazines, greetings cards, some toys, and of course, newspapers. The counter at the far end was a display of a variety of scratch-it cards. Above a cabinet of cigarettes on the back wall was a neon sign that read, 'National Lottery'. The layout was almost identical to that of an Australian store.

Seated behind the counter was an Indian man, perhaps early sixties but good for his age, quite handsome. He wore a grey polo shirt and was scrolling through his phone. He didn't look up when I entered.

Not being there to purchase anything, I made my way straight to the counter and said, 'G'day.'

Startled, the man looked up from his phone.

'Australian?'

This was pure ignorance on my part, but once again, I wasn't expecting his accent to be as broad as Tetley's. He sounded Nottingham born and bred.

'Yeah. I'm Scotty.' I reached over the counter to shake his hand, and he suddenly looked put out as if customer interaction was not allowed.

Reluctantly, he shook my hand. 'Alright?' He didn't offer his name.

'I'm a private detective acting on behalf of Colin Webster, but first I'd just like to say how sorry I am for your loss.'

'You're working for the monster who killed my sister?'

'That's not proven yet; in fact, I believe he's innocent.'

'Innocent? How can you say that?' He rose to his feet.

Not wanting to start our conversation with an argument, I took a moment and offered a casual shrug. 'I'm going to unearth the truth. If that means Colin did it, then so be it, but what if he didn't? What if it's an innocent man who is sitting in Lincoln Prison?'

'Why are you doing this? The police have already got the killer.'

'I realise this is difficult, and I apologise for bringing all this up again. I just wanted to ask you a few questions, if possible.'

The door to the shop opened, and in walked a short, elderly Indian woman. She approached the counter. I stood to one side to let her pass. After picking up a copy of the *Nottingham Evening Post*, she put the exact change on the counter, turned and walked out of the shop. Not a single word was spoken.

'I've told the police everything I know, which wasn't much. Janita and I hadn't spoken for quite some time before ….'

'But didn't she come to see you a few days before she disappeared?'

Realising I'd read the police report, Javed shrugged. 'So?'

'So, why would she come and see you after you hadn't spoken for so long?'

'She wanted what she always wanted, pal …' Anger tinged his tone.

This was good. My simple questioning was having the desired effect, and it was immediately clear that there was more to the jaded relationship between the siblings than Javed had told police. But I had to be careful. I was getting dangerously close to being thrown out of the shop. 'And what was that?' I asked, adopting a more sympathetic tone.

'Money, of course.'

'Family money? Or ...'

'What do you mean, family money?'

I'd remembered reading how important family is in the Indian culture and how the wealth is shared with parents and siblings. 'Well? Was there an inheritance she was entitled to? Or ...?'

'The family owed her nothing!' His voice was rising steadily. 'She threw all that away when she brought shame on us!'

Now we were getting somewhere. I nodded knowingly. 'With her profession, you mean?'

'*Phf* ... profession.' His eyes searched the walls aimlessly as he fought to control his anger.

But I needed to push on. 'Did you give her more money?'

This seemed to strike a nerve, and his face hardened. 'Why on earth would you ask me that?'

'Well ... I don't know. She *was* your sister, all said and done.'

'No, she wasn't. My sister walked out on us when she was sixteen years old.'

'Weren't you worried when you didn't hear from her for so long?'

'No ...' He took a moment to regain his composure. 'It wasn't the first time ... prior to her coming into the shop that day, I hadn't seen her for about five years.'

'But you knew she was still in Nottingham, surely?'

'Not really. How could I?'

'What did she say to you that day when she came into the shop?'

He sat back down and took a deep breath. 'Just that she was going overseas.'

'Is that why she needed the money?'

He nodded. 'She said if I gave her 100k, she'd be out of my life forever.'

'A hundred thousand pounds? Wow! That's a lot of money. Did you give it to her?'

'Of course I didn't. I don't have that kind of money lying around. She stormed off … and I never saw her again!'

And there it was. That something I'd been looking for. Don't ask me how to describe it; all I can put it down to is a detective instinct that I'd honed over the years after speaking with hundreds of witnesses. It was the micro glance that could easily have been missed, the shuffle in the seat, and the declining tone as his voice trailed off when he said, 'and I never saw her again' that told me there was more that he wasn't telling me. Was it sadness at never seeing his sister again? A subtle intrinsic joy? Or relief?

'Did you think she'd gone overseas?'

He nodded but remained silent.

'You never thought of trying to find her? Or …?'

He shook his head. 'No. It was good riddance!'

'So, how long have you had the business?' Changing tack, I asked cheerfully, looking around the shop.

'I think I've said enough. I'd like you to leave now.'

'Sure, sure. I understand. It's only to be expected for you to be in shock after losing your only sister.' I was gauging his reaction closely.

The nonchalant shrug. He was either a good actor, or he genuinely didn't give a damn.

'I'll call the police if you don't leave now.'

'Okay, mate. No worries.' I handed him one of my temporary cards. 'Here are my details. If you can think of anything else, or if you just feel like talking, you can reach me on this number.'

He didn't take it, so I placed it on the counter. 'Okay, thanks again,' I said, backing out of the shop.

Stepping out onto the pavement. I got a good view of the pub across the busy road where I'd left Tetley and Elvis. Checking my watch, it was 2.00 pm. They'd be well into it by now. For a fleeting moment, I considered joining them, but I took a stroll instead. There was a row of shops—a Co-op and a small bottle shop with a sign that read 'Beer Off'. Next to that was a laundrette. The sign above the frontage caught my attention—Sharma Laundry. *Hmm, I wonder.* Was this business also owned by Javed? If so, how many others did he have? He'd given me the impression that he wasn't a wealthy man. This was something I'd need to check out.

<h1 style="text-align:center">18</h1>

At the end of the shops was a servo. Mentally, I was correcting myself as I did when I saw the bottlo. Tetley's voice in my head said, 'Off Licence'. Now he was telling me the servo was a petrol station or a garage.

Soon I realised I was back at the bottom of Bobbersmill Road, so, crossing at the zebra crossing, I took a gentle stroll back up the street.

It was still early afternoon, which meant there was plenty of time to pay a visit to another of the players. Checking the list on my phone, Les Lane, the stonemason, was the closest, so I made the decision to go to see him.

Did nursing homes have visiting times? Hmm, I'd better call first.

Forest Fields was a five-minute drive from Bobbersmill. I Googled the Forever Green Care Home, got the number, and called them.

'Are you family?' The friendly female voice on the phone asked.

'No, I'm a private investigator, I—'

'It's family only, I'm afraid. Mister Lane is ever so poorly.'

'I just wanted to ask him a few questions.'

'I'm ever so sorry, duck, but Mister Lane's been suffering with dementia for the last few years. He hasn't been lucid for quite some time.'

'I see.'

'He'd be of no help, I'm afraid, but his family is here with him now.' She lowered her voice. 'We don't expect him to last through the night.'

'Oh, I'm sorry to hear that. Thanks for your help.' I hung up.

Driving out to a place called Broxtowe saw me turning right at the bottom of Bobbersmill Road, and although the streets were well signposted, Doris kept me up to date. 'Turn left onto Aspley Lane in two hundred metres.'

'Thanks, Dorey.'

After a twenty-minute drive through reasonably thick traffic, I found myself in what I'd come to recognise as a typical council housing estate. Houses were not unlike our base on Bobbersmill Road, but a little more utilitarian perhaps—red brick, unkempt front gardens, the usual wheelie bins lined up along the pavements, cars parked on either side of the street.

Sheila O'Donnell's house was at the end of a small cul-de-sac. When turning into the crescent-shaped street, I immediately noticed that there were no cars parked along the kerb. Number 56 was the left house and what we would call a duplex. Here it was a semi-detached, but the entire front of the white stucco building was paved with no dividing fence, giving it the appearance that it had been converted into a single dwelling. On the paved area were three cars: a late-model BMW, a Mercedes and a Jaguar SUV. Very nice.

Swinging around the circular street, I parked in front of the house while being careful not to block in any of the vehicles.

As soon as I stepped out onto the pavement, I was met by a beefy guy with short, cropped hair and tattoos around his neck and the length of his arms. He wore an Adidas T-shirt and jeans.

'Can I help you?' he asked. His accent, I guessed, was eastern European.

'Yeah, hi. I'm here to see Sheila O'Donnell.'

'Is she expecting you?'

'Not really, no, but I've come all the way from Australia to see her.'

'What's it about?'

The situation brought back memories of dealing with the Brennans—Mick and his mother, Moe. Mick Brennan was the president of the outlawed bikie gang, The Wasps. Moe was the well-protected matriarch who actually placed a curse on me. But that's another story.

'I have some information that she might find of interest,' I lied.

'What kind of information?' He was clearly blocking my path.

'I'm afraid I can only share that with Sheila in private.'

He narrowed his eyes and regarded me for a moment, then said, 'Wait here.' Turning, he headed off to the far-left side of the house, where I guessed the front door was.

A few minutes later, a high-pitched cattle whistle snatched my attention. Looking up, I saw old mate gesturing to me with one hand to approach the side of the house.

'I need to search you,' he said before letting me go any farther.

'Are you serious?'

'Do I look like I am joking?' His stare intensified.

Reluctantly, I held up my arms and allowed him to pat me down.

'Right, any funny business and you'll have me to deal with. Do you understand?'

'Loud and clear.' Bloody hell, I wasn't expecting this. I'd assumed I'd be visiting an elderly widow in the retirement phase.

'Follow me.'

As I suspected, the house had been knocked into one. What looked like a nicely maintained council house from the outside was a different story on the inside. Extensive renovations had created a large open-plan space. We were standing in a big kitchen diner with a similar layout to Donna Simpson's house, and the same kind of extension to the back with bifold doors. Two large guys, that I can only describe as thugs, sat at the kitchen bench drinking coffee. Both eyed me suspiciously while ignoring my friendly nod.

'Through here,' old mate said, without looking back.

Following him along the length of the room, and through a double French doorway, I found myself standing in a tastefully decorated living room with a baby grand piano in one corner. Internally at least, the house was a mansion by all standards.

Sheila O'Donnell was not what I expected at all. Yes, she was probably in her mid to late seventies, but a frail old widow she was not. Seated on an exercise bike by an open patio door and with a view of the well-kept garden, she chewed gum while pounding her head to a beat that only she could hear through her EarPods. She wore tight-fitting leopard print gym pants and a Taylor Swift singlet. Marilyn Monroe blonde hair, and gold chains around her neck and wrists swished and swayed as she pumped hard on the stationary bike. When she saw me, she immediately stopped pedalling, let go of the handgrips, threw herself back, and gasped a lungful of air.

Old mate was just about to announce me when his words were cut off by a heavily ringed finger with a bright red fingernail.

'Wait,' she hissed, then began peddling again but much slower. 'Cool down first. Fetch me my drink, Brinny.'

Old mate, or Brinny, Brin perhaps, left the room.

Sheila removed her EarPods, surveyed me momentarily, then grinned.

'Australia, eh? What can I do for ya, gorgeous?'

I was either going to get kicked out there and then for revealing that I'd lied to get in, or that slight grin may have worked in my favour. 'I'm a private investigator, and I'm acting on behalf of Colin Webster.'

'A private detective? Uh, God …'

'I wondered if I could ask you a few questions?'

Brin returned holding a tall plastic cup with a lid on it. He marched across the room and handed it to his boss. 'There you go, Misses O'Donnell.'

'Thanks, love. You can leave us now.'

He actually bowed his head before backing up and leaving the room.

Sheila stopped pedalling and climbed down from the bike, her thick makeup remaining undisturbed beneath a sheen of sweat.

While shaking the milky liquid in the cup, she asked, 'So, have you got a name?'

'Scott … Scotty Stephens.' *With the James Bond line again, Twat!* Tetley's words chastised in my head.

'Scotty … hmm. I like that.' She gestured for me to follow her out through the patio doors and into the garden, which I did. We took seats at a wrought-iron table and chairs. A gardener, who just happened to be around six-foot-six with an uncanny resemblance to Jason Momoa, delicately trimmed the manicured privet hedge with a pair of secateurs.

'Okay,' Sheila said, with an expression that was hard to read. 'I can either help you or kill you. What's it going to be?'

<h1 style="text-align:center">19</h1>

Grinning, Sheila broke the awkward silence. 'Would you like a cup of tea, duck?'

'Sure, that would be great,' I said, sensing it would be rude to decline the offer.

'Put the kettle on, Ivan,' Sheila called over my shoulder.

Turning, I realised that the two men from the kitchen had joined us and were seated at a larger table just within earshot. One of them rose to his feet.

'Milk with two sugars,' Sheila added. She didn't ask my preference, so I assumed I was getting the same.

'So, Mister Scotty from Australia, tell me again why you're here.'

The Nottingham accent was just as strong as anything I'd heard so far. Sitting there in the quiet, the two of us in one back garden, I couldn't believe we were in Broxtowe—the rough housing estate I'd heard so much about. It could just have easily been Wollaton, or even The Park Estate. But although the situation was very similar, I was a million miles from Moe Brennan and her house in Nerang.

'How familiar are you with the Janita Sharma case?' I asked.

'You're wondering if I killed the woman who was shagging my husband and buried her in the wall of their little love nest.'

I shook my head. 'No … well … unless you did?'

Sheila burst out laughing, and the phlegmy wheeze told me she was once a-pack-a-day gal. 'I like you, Scotty. So how come you're a PI? Wouldn't they have you in the police force?'

'I used to be a copper but gave it all up.'

Ivan returned with a single cup and saucer. If the clue in the name wasn't enough, he didn't need to speak for me to know he was from Eastern Europe—dark, slicked-back hair, wide-set jaw, not quite a unibrow but very close. He wore an orange floral shirt, beneath a tan leather jacket, and flared brown trousers, but the pleasant 1970s attire was cancelled out by his fixed, I'm-gonna-tear-your-head-off stare.

'This is Ivan, Scotty,' Sheila said. 'He doesn't like you like I do. Ivan doesn't like anyone.'

'G'day, mate.' It was a pathetic attempt on my part to lighten the moment and was met with an even deeper frown that reunited the brows. Ivan grunted and moved back to the other table.

I needed to push on. 'So, you knew your husband was having an affair?'

'The only thing I didn't know was when he wasn't. He was Declan O'Donnell, and he couldn't keep his dick in his pants.'

'Did you know about Janita and the house that Declan had purchased?'

Sheila dismissed the question with the wave of a hand as if she were wafting away a fly. 'She was just the latest in a long line ...' She leaned forward and lowered her voice. 'You see, we had an agreement, Declan and me.' She used her chin to direct my attention back over my shoulder. 'He had his girls, and I had my boys!'

'Right, so you didn't care that your husband was secretly setting up a love nest?'

She shook her head and took another swig of her sports drink. 'No, I only found out a couple of weeks ago when the coppers came knocking.'

'So that was the first you ever heard about this?'

'It was.' She eyed me up once more, but I sensed the suspicion was no longer present; her expression was more as if she were considering a side of beef at the butchers.

'I understand you have a son?' I asked, wanting to keep the momentum going.

Her face lit up. 'Yes, I do. Little Rodney.'

'And he lives in London?' This was basically all the information I had on the son, apart from the fact that he'd worked for his dad for a few years before moving south and buying a pub.

'He does. He lives with his … partner.'

I hadn't noticed that she'd had her phone tucked into the back of her gym pants. Retrieving it, she tapped the screen and scrolled with haste.

'There you go,' she said, handing me the phone. 'That's him when he was ten.' The picture showed a smiling, freckle-faced kid with a shock of red hair.

'He's a good-looking lad. How old is he now?' I was well practised at swaying a conversation towards familiar ground while at the same time taking control. Or so I thought.

'You're a clever bugger, aren't you, Scotty?'

'What do you mean?'

'I can see what you're doing …'

'You can?'

'A bit of flattery goes a long way.'

Realising it was a waste of time to deny it. I was busted. 'I know how it looks, but I mean it.'

Sheila grinned and put the phone down on the table.

'So how come Rodney went to London? I would have thought there was plenty of opportunity for him here.'

'Hmm …' Sheila sighed. 'He never got on with his dad. Well, that's not strictly true. His dad never got on with him.' She took a mouthful of her drink, and I wondered how long it had been since she had stopped smoking. I imagined she had once been a chain smoker who possibly had a health scare recently. 'Rodney tried so hard, too hard perhaps. But Declan rejected him time after time.'

'Why was that?'

She leaned forward again and lowered her voice. 'Declan never believed Rodney was his.'

'Oh … right …' *Tread carefully, Scotty.* 'And … was he?'

Sheila laughed out loud again, throwing herself back in her seat. 'You've got some bloody balls, lad. I'll give ya that.' She finished her drink. 'Of course he was. Rodney just took more after my side of the family than his dad's, that's all. Ginger hair, fair-skinned. He wasn't a tough guy like Declan; in many ways, he was quite effeminate. Declan, of course, hated that and would taunt him any chance he got. The gay boy, wally woofter, shirt lifter, all those horrible terms. I would have killed the bastard if I could.'

'How did your husband die?' I'd read the police report. Declan was shot in a gangland drive-by, but I wanted to gauge the widow's reaction to such a sensitive subject.

'Shot dead,' Sheila said solemnly. 'In front of this very house.'

'Do you know who did it?'

'I have my suspicions, but …'

I got the impression that the demise of her husband was no big deal, and I couldn't help wondering if perhaps she was behind it.

She rose to her feet. 'Well, that's all we have time for, I'm afraid, love. It's approaching Friday night. I've got two nightclubs to run.'

Standing, I offered my hand, which she shook. 'I really appreciate your time, Sheila. Thank you for talking with me.'

She smiled, flicked her head to one side and, like an obedient guard dog, Ivan rose from the other table and marched towards me.

'Ivan will show you out.'

'Great. Thanks again. See you.'

'Uh, I hope so, Scotty. Let me know if you want a good night out while you're here. I can arrange that.'

'I will. Thank you!'

20

What had taken twenty minutes earlier that afternoon, now took an hour to drive from Broxtowe to Bobbersmill in Friday afternoon traffic. I was feeling tired but was happy with what I'd achieved so far. First, beating the jet lag felt like a real accomplishment. Morris of the Good Old Boys, who swam at Kirra Beach every morning, had explained how important it was not to nap for the first couple of days. Even though your brain may have still thought it was 6.00 am, when it was actually 10.00 pm, you needed to fall in with the local time, which is what Elvis and I had done. Morris offered a warning though, that the effects of jetlag were worse on the way back home; it was something to do with flying into the light, travelling forward in time. We'd see.

After the second day here though, I was feeling weary, and I was hoping Tetley hadn't made plans for a big Friday night. If he had, I'd be abstaining. My plan now was to get back to Bobbersmill, update the whiteboard and go over the information I'd harvested so far, then give Jenny a call, and have an early night. We weren't scheduled to travel up to Lincoln Prison to see Col until Monday morning, so we had the weekend in front of us for any shenanigans that Tetley may have had planned. He did mention yesterday that he had a surprise for us on Saturday afternoon, but I was hoping to do a little more work, if possible, too. But for now, getting back through the horrendous traffic was my number one priority.

Leaving the Jaguar on the street overnight was a definite no-no. Both Carol and Tetley had insisted that it must be returned to the garage every evening. The turning space out the front of the row of garages was a little tight, and it took me a while to manoeuvre the large car so that I could reverse it into the tiny shed.

The front door wasn't locked, so I entered the house on Bobbersmill Road. The only sound was from the TV in the front room.

Carol looked up and smiled when I entered the room. 'Ay up, duck. Are you alright?' She lifted the TV remote in one hand and pressed pause, the face of a quiz show host freezing on the screen in a distorted shimmer. 'Where's the lads?'

'What? Aren't they here?'

'No. I haven't seen them since you all went out at lunch.'

Oh no. That probably meant they were still in the pub. If so, they'd be steaming by the time they got home. 'I had to do some work. Left them in the pub.'

Carol grinned and rose from the sofa. 'Do ya want a cup of tea, duck?'

'That would be great.' I followed her into the kitchen, and she filled the kettle from the tap and placed it on the stove.

'So how are you getting on?' Carol asked, beckoning me to take a seat at the small breakfast table. 'Have you spoken with anyone yet?'

'Yeah, it's going good actually.'

'Great, you can tell me all about it, but first I bet you're hungry, aren't ya?'

Come to think of it, I hadn't eaten since lunch. Checking my watch, it was 6.00 pm. 'I am a bit, Carol, but I don't want to put you out. I can get somethi—'

'Don't be daft. I've made a casserole. It won't take a minute to warm it up.' Without waiting for my reply, she opened the fridge and produced a glass casserole dish.

'Thanks, Carol. That'll be awesome.'

After scooping out a generous portion onto a plate, she put it in the microwave and danced her fingers over the keypad. Then she industriously went about carving two thick slices of bread from a loaf and buttering them. In silence, I watched through the microwave door at the dish rotating inside. After it went *ping*, a plate of steaming meat and vegetables was placed before me.

'You bloody ripper, Carol. This looks amazing.'

Carol smiled as she completed the service with a mug of tea. 'You are very welcome.' She sat in the chair opposite me and said, 'So, what's been happening?'

While I ate the delicious meal she'd prepared, I filled her in on what I'd been up to that day.

She sat quietly listening, not interrupting me once. When I'd brought her up to date, she asked, 'What are your thoughts so far, Scotty?'

'I want to be honest, Carol, I haven't come across anything yet that contradicts the police report. It's not going to be easy. Basically, the entire case is resting on the witness' testimony. Until I can speak with him, I can't get an accurate picture of what really happened that night because apart from Colin, he was the only one there.'

'Apparently!' Carol threw in.

'That's right. Apparently.' I reached across the table and took Carol's hand in mine. 'Don't worry, we're going to sort this out. We both know Colin is innocent.'

At that moment we heard the front door open and in breezed Tetley and Elvis. After staggering down the hallway and into the kitchen, giggling like naughty schoolboys, Tetley plonked a large, wrapped package down on the table and announced, 'Fish and chips for dinner!'

'Uhh, ya daft bogga,' Carol said, rising from the table. 'I told you I'd made a casserole.'

'Did ya?' When Tetley was drunk, he seemed to lose the use of his neck, so instead of turning his head, his whole body turned as one.

Elvis slapped a hand on my shoulder. 'Alright, mate?'

'Not as good as you by the looks of it.'

'We've had a great afternoon, haven't we, Tet?' He directed a somewhat glazed glance towards his partner in crime.

'Fuckin' ace,' Tetley said, leaning over the table and unwrapping the parcel. 'Ger us some plates, mam.'

Carol playfully slapped him on the arm and retrieved two plates from an overhead cupboard.

'Get Scotty one.'

'No, I'm good, mate,' I said, holding up my hands in surrender.

He shrugged and scooped handfuls of chips onto the two plates, which he then topped with two of the three pieces of battered fish. 'More for us, Elv.' He passed one plate to Elvis and without sitting, they both dug in.

'So, where you bin all afternoon?' Tetley asked with a mouthful of fish, and grease running down his chin.

'Working, mate.'

'Yeah? Find out anything good?'

'Maybe. I'll tell you all about it later, eh?'

'Yeah, no worries.' He outstretched his left arm so he could see his watch. '6.45. Right, we've got half an hour.'

'What?'

'It's Friday night. We're goin out, mate.'

'We're bloody not!'

'Oh, come on.'

Looking over at Elvis, I knew what stage he was at. From 1 to 10 on the I'm-fucked scale, he was nudging a 9.9. After his feed, he'd lapse into a self-induced coma. Tetley was probably around an 8.

'You blokes aren't going anywhere,' I said, sharing a knowing grin with Carol.

And they didn't.

21

The lads didn't go out again that night. Of course they didn't. Elvis went upstairs to get changed but never came back. Tetley did get changed but then fell asleep on the sofa while waiting for Elvis.

This worked perfectly in my favour because although I was tired too, I still had work to do.

The pictures of the victim and Colin sat at the top of the whiteboard. These were needed as a constant reminder of why I was there, and what my objective was. For Colin, I needed to prove his innocence because there was still no doubt in my mind that he hadn't done this. For Janita, the object was to find out who really killed her and why. So far though, I had nothing.

Looking down the list of names I'd made earlier, I wasn't sure of the terminology to use when describing these people. Apart from William Henley, they weren't witnesses, and they weren't suspects. People of interest? The term I often used was *the players*. Using an old household rag, I wiped out the list after deciding to rearrange it in the order I'd met them.

William Henley went at the top. Standing back from the board, I focused on the name and let my mind go to work. He was a strange chap, no doubt about that. The vision of him crouched behind the fence suggested that was normal behaviour for him. This didn't mean, however, that he wasn't a credible witness. He claimed to have seen or heard no one else arrive at the property. So what? Surely, he wasn't up all night watching the house across the street. What if the perpetrator had slipped in on foot after Col had left? According to the police report, the key to the property was left under a stone in the garden for the trades to use. Who would have known about it? The builder and his lad, obviously, and the stonemason and his labourer, no doubt. Did Sheila? Declan's son, Rodney? But then, of course there was the other scenario. What if William himself had entered the property after Col had left? I know this isn't completely fair, and this is just an objective opinion stored in my mind and for no one else to hear, but my impression of Henley was of the classic sex offender. Shifty, odd, a loner. His bio stated that he'd lived in the house all his life with his mother, who passed away last year. He had a clean record but was known to the police from frequent phone calls relating to complaints, usually about his neighbours. I definitely needed to speak with Mr Henley, but I knew how hard that was going to be. The necessity to meet with him on his terms set my mind a task on how to achieve this. I'd think of something.

Next on the list was Donna Simpson. A character witness for the victim, but was there more to her relationship with Janita than she was letting on. She mentioned that Janita owed her money but didn't say how much. From the perspective of a middle-class stay-at-home parent, she merely brushed it off as insignificant, but would that perspective have been different for a young working woman thirty years ago? What if the amount owed to her was substantial? Could it have been enough for her to approach the victim, knowing that she was about to leave town forever? I guess it all depended on the amount, and I was kicking myself for not pushing the matter further. I'd call her in the morning. As usual, my imagination created a visual scenario.

The silhouette of a young woman walking down a tree-lined street in the dead of night. She wore expensive high-heeled shoes, a short skirt and a tailored jacket. Over her shoulder was a Gucci handbag. When she approached the property, she slowed her pace to dampen the *clip-clop* of her heels. The front gate was open, so after checking the street each way, she entered the driveway.

What then?

Would she have known about the hidden key? Or did Janita let her in? Let's suppose she found a means of entrance, and let's just say she confronted Janita, things got out of hand, and she killed her. Would she then have the ability to remove the freshly hung sheet metal, wrap the body in insulation, place it in the cavity and then return the sheet exactly how it was? Doubtful. But what if she wasn't acting alone? In her line of business, she'd come across a few shady characters, no doubt. What if she had an accomplice? *Hmm* ... it may have sounded far-fetched, but I wasn't about to rule it out.

Javed Sharma was the brother of the estranged victim. While speaking with him, I got the impression he was talking down to me, as if I were below his class. He was probably wealthy but still worked in the shop. He was well dressed, fit and handsome. What would his motive be for killing his sister? When in his own words he'd exclaimed that Janita had brought great shame on the family, was he referring to her profession or the unpaid loan? I was guessing both. But could Janita have stolen from him just prior to her death? Or was this just a family feud? Either way, could Javed have killed his sister? Possibly.

Next was Sheila O'Donnell. A powerful woman, who you wouldn't cross lightly. Although she claimed that she'd only learned of the situation recently after the body was discovered, what if that was a lie and she'd found out about the love nest? And what if she'd also found out that his latest mistress was pregnant? How would that have affected the family business knowing that the patriarch had a possible heir to replace Rodney? Even in her more mature years, I got the impression there was very little that happened without her knowing about it. The cameras rolled with Sheila's possible scenario.

Of course she wouldn't have confronted the mistress herself; she would have sent one of her boys.

A black Mercedes pulls up at the kerb someway up the street with the headlights off. A tall, wide man of Eastern European descent climbs from the vehicle. He is wearing black jeans and a black leather jacket. His name is Igor (not really, but this helps with my visualisation). In stealth, Igor makes his way along the tree-lined street, careful to remain in the shadows. Romanian secret service in a past life, remaining out of sight is not a problem for Igor. When he reaches the open gate to The Coach House, he quietly slips inside unnoticed.

Would Igor have known about the key? *Ha!* This is irrelevant. Igor Chenkavic, also master thief in a past life, has no need for keys. The ancient lock is easy for him to manipulate. He slips inside the property and makes his way up the stairs without making a sound. The young woman is sleeping on a huge king-size bed. Igor's orders were to act quickly, no questions asked. With his powerful hands around his victim's neck, he easily squeezes the life from her in a matter of seconds.

While assessing the situation, Igor comes up with the perfect plan. Instead of disposing of the body at the pig farm out at Colwick, as was the usual procedure, he decides to leave it right there.

After carrying the body downstairs, he wraps it in pink insulation from a roll that is sitting in the corner. Next, he removes the steel sheet from the freshly constructed wall. This is not a problem for Igor, also master builder in a past life. He places the body inside and then replaces the sheet, entombing the body for the next thirty years. The perfect crime.

Alright, I may have gone a little overboard with Igor, but the scenario was a strong possibility.

The only reason I was placing Declan O'Donnell next on the list, and not at the top, was because I hadn't met him, and there'd be no chance of that happening.

The same scenario as Igor's, also worked for Declan. The only difference was that he would have known about the key, so he could have easily entered the property unannounced and unseen. Or indeed sent someone like Igor to do the job. Motive? Did he find out that Janita was going to leave him? Did she steal from him? Did he find out about the pregnancy? And if so, would having a kid with another woman other than his wife jeopardise his relationship with Sheila and lead to a breakdown of the family business? All of the above, perhaps? I'd need to speak with as many people who knew Declan around that time as possible. Members of his entourage, friends, associates. It meant I'd be entering the dark recesses of the Nottingham underworld, but if it was the only way to prove Col's innocence, then so be it.

22

Carol brought in a cup of tea with a couple of chocolate biscuits on a plate. 'How are you getting on?' she asked, placing the mug and plate on the table. She seemed to have forgotten my request about not entering the incident room, but I wasn't going to push it at that point.

'Good. I'm getting to know the players.'

'Players?'

'The people of interest, people who might have vital information that may have been overlooked.'

'We're so lucky to have you here, Scotty.' She reached out to me and gave me a hug. 'I'm having an early night.' She kissed me on the cheek.

'Goodnight, Carol.' I checked my watch; it was 8.30 pm.

A cup of tea and a quiet place were the perfect combination for my next task. Retreating to the bedroom was out of the question; I could already hear the dull drone of Elvis snoring through the ceiling. Poor Carol, I hope it wouldn't affect her sleep.

Calculating the time in Queensland, it was 6.30 am the following day. Saturday. Jenny would either be asleep or, more likely, having a surf, so I'd need to wait a couple of hours before calling her. Moving into the living room, I settled down into an armchair, turned on the TV and watched a rerun of *Midsomer Murders* followed by the local news.

Then, after almost falling asleep, I dialled Jenny's number.

She picked up on the first ring.

'Hey you!' She sounded much chirpier than the last time we'd spoken.

'Hey gorgeous, how's it going?'

'Good, but I'm missing you already, you bugger.'

'Ditto. How's the surf?'

'Pumping. I've not been back long.'

Jenny lived at the beach in Burleigh Heads, a little further north of Kirra. The surf around the ancient headland there was notoriously good, and I suddenly realised I was missing my early morning surfs.

I spent the next hour giving her a moment-by-moment account of my movements since landing at Heathrow Airport the day before. When I spoke about the case and the players I'd spoken with so far, she quizzed me as I would have expected and asked how I was getting on with Stewie.

'What can I say? He's a fan!'

'A fan?' Her chuckle only added to the patronising tone in her voice.

'Yeah, he knows all about me and the *X* case and that.'

'Wow. Doth thy fame have'th no boundaries.' Sarcasm was also on the menu.

'My bloody oath.'

Her infectious giggle made me even more homesick. 'So, tell me about the witness across the street,' she asked, going back to the case. 'Sounds like it's all hinging on his testimony.'

'That's right. Unless I can speak with him and hopefully find some cracks in his story, it's not looking good.'

'What's the next step?'

'Apart from William Henley, that's the witness, I'm gonna track down as many of the players as I can and speak with them. I'm getting the feeling that there was more to Ms Anita Madison (aka Janita Sharma) than the small amount of information I have. She was planning on leaving Nottingham for good, possibly moving overseas, but it appears she owed a fair bit of money to certain people.'

'Was she fleeing?'

'It certainly looks that way. Uh, and I forgot to mention, she was pregnant.'

'Hmm … the sugar daddy's the prime suspect, surely?'

'I agree, but unfortunately that's not the case. The prime suspect is Colin, because he was the last person to see her alive, and he was in the same house prior to her death.'

'Bloody hell, it's going to be hard, mate!'

'I know.'

'Good job they've got the world's greatest private detective on the case!' The sarcasm again.

'Yep. You know it.' I wasn't about to take the bait.

'How's Elvis holding up?'

'Uhm … yeah. He's good.' A sense of guilt suddenly swept over me. I'd paid very little attention to my best mate over the last two days. He'd just been through a horrendous year. 'How's Cassie?'

'Oh my God. She's pining.'

'Really?' The guilt again. Was Elvis pining too? I didn't have a clue what was going through his mind at that moment, so I decided to spend some time focusing on him the next day.

'She's keeping herself ultra busy.'

'It's only been three days since we left the Coast.'

'I know, she's ringing me up every five minutes with questions about the house.'

Cassie, apart from being Elvis' recent girlfriend, was the architect I'd hired to design the new duplex project I'd commissioned on the site of the old house on Ruby Street in Kirra.

'And that brings me nicely to the bit of news I have …' Jenny said with an air of mystery.

'Oh, yeah. What's that then?'

'I got a message from the builder yesterday afternoon, and guess what.'

'What?'

'We're breaking ground on Monday!'

'You are kidding me.'

'Nope, it's happening, baby. How exciting is that?'

'Wow!' It was a case of mixed emotions. I was ecstatic to learn that work would finally begin on the house, but I was also gutted that I couldn't be there to witness the event.

'Don't worry,' Jenny said as if reading my thoughts. 'I'll record it and send you the footage.'

'Cool. I can't wait.'

It didn't take long for Jenny to tell me what had happened in her life since my departure. Work, work, work, mundane cases, nothing too interesting to report. When the inevitable silence crept in after we'd exhausted the conversation, Jenny said, 'Right then, I'd better let you get off to bed. What time is it there now?'

I checked my watch. It was 11.40 pm.

'A big day tomorrow?'

'Yep. Apparently Tetley's got a surprise for us.'

'Uh, that sounds ominous.'

'My thoughts exactly. I'm guessing we'll be hitting the town tomorrow night.'

'Well, you be careful out there. It's a different world, might be overwhelming for a sensitive lad like you.'

'Yeah, right.' *Cheeky bugger.*

'I'm missing you, Scotty!'

'I know. I'm missing you too, love.'

'Come back to me soon, eh?'

'Will do.'

'Give my love to Carol and Tetley. No doubt Elvis and Cassie have already spoken, but let him know she truly is missing him.'

'I will. Enjoy the surf. I'm totally jealous right now.'

'Of me or the surf?'

'Both.'

'Alright, nighty night. Talk tomorrow, eh?'

'Yep … I love you, Jenny Radford!'

'Love you too, Scotty Stephens. See ya.'

She hung up, and I was left sitting there in silence. Well, not quite in silence. The sound of Elvis' snoring from the bedroom above was louder through the ceiling now. Then I remembered we were sleeping in the same room. 'Bugger!'

23

Sleep eventually came, even though I was sharing a room with Elvis and his snoring. It was picturing Jenny riding a classic right-hander off Burleigh Heads that helped me finally drift away. In her knee-length wetsuit, with her short hair plastered to her pretty little head, the ocean glistening under a cloudless blue sky And the early morning sun beating down from the west. The scenario would qualify as anyone's dream. For me, it was a reality. *How bloody lucky was I?*

The next morning, I was awake before Elvis. The pattern of his snoring had changed somewhat as dishwater daylight streamed around the curtains. The steady rhythm had given way to sporadic grunts and snorts that threatened to propel him out of sleep and onto the ceiling.

'For fuck's sake, Elv. Wake up, man.'

'K, Koor—what?'

'It's time to get up, mate.' I said, rising out of bed.

'Why, where are we going?' he asked with groggy, bloodshot eyes.

'Nowhere. But mate, you need to get that checked out when we get back.'

'What?' He rubbed his eyes and sat up.

'You're bloody snoring, mate. It's not healthy.'

'What do you mean, I don't—'

'Elvis, you bloody do, and you know it.' I grabbed the towel I'd used the day before that was resting over the radiator. 'Get it checked out because it's bad for your heart, sleep apnoea, mate. If not for you, get it checked out for Cassie at least.'

111

'Cassie?'

'Yeah, you can't expect her to put up with that.'

'Put up with what?'

'Ahh, mate, you're bloody hopeless. I'm going for a shower.' I left the room and headed across the landing towards the bathroom.

I had a shower. Well, I say a shower … it was basically me standing beneath a trickle of super-hot water. At least Carol had put the immersion heater on the night before, whatever that might be.

With towels wrapped around our waists, Elvis and I passed on the landing, him heading for the bathroom, me to the bedroom.

'There's no hot water left,' I mentioned in passing.

'You what?'

'No hot water.'

'But …? How? How can there be no hot water left?'

Guessing that Carol and Tetley had had showers earlier, perhaps the old system wasn't designed for any more than a couple of showers at a time, I couldn't help but chuckle at my best mate's forlorn expression. Even in our old house on Ruby Street, the hot water tank was the size of a grain silo. An exaggeration, yes, but we never once ran out of hot water—even after Elvis and Tetley's prolonged showers.

'You'll have to have a pommy wash,' I said, trying to contain the smirk that wanted to explode.

A pommy wash was something that we'd teased Tetley about over the years. The Australian impression of an English person's hygiene was a well-known fallacy. One bath a week, usually on Sundays, a wipe round with the flannel on weekdays. On arrival in Australia, expats were introduced to the shower for the first time; most fled kicking and screaming. Of course, none of this was true, but it was the perfect piss take, an answer to Tetley's constant banter that just kept giving.

'Good morning, Scotty. Did you sleep okay?' Carol asked when I entered the kitchen. She gave me a hug.

'Yeah, not bad, thanks.'

Tetley was sitting at the breakfast table eating a slice of toast.

'Where's Elvis, then? In the shower?' Carol asked.

'Uh … yeah. He takes a bit longer; he's a big lad.'

Tetley smirked knowingly. 'You've used the last of the hot water, en't ya?'

Luckily, after knowing Tetley for so long, I'd come accustomed to the terms he used—'en't ya?' meant 'haven't you?'.

'Yeah.' We burst out laughing.

Carol wasn't amused, though. 'Oh dear, I was worried about that. What's he doing?'

'Having a pommy wash.'

Tetley almost choked on his toast. 'See you bastards, the good old pommy wash reeks its revenge.'

'What would you like for breakfast, Scotty?' Carol asked, ignoring our mischief.

'Uhm …?' Looking at Tetley, I said, 'I'll just have some toast please, Carol.'

'No worries. Would you like an egg on it?'

'Yeah, go on then.'

Although the kitchen was cramped, I took a seat at the breakfast table opposite Tetley. Moments later, a mug of steaming tea was placed in front of me. 'Thanks, Carol, you're a legend.'

Elvis entered the room.

'Ay up, lad,' Tetley said cheerfully.

Elvis grunted.

'What's up, mate?' There was no way Tetley was going to let this opportunity go by. 'You look a bit put out?'

'No, I'm good.'

'Are you sure? You don't look your usual spit and polished self this morning? There's something different about ya. Look, Scotty. Do you see what I mean?'

'Yeah …' I squinted as I regarded our mate's awkward disposition. 'I'm not sure what it is, but yeah, I see what you mean.'

Tetley lifted his nose into the air, and I realised he was guiding us into the routine that he's been the brunt of all these years. 'Can you smell anything, Scotty?'

'Like … sweat, you mean.'

Tetley clicked his fingers and pointed at me in exclamation. 'That's it, spot on, sweaty armpits. *Phoor,* is that yo, mam?'

'No, it bloody well is not me,' Carol said, buttering my toast at the kitchen bench.

Elvis took the remaining seat at the small table and shook his head like a defeated child. He knew exactly where this was heading. It was a routine *he* had orchestrated many times.

'There must be a dead rat under the floorboards or summat, mam.'

'Sean, now stop it,' Carol said, placing a plate with two slices of toast and a poached egg in front of me. 'What would you like Elvis, the same as Scotty?'

'Yes please, Carol, that will be great.'

We sat there, the three of us, like patrons in a truckers' café, while Carol went about her work. I was surprised that Tetley let the situation go when he suddenly exclaimed. 'So, boys. It's gonna be a big day today.'

'What have you got on the cards?' I asked.

Leaning forward, he reached into the back pocket of his jeans and retrieved his wallet. With focused content, while somehow maintaining eye contact with Elvis and me at the same time, he produced something from his wallet. The logo of the red tree above three wavy lines told us what they were right away. Tetley's face burst into a wide smile as he held up three tickets to see Nottingham Forest play Chelsea at the City Ground that afternoon.

'Great, but what's the surprise?' Elvis said, not missing a beat.

'You're such a twat, Elvis …!' was Tetley's reply.

<h1 style="text-align:center">24</h1>

Later that morning, and at the insistence of Tetley, we caught a green double decker bus into town at the bottom of Alfreton Road. And at the further insistence of our bossy mate, we climbed the stairs to the top deck and sat at the back of the bus.

Dressed for the occasion, Tetley wore a Nottingham Forest jersey and a red and white striped knitted scarf under a black Harrington jacket. With blue Levi jeans and cherry red Doc Marten boots, a proper 'Bovver Boy' was he, or so he told us. His two companions, however, were a different matter. Elvis wore a pink 2023 *Cooly Rocks* hoodie with a picture of a 1956 Cadillac Deville on the front, the saggy-arsed jeans that he usually wore while dossing in the man shed, and a pair of tan boat shoes. I may have looked a little smarter in a Billabong sweatshirt, Calvin Klein jeans (half price from the Harbour Town factory outlet) and a pair of squeaky new black and white Nike runners.

We got off the bus on Parliament Street after exiting the roundabout on Maid Marian Way. I'd particularly requested this stop after doing a little research earlier that morning and discovering that Dave Anderson's barbershop was directly across the road from the bus stop.

'Alright,' Tetley said, checking his watch. 'It's 11.30. We'll have one in the Fox and wait for ya. Don't be too long though because we've got a fair old walk to the City Ground. Kick-off is at 3.00 but there's a few pub stops on the way, and we want to have at least one in the TBI (The Trent Bridge Inn) before we go into the game. Okay?'

'No worries.'

We crossed the road together at a pedestrian crossing, and I watched as the pair headed in the direction of the nearest pub, Tetley with an almost military-style march, and Elvis trundling behind with his hands in his hoodie pockets.

A sign behind a single glass doorway read, 'Dave the Barber, short and sweet and straight to the point'. There were no windows that I could see apart from the shops on either side of the doorway. This was explained when I opened the door to be confronted by a stairway.

Dave Anderson was the labourer of Les Lane, the stonemason, at the time of Janita's death. From the police report, I'd learned that he'd abandoned his ambitions of becoming a master in the art of stone, like his mentor and boss, and undertaken a career as a hairdresser instead. After learning the news that morning from Tetley that we were going to a Forest game, I suggested we go a little earlier so that I could pay Dave a visit.

So here I was, climbing a linoleum-covered staircase up to Dave's establishment. The barbershop was a single square room with windows along one wall looking down onto Parliament Street. There were six barbershop chairs along another wall, each with its own sink and mirror. A row of IKEA dining chairs ran along the opposite wall, and a reception desk occupied the remaining side.

A young guy was sweeping hair into a pile in one corner of the room. A girl with purple hair and a ring through her nose was cutting the hair of a young lad in one of the chairs. A guy, perhaps pushing fifty, but dressed casually in a T-shirt and jeans, sat in one of the barber chairs facing outwards, reading a newspaper. When he saw me enter, he jumped to his feet and closed the newspaper.

'Hi. Here for a cut?' he asked, placing the newspaper down on one of the waiting chairs.

'Yeah, please, if that's alright. I don't have an appointment.'

'Ah …' He wafted a hand in a camp manner and said, 'We're not that busy this morning, so all good. Come on.' He led me to the chair where he had been sitting and swung it around.

When I was seated, I ran a hand through my hair, which seemed to be a little ritual we all do at the barbers.

Dave swung the chair around towards the mirror, placed a paper tissue around the back of my collar and wrapped a black cape around me. 'What would you like, just a mullet trim?'

'Hey,' I reacted defensively. 'It's not a mullet, just ready for a trim, that's all.'

'Just a trim then?'

'Yes, please.'

He turned towards the mirror and went about changing the head on a pair of clippers. 'Aussie, eh?'

'Yeah.'

'Over here on holiday?'

'Not exactly.'

'Working?'

'You could say that.'

Lifting the mullet that wasn't a mullet, Dave began to shave the back of my neck with the clippers. 'What is it you do?' he asked.

'I'm a private detective.'

There was a sudden tremor in his hand, and I was glad he wasn't using a cutthroat blade. 'A detective?'

'Yeah … I'm uhm … I'm working on the Janita Sharma case.'

The buzz of the clippers stopped, and he stared at me through the mirror. 'You're kidding me.'

'Nope.'

'Is that why you're here?'

The wobble of my head was more of an uncommitted nod. 'Kind of. Are you Dave Anderson?'

'I've told the police everything I know.' He turned the clippers back on and continued to shave my neck.

'I know. I've read the report.'

'You're working with the police?'

There was a slight hesitation before I answered. 'Yeah.' Of course, this wasn't exactly true. 'Is there anything you can tell me about that morning when you arrived at the property?'

'Not that isn't in the report.'

'So, it was you who inspected Colin's work the next morning?'

'That's right. It was quite normal. Les always insisted that I arrive early at the jobs before him to make sure everything was ready.'

'Did you notice anything at all out of place?'

'No. The worksite was tidy. The guy they'd brought in, Colin, the night before to do the drywall had done a good job, cleaned up the site and removed all his tools.'

'Was there anybody else there?' I already knew the answer and realised I was clutching at straws.

'No.' He turned off the clippers, replaced them next to the sink, picked up a bottle of water with a spray top and sprayed my head while running a comb through my locks.

'Was there anything different at all? Did the drywall look as if it had been disturbed or—?'

'At a glance, no. Because the wall wouldn't be seen once the stone masonry was built, there'd been no need for fancy joins. Basically, the insulated sheets were just screwed onto the framework.'

'So, they could have been removed simply by unscrewing them?'

'I suppose so.'

'And then put back.'

He shrugged nonchalantly and produced a pair of scissors from his row of tools next to the sink.

'If there is anything you can think of—anything at all—it would be of great help, because I believe an innocent man is sitting in jail at the moment.'

Dave frowned as if in contemplation. 'There is just one thing I forgot to mention.'

'And what's that?'

'Shit … I probably should have mentioned this to the police. It completely slipped my mind.'

'What did?' I'd been in this situation many times before. Speaking with a possible witness in a familiar environment could often prise out that little bit of information that may have been forgotten when making a statement in the threatening environment of a police station.

'Les also always insisted on having a latte there ready for him to consume at the beginning of each morning. Thirty years ago, that habit wasn't as common as it is nowadays, so finding a coffee shop wasn't as easy back then, but I found one at the top of Derby Road on Canning Circus. I only had about twenty minutes before Les was due to arrive, so I headed off in my van.'

'And?' I asked, eager for him to continue.

'Well, just after I pulled out of the driveway, I saw another van approaching from the opposite direction. After it passed, I watched it through my rearview mirror and it turned into the driveway of The Coach House.'

'Did you recognise the van?'

'I did. It was Bill Anderson's.'

'Bill Anderson the builder?'

'The same.'

25

It was the first bit of useful information I'd received so far, but as I pondered on the information while descending the stairs and making my way back onto the street, I wondered if it was relevant. Bill Anderson was the principal builder; it was he who had contracted Colin. Would it be feasible for him to check the site before the stonemason arrived to finish it off? Possibly. The problem was that Mr Anderson had passed away some years earlier and had left no written statement. Would his son have known? There was no mention of it in the report, so I made a mental note to ask Tony, Bill's surviving son, when I got a chance to meet him.

According to Tetley, The Fox was on the same side of the road as Dave's barbershop, and only a short walk. I was heading briskly in that direction when my phone rang. There was no caller ID, but I answered it anyway.

'Hello.'

There was a pause and, assuming it was one of those annoying overseas marketing calls, I was about to hang up when a man's voice said, 'Is that the Aussie who's poking his nose into other people's business?' The voice was deep and gravelly.

'Who is this?'

'My name's Tommy Stokes. And I need to speak with you.'

'Okay.'

'Tell me where you are, and I'll send a car.'

'What's this about?'

'You know very well what it's about. Where are you?'

'I'm just heading down Parliament Street.' I was outside The Fox Hotel, the place where I was to meet Tetley and Elvis.

'Ah, you're literally one street away. Can you see the Theatre Royal?'

There was a white palladium-style building in the distance on the other side of the road. 'I think so.'

'Head towards it, cross the road, then turn left into Wollaton Street. On the right-hand side, you'll see Madison's nightclub. Buzz the intercom and tell them you've got an appointment with Mister Stokes.' He hung up.

Was I intrigued? Of course I was. Should I still go into the pub to rendezvous with my mates? Or see what this Stokes chap wanted first? *Hmm.* As I was making my mind up, my phone rang again. A picture of a scrawny, white arse on the screen told me it was Tetley.

'Where the hell are ya?' he demanded over the busy pub background noise.

'Something's come up. I'll need a bit more time.'

'Okay, we're gonna head off down to The Meadows. We'll see you in the TBI (Trent Bridge Inn). You might need to get a cab. You'll get one at the Market Square in the centre of town.'

'No worries, I'll see you soon.'

Madison's stood on a corner block beneath a four-storey office block. At the side of an underwhelming entrance was an intercom with a single button.

'Hi, I've got an appointment with Mister Stokes.' There was a slight buzz as the door lock released, and I stepped inside. Dim lighting barely lit the dark, rectangular foyer. There was a counter with a cloakroom behind it, ladies' and gents' toilets opposite, and a double doorway at the end, one of the doors ajar. Inside, the room was spacious, with a bar running the length of one side, a dance floor in the middle, and tables, chairs and booths around the outer walls. There was a DJ's podium at the end of the dance floor with a stack of audio equipment, and of course an enormous glitter ball hanging among a bunch of lights.

A middle-aged, stocky gentleman was sitting in one of the booths. He wore a tight-fitting, two-tone suit. His head was wide, and so was his neck. Short hair, thicker at the top, gave me the impression it was a toupee. But on closer inspection, it was more likely he'd undergone some kind of enhancement—a hair transplant perhaps.

When he saw me, he beckoned me over with a chunky hand. There was a significant gold ring on his wedding finger, which I recognised as a South African Krugerrand.

'Scott. Over here, son. Take a seat.'

Stokes sat on the left-hand side of the booth. On the table was a plate with what looked like a fried egg sandwich and a butter knife. There were condiments, salt, pepper, and tomato ketchup, as well as a tall Bloody Mary.

As I approached, he stood and held out his hand. When he grasped my hand, he pulled me towards him with a vice-like grip, knocking me off balance while holding me there in limbo. 'Tommy Stokes.'

'Hi, I'm Scott Stephens. Scotty.'

'Take a seat, Scotty.' He released his grip and gestured to the seat opposite him.

When I perched on the edge of the seat to his right, Stokes worked industriously on the sandwich. 'You can't beat an egg sandwich, Scott. It's got everything in there you need.' He peeled off the top slice of bread. 'It has to be white bread. None of that brown stuff or poncy multigrain.' With the butter knife, he carefully pierced the yolk and spread it across the sandwich. 'It's very important to break the yolk first, otherwise you're going to end up wearing it.'

While he worked, I was analysing his character. He was a hard man, no doubt about that. A boxer's nose. Ruddy skin with a network of fit-to-burst capillaries. Under his jacket, he wore a white, open-collar dress shirt and a thick gold chain. His choice of cologne was almost overpowering.

'What's this about, Mister Stokes?' His demeanour demanded the formal address.

Holding up a hand as if stopping traffic, he proceeded with his task. After spreading a thin layer of tomato sauce over the egg and sprinkling salt and pepper on it, he carefully replaced the top slice of bread. He then cut the sandwich from corner to corner with the butter knife. Momentarily, he sat back in his chair, raised his chin and took a breath of air before lifting the sandwich and taking a bite. 'I want to put an end to these rumours,' he said with a mouthful of food.

'Rumours?'

'About me, and that night.'

I didn't have a clue what he was on about, but didn't let on. 'Ahh, right. I see. That night.'

'Yes. Regardless of what you've heard … I didn't kill that girl!'

26

When the sandwich was finished, Tommy swilled it down with the Bloody Mary. Sitting back in the booth once more, he produced a toothpick from his inside pocket and regarded me for a few moments through squinted eyes. 'So, an Aussie, eh? From the Gold Coast.'

'Yep.' I wasn't sure where he'd got his information from, until he said, 'Bit of a celebrity over there, I hear.' He was using the toothpick now as he spoke. 'I Googled you earlier. Bloody hell. There's pages and pages of stuff about you. You've even got a Wikipedia page!'

I was blushing as I never did get used to being praised.

'I hear you paid Sheila a visit yesterday.'

'Sheila O'Donnell. That's right.' *Of course. Was Sheila Tommy's boss?*

'So, you reckon this builder chap they've got banged up is innocent?'

'I do, and I'm over here to prove it.'

'Hmm …' He was digging deep with the toothpick. 'That might cause us a few problems, Scott.'

'How come?' I was resisting his intimidation.

'This case is something that needs to go away.'

'Right … I see. So, your boss has instructed you to have a word. Persuade me to back down?'

'My boss?' His confusion triggered a temporary stall in the oral mining project.

'Sheila.'

His laugh was deep and loud. 'Sheila ...? You think Sheila's my boss?' He rocked his head back and continued to chuckle like a moped engine on idle.

'You work for her, don't you?'

The laughter abated, and he directed a fierce stare in my direction. 'I don't work for no one!'

'But this club, and whatever else Declan left behind, it all belongs to Sheila, surely?'

'No, son. You're way off. Sheila might think she's in charge, but there's only one person running Nottingham.' With his stubby index finger, he tapped himself on the chest. 'And that's me.'

'So, you're saying you took over from Declan when he passed?'

'Before then even. I'd been running the firm for years.'

'How did you two meet? How did it all begin?'

He sat back again and seemed to relax. 'We met when we were both bouncers on the door of Yates's Wine Lodge. A couple of real hard bastards we were.'

Over the next half hour, he told me how he and Declan O'Donnell rose through the ranks of the Nottingham underbelly. First they took over the security company that they worked for, then added to a growing portfolio—properties, small businesses (tattoo parlours, launderettes, taxis, and a towing company). And of course, the rackets, including a substantial money laundering operation as well as the escort agency. Then came the pubs and finally the nightclubs. There seemed to be no reluctance in sharing this information; it was as if he were boasting.

'From about 1986 until Declan's passing a few years ago, we ran the city together. He was the frontman; I was the bloke doing all the work in the background.'

'Sounds like you harbour some resentment.'

'Nah,' he wafted the accusation away with his hand. 'Since Declan's passing, I'm the man. I run this fuckin' town.'

'So, what about Sheila? Where does she fit into all of this? She owns this place, doesn't she?'

'No. She doesn't even own the house she's living in.' He suddenly raised a finger in caution. 'She doesn't know that though, and she must never find out. Declan left everything to me in his will, but with one stipulation—that Sheila be looked after for the rest of her life.'

'And she's got no idea?'

'No, she's got a little accountant who goes over the books with her every month, showing what a handsome profit she's making from all her business ventures. What she doesn't realise is that her little accountant works for me. The books he's showing her are fake.'

'Really?'

'Don't get me wrong; she's got a healthy bank account, one that will keep her in Gucci and Louis Vuitton handbags for as long as she lives. *And* she's got her boys, so she's happy.'

'What about the son?'

'Rodney?' A wry smile deepened the creases around his mouth. 'He's taken care of too.'

'How come he doesn't work for the firm?'

'He never had it in him. He wasn't anything like his dad.' Tommy leaned in and lowered his voice. 'A bit soft if you know what I mean. Declan didn't even believe he was his son.'

'Really?' Although Sheila had mentioned this, I didn't let on.

'Declan had promised Sheila that he'd be leaving everything to her and the lad, but he actually left them nothing. It was me who helped the lad out. I always felt a bit sorry for him.'

As information went, this was gold class, but I wanted to sway the conversation back to a comment that Tommy had made earlier about his involvement on the night of Janita's death.

But as if sensing a tactical manoeuvre, Tommy raised a hand and flicked his fingers.

A man immediately appeared from behind the bar—short, balding. He approached the booth with an air of dread. 'Yes, Mister Stokes?'

'How are your pipes, Trevor?'

'Perfect as usual, Mister Stokes.'

'That's good to hear. Line them up then.'

My questioning frown invited an explanation.

'I won't stand for shoddy management, Scott. This is a quality establishment, so the beer has to be worth the two quid a pint extra we charge.'

'Okay.'

'It's all down to the pipes. Have to be cleaned regularly and maintained.'

Trevor returned carrying a tray with a variety of beers in pint glasses. Carefully, he placed the tray on the next table, removed the empty plate and condiments from our table, and then set the glasses out in a row in front of Tommy. Each glass bore the brand of the brewery. There was Carling Black Label, Shipstones Ales, Home Ales, Mansfield Bitter, Kimberley Ales, Guinness, and an IPA called Little John.

Tommy lifted the glass marked 'Carling Black Label'. After sniffing it loudly, he took a sip and swilled it around his mouth. Anyone would have thought he was tasting the latest batch of fine wine. 'Hmm, not bad for a foreign beer.' He placed the glass back on the table and then slid it over to me. 'Try that, Scott.'

Lifting the glass and taking a taste, I had to admit, it wasn't bad.

'This is where we're way ahead of the other pubs and clubs. They don't clean their pipes, Scott. Do you know what I mean?' Tommy said as he lifted the next glass. 'I hate this stuff,' he said before taking a sip of the Shipstones Bitter. 'It's alright if you need a clear out,' he added, placing the glass down.

'Eh?'

'You know, if you're a bit clogged up, this'll get it moving.'

Remembering the taste of this particular beer from the day before, I too only took a cautious sip, and although the same malty taste was present, I had to agree that this one was crisper, perhaps fresher.

We continued with the ritual through the rest of the beers, with Tommy offering a brief history of the local brews.

'I'll not have too much of this new homebrew shit in the place,' he said after setting down the IPA. 'We're trying it out because I just took a substantial share in the Robin and Marian Brewery.'

Sharing his dislike of the new, overpriced and overrated brews that seemed to be everywhere nowadays, I reluctantly took a sip. It was … okay.

Tommy lifted a hand and flicked his fingers. Like a genie summoned by his master, Trevor appeared from nowhere.

'Very good, Trevor, as usual.'

'Thank you, Mister Stokes.'

'What was your favourite, Scott?' Tommy asked, redirecting his attention to me.

'Uhm … the Carling, I guess.'

'Fetch us two pints of Carling Black Label then, please, Trevor.' Tommy said.

Trevor retrieved the tray of drinks, backed away once more and disappeared behind the bar.

My phone buzzed in my pocket. Retrieving it, on the screen was exactly what I expected to see—the picture of Tetley's arse. At least Elvis wasn't calling me. There was a huge distinction between their bum pics. It was 2.30. *Shit.*

Noticing my hesitation, Tommy asked. 'Do you need to get that?'

'Uhh, no, she'll be right.' I was in need of something else at that moment.

'I need the loo, but.'

Although I'd seen the gents when I came in, Tommy pointed towards the exit. 'Just through there.'

After relieving myself in the spotless facility, I called Tetley back. There was no answer, and I imagined him and Elvis being carried towards a heaving stadium by a sea of red and white, very loud, Nottingham Forest supporters. So, I quickly typed a message. Will be there for kick off.

When I returned to the booth, there were two fresh pints of Carling.

'I've really got to go, Tommy.'

'Bullshit,' he said, gesturing for me to return to my seat. 'Not until I've told you everything you need to know about that night.'

It was an opportunity I couldn't miss. Reluctantly, I sat, lifted the glass and said, 'Cheers!'

27

Unfortunately, Tommy seemed to want to talk about anything else but that night as we drank our beers together. My attempts at swaying the conversation back to the evening in question were deflected with a history lesson of his beloved town. It wasn't all trivia, though. He shared some interesting anecdotes about Declan O'Donnell and some of the things the pair got up to during their rise to infamous glory.

'Tommy, I've got to go, mate.' Rising to my feet, I'd made the decision. I was bluffing, of course. There was no way I was going anywhere until I'd got the information Tommy had hinted at, but I needed to move things along.

'Course you do.' He stood, buttoned his jacket and gestured for me to lead the way. Making our way towards the exit, he called over to the bar manager. 'Well done, Trev. I'll see you next week.'

It was notably warmer when we stepped out onto Wollaton Street. Silently, Tommy marched back in the direction I'd come earlier, but just before we reached the Theatre Royal, he took a left.

'Where are we going, Tommy?'

'To Isabella's.'

He was setting a steady pace, and I needed to skip in line to keep up. 'Who's that?'

'Not who. What. Isabella's is my other club. It's just up here.'

As we walked, Tommy continued to give me a history lesson, pointing out buildings of interest. Behind the Theatre Royal was the Royal Centre, where the Emporium Theatre once stood. Behind the Theatre District was an opposing utilitarian building. Tommy informed me it was part of the University of Nottingham but would always be known as the Trent Polytechnic to the locals.

Soon the road narrowed, and we turned into an arched, cobblestoned alleyway. At the end of this was a closed, double wooden doorway, kind of like a barn door with no windows. Brass coach lights on either side of the entrance and a switched-off neon sign above it told me we'd reached Isabella's nightclub.

Like a scene from a 1930 speakeasy movie, Tommy tapped a secret code on the door. Immediately, the sound of a bolt being pulled aside was apparent, and one side of the door opened. A tall, stocky man with a black goatee poked his head out (Igor perhaps?), then stepped aside, allowing us to enter.

Inside, the club was similar to Madison's, only not as classy. A dark interior, lots of mirrors and brass with black and red upholstery. It was a typical nightclub where kids went to dance and get shitfaced on the weekend.

We took seats at a table opposite an expansive bar. Igor perched himself on a barstool, warily keeping his eyes fixed on me.

A young Indian man appeared wearing a white shirt that was at least two sizes too big for him, with stiff collars that seemed to have a mind of their own.

'Mister Stokes. It's great to see you again.'

'Good to see you too, Pavis. How are your pipes?'

'Good as usual, Mister Stokes.'

'That's good to hear. Line 'em up then.'

It was obviously a chore that Tommy undertook at least once a week, and I could tell he enjoyed it.

Checking my watch, I realised I'd missed kick off. It was 3.05 pm. Tetley would be pissed off, but hopefully I'd have a good excuse, if only I could tie Tommy down and get the information he kept hinting at.

'So, you were telling me about that night, Tommy.'

'What night?'

'The night Anita Madison died.'

His face suddenly turned solemn. 'Oh, that's right.'

Annoyingly, Pavis appeared with the tray of beers and then went about setting them up before his boss.

Tommy launched straight into the ritual, sliding each glass over to me after he'd tasted it. 'He's not as good as Trevor; needs a kick up the arse from time to time.'

The beers, some different brands from the last ones, didn't taste too bad to me except for the last one—a different IPA called Will Scarlet. Cloudy and a little vinegary, Tommy had already exhibited his distaste for it before passing it on to me.

'That tastes like goat's piss,' he cussed. Lifting his hand, he flicked his fingers as before, and Pavis returned to the table. 'What's this shit, Pav?'

'It's that new IPA you wanted us to try, Mister Stokes.'

'Your pipes aren't clean, lad. Look at it.' He held up the glass, emphasising the murky liquid inside.

'No, that's how it is, Mister Stokes. It's supposed to be like that.'

'Get rid of it. It's shit.'

'Yes, Sir.'

'And take this as a warning, youth. I'm watching you.'

'Yes, Sir.' The poor chap backed away.

'You see, Scott. You might ask yourself, why does he bother? And I sometimes ask myself that very question. I mean, this place isn't what it used to be. Full of bloody students nowadays, but they're still paying punters. And I'm all about quality, do you know what I mean?' He then barked an order towards the bar for two pints of Fosters. I guess I wasn't going to the game.

When Pavis had set down the drinks and returned to the bar, I leaned in and lowered my voice. 'So, you said you have some information about that night, Tommy.'

'Yes … I do.' He took a sip of his beer. 'Contrary to what you may have heard, Scott. I didn't do it!'

I'd heard nothing of the kind. In fact, before this morning, I'd never even heard of Tommy Stokes. But of course, I wasn't going to tell him that.

'Don't get me wrong. I would have rung her scrawny neck if I'd found her.'

'You went looking for her? Or—?'

'Declan had got wind of her little plan, you see. And he found out she'd been stealing from him.'

'So, he wasn't too happy?'

'More than that. When people crossed Declan O'Donnell, they disappeared, never to be seen again—or perhaps in some future archaeological dig if you know what I mean.'

'Did you go to The Coach House?'

'It was on my way home. I live in The Park, not far from Cavendish Avenue. I was meeting a potential Misses Stokes number two that evening, so I was keen to get back out.'

'Was Anita there?'

'Nah, of course she wasn't. That would be the last place she'd go—or so we thought.'

'What happened when you got to the property?'

'Nothing. I didn't even go in. The lights were on, and there was activity inside. The builder was mixing some kind of cement or whatever it was.'

'Did you approach him?'

'No. Like I said, I didn't even go inside. She wasn't there as far as I was concerned, so I headed home.'

'It's funny because the man across the street never mentioned that he'd seen you. Apparently, he misses nothing that happens on that street.'

Tommy grinned. 'He missed me, didn't he?' He sat back in his chair and put his hands on the table. 'So, as you can see, I didn't do it.'

28

I should have left after the taste test, gone to the game, saw the second half at least. But something told me that Tommy had more to offer. I'd let Tetley down, but I was pretty sure he'd understand once I explained how important the day had been for the investigation. Tommy seemed to be open to my questioning, so over a couple more pints of Fosters, I pushed on, changing tact slightly.

'I read in the police report Declan died in 2019, but there was very little information about how he'd died.' A lie, of course. I already knew he was killed by multiple shots from a drive-by shooting outside his home in Broxtowe.

'The killing took place in broad daylight.'

'Really? Wow!' Elvis always said I could have been a great actor.

'And the killer was never found?'

'No. No witnesses, no clues, apparently.'

'A rival gang?'

'Well, that's the strange thing, Scott.' *Was the twitch that had suddenly appeared a nervous tick, or a product of grief?* 'There were no issues at all with the other families at that time; in fact, Declan had drawn up a truce. For the first time, we were all working together—Leicester, Derby, Mansfield. There were no grudges.'

'Could it have been someone in the inner circle?'

Tommy lifted his pint and silently took a sip without taking his eyes off me. 'What do you mean?'

'I don't know. Sheila? One of the employees? The girls? You?'
The last part was a throw-in, which I probably should have given
more thought to.

'You think I killed Declan?' His eyes welled up.

'No, no … disregard that.'

'He was my brother!'

'Right, I'm sorry. I—' *My* twitch was definitely the nervous
kind. 'I'm just curious why you never actually followed through.
It looks like the police cared little about Declan's death.'

'I thought you said you knew nothing about the killing.'

Bugger. I'd slipped up. 'I only know what I've read in
the newspapers.'

'Maybe I did follow through. Maybe justice was served.'

'And did you?'

A subtle shade of embarrassment crossed Tommy's face as
he shook his head. Then, as if a light switch was flicked on, he
suddenly perked up. 'Hey, you're a detective.'

My quizzical frown said, 'So?'

'So, you can open an investigation.'

The frown deepened. 'Into …?'

'Into Declan's death.'

I was about to decline when he said, 'Name your price.'

'I don't really think—'

'And I'll pay all of your expenses. I bet it was expensive flying
all the way out from Australia.'

'Well, yeah, but—.'

'How would you like to fly back business class?'

'Business class?'

'You find out who killed Declan O'Donnell, and I might even
upgrade you to first class.'

Bloody hell. It was madness. There was no way I could take on
another case. The one I had was proving impossible. I was already
feeling as if I were in too deep. But it was none of these thoughts

that filled my mind as I shook Tommy's hand. Name my price and fly business class home—possibly first class? I was in.

'Okay, I'll need all the information you have. I'll need to speak with everyone involved with the case, no matter how small their involvement might seem.'

'Yep, I can arrange that.'

By the time I left Isabella's nightclub, it was 4.40 pm. Although there'd be a few minutes left of the game, there was no way I could get to West Bridgeford on time now, so I took a stroll back the way I'd come earlier with Tommy, until I reached the Theatre Royal. Once I crossed Parliament Street at the busy intersection, it may have seemed like I was roaming aimlessly, but I was following the directions Tetley had given me to the Market Square earlier.

Opposite the theatre was Market Street. A slight decline took me down to the centre of town. The Market Square was an open slabbed area surrounded by shops of different periods—modern, mid-century and medieval. At the far end of the square stood the Council House, an enormous palladium-style building made of white stone, with an impressive grey-capped dome. The clock in the dome said 4.45. At that moment, a loud, deep bell rang across the square, scattering a flock of pigeons as it did every fifteen minutes.

Double-decker, green and cream buses trundled in all directions around the square, and at the opposite end to the Council House, there was a modern tram waiting for departure.

I needed to get back to base and update the whiteboard, but there was no hurry, so after realising I was hungry as hell, I decided to have a bit of a look around. Walking towards the Council House on the left-hand side of the square, I crossed King Street and immediately saw a familiar face. Stood in the centre of a paved area, with his victorious hands held in the air, was a bronze statue of Tetley's idol, the man he often talked about—Nottingham Forest's greatest manager, and the best coach the England squad never had—Brian Clough.

The shops around the side and back of the Council House were still quite busy. A crowd of people adorned with plastic shopping bags and strollers seemed to be travelling in the same direction. An arched entranceway on the side of the Council House led me into a quaint arcade. Glass shop fronts with brass fittings were a reminder of a prosperous bygone age, as too were many of the old buildings that surrounded the square.

When I exited at the back of the building, I came across a Pret A Manger. Five minutes later, I was seated at one of the outside tables with a cheese salad baguette and a cup of coffee. My phone buzzed in my pocket, and I realised it was still on silent. Tetley's white arse adorned the screen.

'Hey, mate,' I said with a mouth full of food.

'What the hell happened ta yo?'

'Sorry mate. I got held up.'

'What, you've been at the barbers all this time? I know you've got a big head, but fuckin ell!'

A brief explanation of my afternoon and my meeting with Tommy Stokes soon calmed him down. I didn't tell him, however, that I'd agreed to look into Declan O'Donnell's death. 'How was the game?'

'Bloody magic! Two nil. Youuuu redddddddds!'

'Great. What are you doing now?'

'Just gonna have another pint in the TBI, then head back. Where are you?'

'Uhm … I'm just heading back now.' It was a half-truth; I'd be heading back after I'd finished my coffee. The last thing I wanted to do now was get on the piss.

'Okay, we'll see you at home. There'll be plenty of time to get changed and head back out.'

'Back out?' I'd envisioned updating the whiteboard before giving Jenny a call and turning in for an early night.

'It's Saturday night, lad. And Forest's had a win. We're out on the town, buddy.'

'What, here? In town?'

'Yep, see you soon. He hung up.'

29

I ended up getting a cab back to Bobbersmill from a taxi rank at the side of the Market Square.

Carol, bless her heart, was reading a spy novel but was glad for the interruption when I arrived home. After a little chat and bringing her up to speed on the investigation so far, I retreated to the incident/dining room and set to work on the whiteboard.

Under Tommy Stokes, a name I'd never even heard of before that morning, I wrote a list of dot points, in no particular order. These were just things of importance that Tommy had said, such as him being in charge of the firm and not Sheila, and Declan's feelings towards his son, Rodney—things I felt the need to follow up on. Tommy had given me more information about the case than I'd had so far, and I couldn't help wondering why he'd been so generous with his knowledge, and why he was so happy to share it with me. How did he get my number? And how did he even know I was in Nottingham? Was he telling the truth? Or was he spinning me a yarn to put me off the scent? He was hard to read and, excuse the expression, but he came across as being a bit thick. A typical punch-drunk thug. But I reckon there was more to him underneath the tough exterior—an astute businessman, perhaps, with a keen mind.

Then Rodney, Declan and Sheila's son came to mind and I decided to give him a call. After dialling the number he'd provided on his police statement, I waited patiently as the phone rang out. And there was no answering service, so I decided to keep trying over the next couple of days.

Standing there in silence, the room gradually growing dim with the onset of dusk, a blackbird in full song serenaded the end of the day from the back garden.

Then I heard the front door fly open. And all hell broke loose.

'Not, Not, Not, Not Nottingham, Nottingham, Nottingham. Youuu Redddddds!' Tetley came bursting into the room, followed by Elvis. 'Here he is. What happened ta yo?'

'I got waylaid.'

'You missed a crackin' game, din't he, Elv?'

'Yeah, cracking,' Elvis said with somewhat less enthusiasm.

'Two nil. Third on the ladder now, lad!' Tetley added, beaming.

'Great.'

Carol appeared in the doorway, and Tetley gave her a big, boozy hug. 'Ay up, Mam. We won!'

'Lovely. I'll put the kettle on.' She backed out of the room.

'No time for that, Mam,' Tetley said, checking his watch and then industriously rubbing his hands together. 'We've got to get ready and head back out.

Elvis exhaled and deflated slightly at the same time. I was guessing he was knackered.

'Do we have to go out, Tets?' I asked.

'Of course, we bloody do. It's Saturday night and your first weekend in Nottingham.'

'I've had a busy day.'

'Good to hear. You can tell me all about it tomorrow morning, but for now, get your glad rags on, we're guin' down town!'

There was no arguing with him.

Elvis and I reluctantly retreated to our bedroom to get changed.

'Bags first shower,' Elvis said.

'No worries. How was the day?' I asked, rummaging through the wardrobe.

'Yeah, it was good. Amazing atmosphere at the game. I got to meet a couple of Tetley's mates.'

'Yeah? What are they like?'

'Mental, just like him.'

Stripped down to his undies, Elvis wrapped a towel around his waist and left the room, heading across the landing towards the bathroom. Two minutes later, he was back. 'There's still no hot water.'

'What?'

'You heard.'

'No hot water?'

'Nope.'

'Shit.'

I went downstairs to find Carol back in the front room reading her book. 'Hey Carol, uhm, there's no hot water for a shower.'

Carol blushed and giggled. 'You're not on the Gold Coast now, Scotty. It's one shower a day here, if you're lucky. A lot of folks don't even do that.'

'Can we flick the heater on?'

'It wouldn't be hot until the morning. I'll boil the kettle and put the big pan on so you can have a wash.'

'Thanks, Carol.' Returning to the bedroom upstairs, I found Elvis sitting on the edge of his bed waiting.

'What did she say? Can she put the heater on?'

'No, she's boiling some water.' I couldn't help but smirk.

'Mate, I didn't get a shower this morning. I've been at a football game all afternoon, I've been in the pub, and I've walked bloody miles. I stink.'

'Yeah, you're not wrong.' It wasn't noticeable, but I wasn't going to miss the chance for a cheap shot.

'What are we going to do? We can't go out tonight like this.'

'Yeah, we can. She'll be right.'

Shortly after, Carol called up from the bottom of the stairs, asking us to fetch the hot water.

Elvis had a full-body wash in the small bathroom sink. I could hear him from the bedroom, splashing water all over the place, throwing it under his armpits and around his neck. 'Bloody ridiculous this is,' he cussed as he washed.

Thankfully, he hadn't used all the water, and it was still reasonably hot when I poured the last of it into the sink. It didn't take me long to wash my bits. After some deodorant and a splash of cologne, I was good as new.

We both wore jeans and polo shirts, mine blue, Elvis' white. With our best shoes on, we felt more than dressed up enough to hit the town. When we went downstairs, however, we were left feeling a little underdressed when we saw what Tetley was wearing.

'Bloody hell, where are *you* going? To a wedding?' Elvis asked.

Tetley wore a pair of beige chinos, a shirt, a tie, and a blazer, and he smelled of Brut deodorant. 'We're goin *out-out*, lad!' He was in the kitchen, and so too was Carol, who was washing dishes in the sink. 'Look at uhm, Mam. Typical bloody Aussies. I'm surprised you didn't wear your thongs, Elvis.'

'You're more of an Aussie than you think,' Elvis fired back. 'At least you said thongs and not flip-flops.'

'Deary me, I don't know. What're we gonna do we 'em, Mam?' As usual, whenever Tetley had a drink, his old Nottingham accent was as sharp as his wit.

'They look lovely,' Carol said, turning from the sink. 'Leave 'em alone.'

Tetley checked his watch. 'Come on then. It's time to roll. We're meeting Dodgy and Motown at 7.00.'

30

When Tetley had said The Fountain was a very popular night spot, he wasn't kidding. The pub was absolutely packed. When the three of us eventually weaved through the crowd with our heads down, the line at the bar was about three rows thick, all jostling to be served while a bar staff of half a dozen wearing the same black T-shirts did their best to meet everyone's needs as quickly as possible.

As we waited for our turn, there was a group of guys to our right, five of them, about our age, but acting like loud teenagers. The loudest of the group, a stocky lad with short, cropped hair and a Hawaiian shirt that was two sizes too small, saw us in the line and suddenly shouted at the top of his voice, 'Webby!'

Tetley stuck a solidarity fist into the air and yelled back, 'Dodgy!'

Elvis and I shared a glance that said, 'Webby?'

Dodgy waded through the crowd and threw his arms around Tetley. 'Ay up ya little fucker, how's it goin?'

'I'm alright, Pal, ya sen?' Was this Tetley speaking in his native tongue? He'd always had an accent, but this was fully blown Nottingham slang.

'Not bad. What ya drinking?' Dodgy said.

'Dodge, these are me mates from Australia,' Tetley said. 'This is Elvis.'

'Elvis, the king himself,' Dodgy said, taking Elvis' hand and shaking it wildly. 'We've heard a lot about you, lad.'

'And this is Scotty.'

'The detective?' Dodgy's eyes opened wide as we shook hands. 'Bloody hell. It's good to meet ya, pal.'

By this time, the rest of the group had pushed through the crowd. Like Dodgy, they were all excited to see Tetley and gave him a hug, except they didn't call him Tetley; instead, they greeted him with 'Webby'. And thinking about it, it made sense. Webby was obviously short for Webster. Sean Webster.

The four remaining lads were introduced to us as Motown Mick—a tall, skinny lad wearing a white Fred Perry polo shirt, tight Levi jeans, and black and white Adidas Samba shoes. Then there was Fred. He was a handsome black guy with the whitest teeth I'd ever seen in my life. Next was Terry, a short, balding lad. He wore a Nottingham Forest shirt and tracky pants. And last was Joe. Joe had short, blond hair and wore horn-rimmed glasses perched on the end of his nose, forcing his head to constantly tip backwards.

'Me name's Dave really, but these fuckers have called me Joe since infant school.'

'Why Joe?' I asked.

'Joe Ninety.'

I didn't know who Joe Ninety was but had to smile when the group burst into song.

'Joe Ninety, dah, dah, dah, dah, dah, dah, dah, dah, dah, dah, dah … dah!'

'I'll tell ya later,' Tetley said.

'Three pints of Fosters, is it?' Dodgy asked.

'Yeah, mate,' Tetley replied.

'I can't drink that piss, I can't,' Dodgy said over his shoulder as he joined the queue. 'It's not proper beer, is it?'

'No, yo stick ta ya Shippo's lad,' Tetley said. 'Ya give us all the shits any road so ya may as well 'av 'em en'all.'

Dodgy worked his way to the front of the bar surprisingly quickly and ordered our drinks.

'Why do they call him Dodgy?' Elvis asked Tetley.

'Cause he's a dodgy fucker,' Tetley replied.

I was about to question this more when Fred lowered his head to my ear.

'So, is yous that detective, den?'

'Yeah. That's right.'

'That's cool innit? Are ya gonna help Colin?' His accent was a multicultural mixture of English and Caribbean.

'I am, mate. That's what I'm here for.'

'Cool!'

'Do you get soul music in Australia?' Mick asked, changing the subject completely.

'Uhm, yeah, of course.' *Did we?*

'Motown?'

'Yep.' I wasn't super familiar with the genre, but I was a big fan of the Jimmy Barnes album, *Soul Deep*; however, I wasn't about to own up that that was about as far as my knowledge went.

'Yeah, I've heard they've got a thriving soul scene in Aus. I want to get down there one day, but it's bloody hot, init?'

'Depends on when you go and where,' I said, waiting patiently for Dodgy to return with the drinks.

Joe pipped in. 'What about the spiders and the snakes? How do you even leave the house in the morning?'

'Ah, it's not what you think,' I assured him.

Joe went into a detailed account of the number of venomous spiders and snakes that inhabit Australia.

'Yeah, but you never see them, mate. Especially at the beach.'

Fred pipped in. 'The beach? Sharks though, init?'

I realised there was no convincing these guys; they'd already made up their minds that Australia was the most dangerous place on Earth.

'Do you surf, Scott?' Joe asked.

'Yeah, most mornings.'

'Fuckin ell, mate,' Fred said. 'En't ya seen *Jaws*?'

Thankfully, I was rescued when Dodgy returned carrying three pints of beer. 'That's thirteen pounds eighty!' he said as he handed me my beer.

'Eh?'

'For the beer.' He frowned and lowered his jaw. 'You don't think I go around buying strangers bloody drinks all the time, do ya?'

'Uh, no. I suppose not.'

Elvis and I shared another glance. Was this an English tradition that Tetley hadn't told us about? Didn't the English buy each other rounds?

Tetley burst out laughing. 'He's messing we ya, Scotty.'

'Oh …' I should have realised. To us, Tetley was the king of banter, but here in his natural habitat he was probably just second-rate.

'Your face,' Dodgy said as the group joined him in laughter directed at me and Elvis. 'Ya gonna have to get used to us, lads. Right, piss tekers, we are.'

I was kind of getting used to the accent and the phrases they used. 'Tekers', meaning: takers. It wasn't that hard to understand as long as you followed along with the context.

'So, tells us all about the Gold Coast, then lads,' Dodgy said after we'd all made our way from the bar and found a spot in the corner of the room.

Averting my eyes to Elvis, they said, 'You can take this.' His eyes said the same.

'It's only the best place in the world,' I said, taking on the challenge.

'As nice as Benidorm, ya reckon?' Mick asked.

'I've never been to Benidorm, and I'm sure it's very nice, but yeah, I'm pretty confident that it's better than Benidorm.'

'It's hot though, int it?' Mick repeated, more as a statement than a question.

'The temperature's actually perfect all year round—'

'Sharks though, init?' Fred interrupted.

'And the spiders and snakes,' Joe added.

I was wasting my time.

'So, are you gonna find out who killed Javed's sister?' Mick asked, changing the subject once again.

'I'm hoping so. Do you know Javed, do you?'

Mick offered a nonchalant shrug. 'Only from the paper shop at the bottom of Alfreton Road.'

'What's he like?'

The same shrug again. 'He's alright.'

'Did you know the sister?'

'Hey, look at him. He's doin' it!' Dodgy exclaimed. 'He's doing his detectivin'.'

'That's what he's here for,' Tetley said, coming to my defence.

'Did you?' I continued.

'No, we were only kids when she went missing.'

Then Fred pointed behind us and said, 'Isn't that Javed over there?'

31

'Javed ...? Javed Sharma?' I said, competing to be heard over Depeche Mode.

Nursing a double whisky, and leaning against the bar, he turned his head and squinted in my direction. 'Do I know you?' Clearly, he'd already had a fair bit to drink.

'It's Scotty. Scotty Stephens. We met yesterday at your shop.'

'Oh, that's right.' He swayed backwards and forth as he left the security of the bar and stood up straight. 'The private detective.'

'We didn't hit it off too well yesterday. Mate, I'm just here to find out who really killed your sister.'

He threw back a mouthful of whisky. 'You don't get it, do ya?'

'Get what?'

'I killed her, you idiot!' He finished his drink.

'Eh?' Getting the impression that he was about to leave, I stepped up to the bar, so I was right beside him. 'What are you drinking?'

He raised his chin and breathed through his nose, regarding me with cautious eyes. 'What do you want?'

'You look like you need someone to talk to.' I knew a man trying to drink away his problems when I saw one.

'Teelings. A double.'

The young barmaid looked at me warily as if to say, 'I think he's had enough.' My 'she'll-be-right-mate' nod was offered as reassurance that I'd look after him. I wasn't a whisky drinker, but I ordered two doubles and handed one to Javed.

Looking around, I noticed an empty booth in the far corner. 'Over here, mate.' With a gentle hand on his shoulder, I steered Javed towards the booth and sat him down. Tetley and Elvis were deep in conversation with the Nottingham lads, talking shit, no doubt, so I didn't feel too bad about breaking away from them.

'What do you want, man?' Javed asked wearily. 'The police have already grilled me.'

'I know. I'm guessing you didn't tell them what you just told me, though.'

'What's that?' His deep frown told me he'd already forgotten what he'd just said.

'That you killed your sister.'

He sculled half of his drink. 'I've told no one that.'

'Why'd you do it?'

'Because she didn't really want my help. It was just another scam. She already owed me money from two years ago. "This is different this time, Javed. I need to get out, away from here. They're going to—" "Shut the fuck up!" I yelled back at her. "I've heard it all before, Janita." "Please, Javed. I need your help." "Get the hell out of my shop and my life!" She burst into tears and stormed out of the shop. And that was the last time I ever saw her.'

'So, you're not saying you physically killed her.'

'As good as.' Tears welled in his eyes and his bottom lip began to tremble. 'I should have helped her. Could have ... didn't.'

'What happened between you two? How did she become estranged?'

'You do know what she did for a living, right?'

'She was an escort.'

'That's just a fancy name for a prostitute. A whore.'

'But she was still your sister.'

'No. She brought shame on the family.'

'Was she banished?'

'Our parents died in a car crash when we were still kids, so I became the patriarch at a very young age.'

'Right, so you were calling the shots.'

'No … it was my duty to continue with our traditions, our family values. The family already owned a substantial business, the shops, launderettes, taxis. I had to step up and keep it all going.' He finished his drink.

'What about Janita? What was her role?'

He took another deep breath and looked into the distance. 'It was simple. All she had to do was marry a respectable Sikh boy and have lots of children.'

'But she was never going to do that.'

'No.'

'Would it have been an arranged marriage?'

'Yes … that was something the parents would usually organise, but it fell on me along with all the other responsibilities I'd had thrust upon me.' He was getting twitchy, and I realised he needed another drink. I didn't want to leave him there on his own, and the bar staff were way too busy to catch my eye. So already having the pint that I'd left with Elvis, I slid over my untouched glass of whisky.

Javed took the drink and then squinted hard at his watch. 'I should go. I've had way too much to drink.'

'Just have the one more, then I'll call you a cab.' It was irresponsible of me, but the situation called for it.

His squint deepened. 'Who the fuck are you again?'

'Scotty, remember?'

'The Australian … you were a friend of Janita's.'

'That's right.' I obviously wasn't, but I was happy to go along with it. 'You were telling me why you fell out.'

'She wasn't interested in marriage. Said she would eventually, but first she wanted to start her own business. A boutique in town.' He lifted his glass but didn't drink from it. His eyes had wandered into the past. 'Reckoned she'd already saved most of the money and that an opportunity had come up, a lease in Hockley.'

'So, you gave her money.'

He nodded and sipped his drink.

'How much?'

'Twenty thousand!'

'Wow, that's a lot of money. Then what happened?'

'As far as I knew, there was never any shop. I didn't know where she'd gone. She wouldn't answer her phone. The next I hear, she's mixed up with Declan O'Donnell.'

'Did you know about the house in The Park?'

There was a definite hesitation before he shook his head.

'Did you get a chance to confront her?'

'No, I tried, but at that point you couldn't even get close to her. She'd become Nottingham's first lady.'

'So, what did you do?'

'What could I do? It was a family loan, a handshake. So, all I could do was disown her.'

It all made sense. A family with traditionally strict religious values. Javed was the patriarch, the father figure, and his younger sister had not only turned her back on the religion, the family and their traditions, but she'd borrowed money from him with no intention of paying it back. What I needed to understand though was the reason for his current state of mind. Had the discovery of his sister's body hit him hard? Understandable, of course. Had he really believed that Janita had left Nottingham behind all those years ago, in search of a better life? *Hmm.* I needed to dig a little deeper. 'So, then she turns up again a few years later asking for more money?'

'Yeah. Something like that. All apologetic of course, said she'd pay me back the 20k in full.'

'How would she have done that?'

Staring sombrely down at the table now, he shrugged.

'Did you lose your temper?'

'Of course I did.'

'Did you … hit her?'

He raised his head and glared at me with bloodshot eyes. 'No. I was mad, but I would never …'

'Did you give her more money?'

'No. Just told her to fuck off and never come back.'

'And now you're feeling guilty for not helping her.'

He nodded and took another mouthful of whisky. 'I could have.'

'You helped her before, and look what happened then.'

'That's right, but … this was different. She was scared. I see that now, but I was still angry at her.'

'Of course you were.'

'I knew she was seeing O'Donnell. She said … she said he was going to kill her if she didn't get away.'

'But you didn't believe that.'

'No. She disgusted me, in her fancy clothes and her high heel shoes—' He lifted a hand to his mouth to prevent a sob.

'You were working your arse off with the business, doing the right thing, and here she was living the life you could only dream of.'

He shot me a defensive glare, and I worried I was overstepping the mark.

'But you still loved her,' I quickly added sympathetically.

'I thought so … perhaps, but … then she stole from me, and I hated her!'

'More money?'

He nodded and returned his stare to the table. 'Two hundred and fifty thousand pounds!'

'Wow, a quarter of a million quid. How?'

'It's time for me to go.' He stood and headed for the exit.

32

Sunday morning should have heralded a much-needed lie-in, but with the unofficial Guinness World Records holder for the loudest snore in the next bed to me, there was no hope of that. To be honest though, I was never really into sleeping in late. I was a surfer, an early riser. There'd be no surf that morning, though. The nearest beach was over a two-hour drive away, but even there, there was no surf. The nearest decent breaks were down in Cornwall, around a six-hour drive away. I suddenly realised how much I was missing Kirra—the apartment at the beach, the sunshine, the people.

It was 6.00 am when I rose from bed, dressed and headed downstairs. The house was quiet (apart, of course, from the sound of Elvis' snoring). Out on the street, however, was a different matter. Church bells rang out in the distance, calling the faithful to worship. When I stepped out of the front door, the endearing sound seemed to draw me towards it.

Although it wouldn't be the same as a stroll along the Coolangatta promenade, a walk in the fresh air would still do me some good, so off I set heading up Bobbersmill Road. The church soon came into view—a quaint Victorian redbrick building with a steeple. As I approached, the sound of the bells grew louder, and I wondered if there were people inside, pulling on ropes to create the sound, or if it were a sound recording. To my surprise, I later learned it was the latter.

As far as I knew, we had nothing planned for that day. Sunday was the day of rest, according to Tetley, but I suspected we'd still be paying a visit to the pub at some point. To be honest, apart from watching TV, I couldn't think of much else to do, unless an excursion was on the cards. I quite liked the idea of that—a tour of the local historical sites, Nottingham Castle, Sherwood Forest, Trent Bridge Cricket Ground. Making a mental note, I decided that when I got back, I would talk to Tetley about arranging a day for sightseeing.

My phone call to Jenny had been short and sweet the previous evening, basically because after returning from our night out, I was bushed. But it had been a pleasant night. Elvis and I both enjoyed meeting Tetley's mates. But it was my conversation with Javed Sharma that stood out in my mind the most. The revelation that Janita stole a substantial amount of money from him, and the fact that there was no mention of this in the police report, was highly significant. Why hadn't Javed told the police about the theft? Was it because it would have implicated him in the case? It certainly gave him a motive, so a call to Stewie was warranted, and a promotion on the whiteboard was called for, moving Javed's name higher up the list.

Radford Road. Seeing the name made me smile, reminding me of my fiancée, Jenny Radford. The multicultural hub of Hyson Green was quiet as I strolled past a variety of closed shops and businesses, an Asian supermarket, a second-hand furniture shop, a record shop with a poster of Bob Marley in the window, a ladies' hairdressers, an exotic fruit and vegetable store, a barbershop, and an off-licence to name a few. On the other side of the road were a huge Asda supermarket and a service station. Next to that was a pub called The Cricket Players, facing which was another old church, a stone building looking older than the one on Bobbersmill Road.

At the junction at the bottom, there was a NatWest bank on the corner of a tree-lined road. Turning left, I noticed the houses were bigger, still side by side, but three storeys high with large bay windows. Strolling a little farther, I reached an open park, which I recognised from Tetley's descriptions as The Forest, the home of the famous Goose Fair, an annual event in October which saw travelling fairs from all over Europe converge on Nottingham for a week. Although a large part of the park was bitumen, forming a 'Park and Ride', the rest of the space comprised football pitches and cricket ovals. The top edge on a slightly higher elevation was skirted with large oak and sycamore trees.

When I reached the far end of the park, an old wrought-iron fence led into a large graveyard. Checking my watch, I'd only been walking for forty-five minutes, so I pushed on. Exiting the park, I found myself at a busy intersection called Mansfield Road. The traffic there was already building and mostly heading in the same direction. I followed that direction, and fifteen minutes later, I realised why—the road had led me into the city centre. The first building I recognised was the University of Nottingham campus that I'd passed the day before with Tommy Stokes. Next was the Theatre Royal, and before I knew it I was back in the Market Square. Checking my watch, it was still only 7.00 am. Breakfast seemed like a good idea at that moment, so I found a café close to the square and took a seat at one of the tables out the front of the building. A waitress approached me with a pad and pen in hand.

'Mornin'. Ya alright?' she asked cheerfully.

'I'm good, thanks.'

'Ah, Australian.'

'Yep.'

'What can I get for ya, duck?'

Pondering over the menu and deciding to go healthy, I ordered poached eggs and smashed avocado on sourdough.

'Tea or coffee?'

'Green tea, please.' I almost said, "Tah, duck" Maybe next time. The warmth and the genuine friendliness of the Nottingham people that I'd met so far was exhilarating.

The walk back seemed to take a lot longer. Probably because Doris, care of the walking app on my phone, took me another way. I headed up Wollaton Street, and past Madison's nightclub from the previous day. At the top of a hill, I found myself at a busy, but very characterful, intersection called Canning Circus. A row of whitewashed tiny almshouses in a row stood on either side of an entrance to another old graveyard. Just past this, I realised I was at the top of Alfreton Road. A brisk walk past more shops that were now stirring, and I soon found myself outside the Lilly Grand Pub. Five minutes later, I entered the house on Bobbersmill Road.

33

The house was pretty much the same as I'd left it. The familiar sound of Elvis' snoring brought some comfort, and I realised just how much I was missing home. I'd only been away from Jenny, and Kirra, for four days, but being half the world away would have been more difficult if Elvis hadn't been with me. I was standing in front of the whiteboard reading over what I'd just added from the information I'd harvested from Javed the night before. He was certainly racked with guilt; that was easy to see, but was his remorse really the product of not being there for his sister when she needed him? Or did he harbour a hatred towards her for stealing from him? And the big question: could he have killed her and hid her body in the wall? While I pondered over this for a few moments, the floorboards above creaked, and I realised someone was stirring. It wasn't hard to track the movement of that someone padding out of one of the bedrooms and into the bathroom. A few minutes later, a creak on the stairs told me they were descending from above.

'Good morning, Scotty,' Carol said, poking her head around the open dining room door. She had dishevelled hair, and wore a full-length pink dressing gown.

'Morning, Carol.'

'Did you sleep okay?'

'I did, thanks.'

'I'm amazed with that racket going on.' She raised her eyes towards the ceiling.

157

'Yeah, I know. I'm used to it, but.'

'Would you like a cup of tea, duck?'

'Yes please, that'll be great.'

Following her into the kitchen, I sat at the table as she filled the kettle from the sink tap.

Then, after lighting one of the gas rings on the stovetop and setting the kettle in place, she opened the back door. 'Let a bit of fresh air in.' The air was certainly fresh, cool and welcome. 'Did you have a good night last night?' she asked, taking the seat opposite.

'Yeah, it was good. I went for a walk this morning too.'

'Oh lovely. Where did you go?'

'Into town.'

'Into town? You walked all the way into town?'

'Yep. And back.'

'Wow! That's a big walk.'

I guess it was, but that was nothing out of the ordinary for me. While pondering over a case, I'd often take early morning walks and sometimes find myself as far as Currumbin Beach before realising it was time to turn back. My Apple watch informed me on those occasions I'd walked around fifteen kilometres. I hadn't brought my smartwatch on this trip, so I had no idea how far I'd walked that morning.

'Carol, do you know Javed Sharma?'

She frowned and squinted.

'He owns the newsagents at the bottom of Alfreton Road.'

'Oh Javed. That Javed. Yes. Why?'

'How well do you know him?'

'Only as a customer when I go into the shop, usually to get my lottery ticket.'

'What do you reckon to him?'

'What do you mean?'

'Well, is he friendly or …?'

'I wouldn't say he was friendly. You'd be lucky to get a smile or even eye contact.'

'So, you don't know him very well.'

'No … why?'

'Why? You do know he's Janita's brother?'

'Janita? Who's that?'

'Janita Sharma.'

Carol shook her head and shrugged, and I realised she knew very little about the victim.

'Anita? Anita Madison?'

'Oh. The girl in the wall. She was Javed's sister?' The kettle whistled, so Carol rose from the table.

'She was, yeah. Haven't you been in the newsagents since all this happened?'

'No, I haven't been out, remember?' She went about making two mugs of tea.

'But you would have seen the news, surely.'

'No.' She placed one of the mugs in front of me, then resumed her seat. 'I've heard how the media is twisting the story. Just like they did with you, Scotty, in Australia. No … I'm only interested in what my Colin says. And he says he has done nothing wrong, and I believe him!' Her hand shook as she raised the mug to her mouth and gently blew on the hot liquid.

Reaching over the table, I grasped her other hand in mine. 'I believe that too.'

'We'll need to leave bright and early tomorrow morning,' Carol said before taking a cautious sip of tea. 'It's about an hour's drive to Lincoln, but we need to get on the other side of the city first because the traffic will be mad on a Monday morning.'

The stairs creaked in that ascending way once more. I knew it wasn't Elvis because the engine was still idling above, so it must have been Tetley.

'Mornin,' he said groggily as he padded into the kitchen.

'Lift ya bloody feet up, lad,' Carol scolded.

'Steady on, Mam. Had a big night last night.'

'Kettle's just boiled.'

'Great.' Tetley quickly made himself a cup of tea, then stood leaning with his back against the sink. The legend was true. The Brits really loved their tea. It seemed to be an important part of their daily lives, a ritual even.

'Hey, did you know Javed at the newsagents is that poor girl's brother?' Carol said.

'Yeah, of course.'

'I didn't know.'

'You did. I told you.'

'Do you know him?' I asked Tetley.

'Not really. You were talking to him for a while last night.'

'Do you see him out often?'

'No, first time.'

'Have you been in the shop since … you know?'

He redirected his bleary morning eyes back to me. 'Not since Dad was arrested. A bit awkward, you know.'

'Did Col use the newsagent?' My question was directed at them both.

'Bloody ell, he's interrogating us, Mam!' Tetley said laughing.

It was down to Carol to remind him why I was there.

'No. It's too hard to park down there, so he used to use the one at the top of Churchfield Lane. He'd get his paper and his strawberry milk every mornin'.' As if suddenly realising he was talking in the past tense, Tetley took a reflective sip of tea.

My phone rang. It was Detective Stewart Weston. The name on my screen said 'Stewie UK'.

'Hey, Stewie, how's it goin?'

'Good mate, yourself?' I could tell from the background noise that he was driving. Instinctively, I stood and headed for the incident room.

'Yeah, not so bad. How are you enjoying Nottingham?'

'Great. Lovin it. Listen, I've got some important information about Javed Sharma.'

'Really?'

I spent the next few minutes telling him about the money Janita had stolen from her brother.

'That's interesting. Listen, you're going up to Lincoln tomorrow, right?'

'That's right.' *Did he just disregard the information I'd just given him?*

'Well, I've got to go up there too, so I'll be happy to give you a lift.'

'That'd be great, but Carol, Tetley and Elvis are coming too.'

'No worries, there's plenty of room in my car. We'll need to head off reasonably early though. About 8.00?'

'Yep, eight will be good. I'll let Carol know.'

'Cool. See you then.' He hung up.

<h1 style="text-align:center">34</h1>

'So, what's on the cards today, lad?' I asked Tetley after Elvis had joined us.

'Not a lot. Take it easy this morning. Perhaps pop down to the Wheatsheaf at lunchtime.'

The Wheatsheaf, I assumed, was another local pub. Like fried food, we were going to have to curb our drinking. Saturated fat and alcohol in excess were things I usually avoided these days. Unlike when the three of us were living bachelor lives, we were no longer young lads. I was hoping this was just a weekend thing, perhaps a special occasion in honour of our arrival.

'I was hoping we could do a bit of sightseeing,' I said.

'There'll be plenty of time for that,' Tetley said rather dismissively.

'It's a lovely morning. Why don't you take your teas out into the garden …?' Carol said. '… I'll bring you out some breakfast.'

'Yeah, why not?' Tetley said, pushing back his chair.

'No thanks, Carol.' I whispered as I passed her at the sink. 'I've eaten.'

Elvis and I followed Tetley outside, onto a cracked concrete patio. From a round cast iron table and chairs, we had a good view of the neighbourhood and factory chimneys in the distance.

Carol brought out a plate of what looked like toast. 'Fried bread,' she said, noticing my inquisitive expression.

'Fried bread?' Elvis said. 'What's that?'

'Uhm ….' Tetley shot him a patronising stare that we knew from experience was the prelude to a sarcastic comment.

'It's fried bread! There's no real explanation required, dickhead. It's bread that's been fried.'

'I've just never heard of it before, that's all,' Elvis replied.

Two full English breakfasts followed.

'Ya not eatin, lad?' Tetley asked, but he wasn't really interested when I told him about my early morning walk. He was already hooking into a very streaky rasher of bacon.

Apart from the delightful birdsong and Elvis' tendency to hum as he chewed, they ate their breakfasts mostly in silence.

'Have you spoken to everyone yet?' Tetley finally asked, wiping his plate with the last of the fried bread.

'Not quite. There's the builder's son, Tony Patterson. I'm guessing he'll be out working during the weekdays, so I'm planning to pay him a visit one evening. Perhaps tomorrow if we get back from Lincoln early enough.'

'Why not today?'

'I don't want to piss anyone off. Need to get them on side. Sunday for a busy builder is probably his only day off.'

Tetley nodded and then swilled away the last residue of bacon with a mouthful of tea.

'Then, of course, there's Declan O'Donnell's son, Rodney. The trouble is he lives in London. I've tried calling him but there was no reply, so I'll try again.'

'Whereabouts in London?' Tetley asked, sitting up to attention.

'A place called Wandsworth.'

It's only a couple of hours' drive south,' Tetley said.

'Right, so a trip down to London might be on the cards.'

Elvis shrugged. 'Could be a double whammy. Interview a potential witness while having a bit of a break and seeing the sights.'

My phone rang. The picture of Jenny standing under the beach shower at Kirra, looking back over her shoulder, adorned the screen.

'Hey you.' I left the table and made my way down the steps to the lawn. 'How's it goin?'

'Good. What are you up to?' Jenny asked.

'We're just sitting out in the backyard enjoying a bit of early morning sun.'

'Oh, that's right. It's morning over there. Weird.'

'I'm missing you like hell!'

'Ditto.'

'How's the surf?'

Jenny chuckled. 'That's what you're really missing, isn't it?'

'Nah. What's new?'

'Well … I've got some bad news for you.'

'What?'

'You're no longer the Golden Boy.'

'What do you mean?'

'There's a new guy in town … well, Queensland.'

My silence prompted her to continue.

'It's all over the news here at the moment. A detective from America just caught a serial killer known as The Moon. Apparently, there were 12 killings 25 years ago in LA. And this detective, Joe Dean, was the leading DI on the case, but it was never solved after the killings just stopped. Then, apparently, the killer, can you believe, writes a book called *Flirting with The Moon*, and Joe tracks him down to a town in Far North Queensland. And you won't believe where?'

'Where?'

'Candlestick Bay.'

'You're kidding me?' Candlestick Bay was a quaint little seaside town on the Coral Sea Coast, way up near the top end of Queensland. Although I'd never been there, I'd heard all about its natural beauty from Jenny because her brother, Fat Bobby, was the local cop there.

'Nope. And Bobby helped him with the investigation.'

'Wow!'

'So, I'm afraid you're old news now, my old mate. Joe Dean is the new hero.'

The fame I'd enjoyed since solving the *X* case, when a serial killer was terrorising the Gold Coast, had been both a blessing and a curse. A blessing because it opened up a lot of doors, especially when I quit the police force and opened my private detective agency, and not to mention all the free meals and drinks bestowed upon me from the local businesses in appreciation, but it was also a hindrance because there was no longer any privacy in my life. Opening the front door in the morning to a mob of reporters and TV cameras happened regularly. Being recognised in the street and stopped for selfies wherever I went became quite normal. It had waned a little of late, which I was glad for, and now with this new bloke taking the limelight, hopefully I'd be able to get back to a more normal life. But if that was the case, why was I feeling pangs of jealousy?

'And that's not all,' Jenny said.

'What else?'

'Fat Bobby's getting married. In the spring.'

'Oh, that's great news.' I'd never met Jenny's brother. He was Sergeant Robert Radford of the Far North Queensland Police Service. Fat Bobby was apparently a leftover nickname from a time when he was overweight. The most recent photographs I'd seen of him showed him to be tall and in quite good shape. 'Will we be going up for the wedding?'

'Of course we will, you drongo. And you'll get to meet this detective because he's Bobby's best man.'

'Wow! I can't wait.'

We chatted for a good half hour. Jenny filled me in on the case she was currently working on—a gang of youths terrorising the Ashmore area—and arrests were imminent.

After the call, I wandered back up to the house to find that Tetley and Elvis had showered.

'Hope there's some hot water left for you, mate,' Elvis said, tongue in cheek.

'You might have to have another pommy wash, lad,' Tetley said.

35

Monday was the day we'd all been waiting for. The day we'd be going to Lincoln to speak with Colin.

Sunday had been a cruisy day. Yes, we spent the afternoon at the pub. But the scenery was a little different, and so was the weather. The sun had finally made an appearance. The Wheatsheaf at the bottom of Aspley Lane was a pleasant stroll from Bobbersmill Road, and although it sat on a busy junction, sitting outside at large wooden picnic tables drinking lager and eating Walkers crisps was quite relaxing.

That evening, after a large Sunday roast dinner prepared by Carol with proper homemade Yorkshire puddings, I spent some time in the incident/dining room while Tetley and Elvis watched Sunday evening TV with Carol.

Studying the whiteboard in silence, as I liked to do, just standing there as if in deep meditation, focusing on the information in front of me, Col's name was obviously predominant in my thoughts. Although I hated visiting jails, I was looking forward to seeing him, and questioning him, when we travelled up to Lincoln.

Next were the three names of the players I'd yet to speak with.

First on the list was the witness, William Henley. I'd devised a cunning plan to break down the barrier between us, but I would have to wait until Tuesday to put it into place.

Then there was Tony Patterson, the builder's son. According to the police report, he was a young bloke working with his father at the time of the renovation on The Coach House. *Could he have gone to the house late that night or early the next morning to check on Col's work?* Depending on what time we got back from Lincoln the next day, I was planning on paying him an evening visit at his home in Gedling.

And finally, Declan's son, Rodney O'Donnell, who had lived in London since the death of his father. I'd try calling him again, but if that didn't work, perhaps a trip down to London would be warranted.

Once I had spoken with all the players that I was aware of, I could start putting together some of the pieces in order to get a clear picture of what happened on that night.

Then I also remembered my agreement with Tommy Stokes to look into the death of Declan O'Donnell. *Where on earth was I to begin with that investigation?* Being the head of a major crime family, you would have thought O'Donnell would have had too many enemies to count—rival gangs, disgruntled shopkeepers and small business owners who were sick of paying protection money, a community tired of being bullied and living in fear. So, what if someone had hired a hitman? If that were the case, there'd be no evidence, and the culprit would be long gone. I certainly had my work cut out for me, and I was regretting taking Tommy up on his offer.

I somehow needed to work the two cases side by side. To do this, speaking again with the people who knew Declan would make sense, but this time directing the investigation towards the death of the crime lord as well as Janita's sad demise.

Looking at the list of names, I doubted Tony, the builder's son, knew Declan, unless he'd continued to do work for him over the years. Neither would Javed Sharma, the stonemason Les Lane, or his apprentice Dave Anderson. And what about the witness William Henley? Could he have clashed with O'Donnell over the renovations? Or am I forgetting that O'Donnell ran Nottingham with an iron fist? Perhaps everyone on the list not only knew of him but had had a run-in with him at some time or another. *Hmm.* At that moment, I still had to admit I had very little to go on with.

I'd had trouble sleeping that night. And it wasn't just Elvis' snoring, although that didn't help. Normally, by now, after interviewing most of the players, I'd be forming possible scenarios in my head. And now was no exception, but none of them were gelling. If Col didn't kill Janita Sharma (aka Anita Madison), it meant someone else must have gone to the property after he had left. For obvious reasons, there was no time of death reported, so we had no way of knowing if Janita was killed during the night or the following morning. This meant anyone could have gone to the property, and got in and killed her, but then who else besides Col knew she was there? And who could have got into the building without Henley across the street noticing? The scenarios I was contemplating were:

Declan O'Donnell went to the house on the off chance and found Janita there sleeping. Aware that she had ripped him off out of a substantial amount of money, and that she was planning on doing a runner, he killed her and hid the body in the wall.

Or

Tommy Stokes admitted he went to the property that evening, but what if he'd lied when he said he didn't go inside? What if he'd been there after Col had left, and entered the property to find Janita there? Were his instructions from his boss to find her and kill her?

Or

Did Janita's brother, Javed, find out about the property at The Park, and find his sister there on the off chance? Was his anger so great at the theft of his money that he flew into a rage and killed his sister?

Or

Dave Anderson, the stonemason's labourer turned barber, also admitted to going into the property the next morning to check that the necessary work had been carried out before his fussy boss arrived. Could he have also found Janita there? And if so, could he have killed her? If yes, why?

Or

Although I hadn't yet spoken with Tony Patterson, the builder's son, what if he had gone in early that morning? The same, if so, if yes, and why questions applied to this scenario as with Dave. With each scenario so far, there were a lot of ifs and buts.

Or

According to Dave Anderson, he saw Bill Patterson, the builder, arrive that morning after Dave had ducked out for coffee. There was very little information about Bill. He obviously hadn't made a statement because he'd passed away a few years ago. To get a clear picture, I'd need to understand more about his character, what kind of bloke he was. Perhaps his son could fill in a few of the gaps.

Or

It was doubtful, but I wasn't ruling the next scenario out. What if Donna Simpson knew that Janita was at the property, and what if the money she was owed was substantially more than she'd let on? Would she have been capable of killing her friend and hiding her body? Or did she have help?

Or

Was Sheila O'Donnell capable of murder? I would have to say yes, not directly perhaps, but she would definitely have the contacts to carry out a job like this. Thirty years ago, she was a powerful socialite, the matriarch of the O'Donnell empire. She also has a lot of young men at her disposal.

Or (and I know this is the obvious scenario)

What if all the above scenarios are pure fiction, fuelled by one man's testimony? What if it was William Henley, the witness across the street, who, knowing that Janita was in the house alone, crept into the property and killed her in the night? What would his motive have been? Was he a sicko? Or at best, was his testimony worthy of sending an innocent man to jail for the rest of his years?

Like I said, there were a lot of ifs and buts, but it was time to up the investigation, and get some answers to the questions that the scenarios had unearthed.

Sleep was a long time coming that night.

36

Stewie arrived early the next morning just as Carol was putting out the breakfast. To my relief, there was no fried food in sight, just a selection of cereals, a round of toast and fruit juice.

After the informal salutations, Stewie asked if he could have a word with me in private, so we stepped out the front of the house.

'What's up, mate?' I asked, leaning with my back against the front gate.

'I hear you spent Saturday afternoon with Tommy Stokes.'

How would he know that? Were the Nottingham Police having me followed? My frown asked the questions for me.

'There's not much that happens in this town without me knowing about it. I make it my business to keep informed.'

It was the third time I'd heard that phrase since arriving in Nottingham, once from Sheila O'Donnell, then from Tommy Stokes and now from DI Weston. Although Stewie was a fairly high-ranking detective, it's not like he was the bloody police commissioner, so his comment was either an exaggeration or he had inside information. There was a slight arrogance in his demeanour that morning that I hadn't noticed before. Could he be a bent copper as Tommy had suggested? Or was he just a good detective, keeping his nose to the ground?

'What did he tell you?'

'Uhm … that he was at the house the night of Janita's death.'

'What?'

'It took him about four hours to get to the point of the meeting, but yeah. He reckons he was there.'

Stewie narrowed his eyes, and at first, I thought he was going to challenge me, but then I realised he was thinking. 'This is the first I've heard of this. Are you sure?'

I shrugged because no, I wasn't sure. I was only relaying what Tommy had told me.

'We'd never even considered Tommy as part of the investigation.'

'So, you never spoke to him?'

'Not about this. Did he see Anita there?' I noticed that, unlike me, Stewie never used the victim's real name.

I told him everything that Tommy had told me, which wasn't a lot.

'And did you believe him?'

The non-committal shrug again. 'I'm surprised you didn't question him, though, seeing as he's running Nottingham.'

Stewie burst into laughter. 'Running Nottingham? Old Tommy?'

'Isn't he?'

'No, mate. Bloody hell. He might have had some of the limelight back in the day, but Declan only kept him around because he was an old mate from school.'

'But he was second in charge?'

The laugh again. 'He'd have you believe he was running the firm. Nah, he may have thought he was, but no, Tommy was never second in charge.'

The I-don't-really-believe-this-either, humorous smirk that I delivered with the next question was meant as a friendly gesture. 'He told me you're working for him. Surely that's not true.'

The laugh again. 'What do you reckon, mate?'

'I think it's bullshit.' I lied because I couldn't be sure. Tommy seemed quite believable to me.

'Good. Did you believe him when he said he didn't go inside the property?'

'Not really, no.'

'Okay. I think a word with Mister Stokes is on the cards.'

'So, what do you know of him?'

'Like I said, he was a mate of O'Donnell's. Declan looked after him, letting him run some of the businesses. The nightclubs mainly.'

'And now he owns them.'

'Is that what he told you? Sheila and Rodney own all the family assets. Tommy still manages the clubs, but as far as I know that's about it.'

'Hmm, that's the opposite of what he told me. But running a large firm like this would need someone at the helm. Not Sheila, surely?'

'There is no firm, mate. Not anymore, not since Declan passed. Nottingham's run by the McCanns and the Patels nowadays. Times have changed.'

'Tommy asked me to look into Declan's death.' I had debated about sharing this information with the police, but I was glad I did when I saw Stewie's reaction.

'You're what?'

'The shooter was never brought to justice. What happened to the investigation? Was it dropped?'

'It was before my time, but I'm guessing the investigation was buried away in the nobody-gives-a-fuck file.'

'Really?'

'The impression I got was that whoever killed O'Donnell was a hero.'

'But wasn't he maintaining peace with the rival gangs?'

'No. There was a war brewing. New gangs flexing their wings, challenging O'Donnell for the throne.'

'Were there any clues at all as to who might have killed him?'

'Like I said, it was before my time, but I can get you the file if you like. I was still a young bloke in Melbourne when all this went down.'

'That would be awesome.'

'My guess though is that it was a professional hit. A hired gun financed by one of the rival gangs.'

It made sense, but if that was the case, it pretty much made the investigation Tommy had commissioned as a waste of time. 'What do you know about Rodney?' I asked, changing tact slightly.

'Uhm, he moved down to London not long after his dad's passing. Apparently, they never saw eye to eye. Rodney was gay. Declan could never accept that.'

I'd read the interview in the police report, but there was little to read between the lines. Rodney had an alibi for the night of Janita's death and for the time of his father's demise. He was of little interest to either investigation. A peace-loving man, unlike his father, with no history of violence or of even breaking the law. But regardless, I'd decided I'd need to speak with him. 'Could Sheila have had anything to do with it?' My enquiry had inadvertently shifted to the death of O'Donnell, but then I realised this question applied to both cases.

Stewie shrugged. 'Anita or Declan?'

'Both.'

He thought about this for a moment before replying. 'Possibly. If she found out about Anita, she certainly had a motive, but she had an alibi. Plus, I doubt she'd be capable of hiding the body.'

'She could have had help. Tommy perhaps?'

'Ha, Tommy again. I'm wondering if he's been thrown in to put you off the scent. How did he get your number, do you know?'

It was a valid point. How did Tommy get my number? So far, I'd handed it out to: Donna Simpson, Javed Sharma, Dave the barber, and of course … Stewie. 'I'm not sure. He simply said what you'd said earlier.'

'What's that?'

'That nothing happened in this town without his knowing about it.'

The front door opened, and Tetley appeared. 'It's time to go, boys.

Lifting the key fob that Stewie held in one hand, he pressed a button, and the headlights of a black, late model, BMW parked out front blinked in recognition.

37

'Oh, in't this lovely?' Carol remarked as she made herself comfortable on the back seat of the spacious coupe.

'Doin alright for his sen, owd Stewie is,' Tetley remarked, rubbing a hand across the leather seats.

I sat in the front passenger seat, Carol sat behind me, Elvis was on the far side in the back, and Tetley, being the short arse, perched himself in the middle. I was beginning to notice that Elvis was unusually quiet. *Was he pining for Cassie?*

'I've made some egg sandwiches if anyone feels hungry,' Carol said. 'And there's a flask of tea.'

'Of course you have,' Tetley said, grinning.

'Smokey bacon crisps,' Carol added. 'Well, it's a long drive.'

I remembered her telling me it was just over an hour from Nottingham to Lincoln.

'How are you holding up, Carol?' Stewie asked as we headed down Bobbersmill Road, weaving through the avenue of parked cars.

'I'm good, darlin. Thank you. Well, as good as can be expected. I'll be better when Colin's home with us where he belongs, though, and we can go back to Australia and forget about all this.'

Stewie's side glance towards me said, "That's not likely, is it, Scotty?"

'That's why I'm glad Scotty's here,' Carol said, peering out of the window. 'He's going to find the real killer. Isn't that right, Scotty?'

'My bloody oath.' The return side glance aimed at Stewie reinforced the words in silence.

The traffic was heavy as we made our way up Alfreton Road and into town, but once we came out of the city and through The Meadows, it had eased a little. When we passed over Trent Bridge, I got my first view of two iconic stadiums. The City Ground, on the left, was the home of Tetley's beloved Nottingham Forest, and on the right was the more internationally known, at least by us Aussies, as the hallowed cricket ground simply called Trent Bridge.

Tetley said from the back of the car, 'If you're interested, the other stadium you can see there over the other side of the river, that's Meadow Lane, the home of Nott's County.'

I *was* genuinely interested. There was a lot of history there. Although Tetley never spoke about them much, Notts County was one of the oldest teams in the English Football League, and Trent Bridge had seen many a victory and heartache for the Australian cricket team over the years.

'We're at home again next week, Scotty,' Tetley said as we followed a sign heading towards Newark. 'No bloody excuses this time; you're coming.'

'Who are they playing?' Now, a glance towards Elvis was reciprocated with a slight frown as if to say, "Don't encourage him."

'Arsenal.'

'Can't wait.'

The rest of the journey was pleasant. Stewie had no problem putting his foot down whenever we hit an open road. Those stretches were rare though and short-lived, broken either by roundabouts or small townships.

There would only be three visitors allowed—me, Carol and Tetley. Stewie's visit was related to another case he was working on, so he'd be busy interviewing a suspect over a spate of burglaries in the Bilborough area. We'd arranged to drop Elvis off in Lincoln City where he could spend a few hours on his own, strolling around what Carol described as a quaint cathedral town, and that was exactly the impression I got after we'd dropped Elvis off in a narrow, cobblestoned street. Apart from all the bravado, Elvis was a bit of a connoisseur when it came to history and the arts, and although he'd never admit it, I knew he'd enjoy the cultural experience this historical town had to offer.

It was a bit out of the way from the prison, but we had plenty of time. The detour took a mere ten minutes.

In contrast with the town, HM Lincoln Prison was an imposing 19th century building that was never meant to look pretty. The sight of this red-brick fortress with turrets and a castle wall would fill anyone approaching with a feeling of dread.

After working twenty years for the Queensland Police, both in uniform and later as a detective, I was familiar with the inside of a prison—the smells, the sounds, the feeling of desperation, danger and fear that a building like this seemed to harbour.

A young prison guard called Brian Connolly met us, who then escorted us through a series of barred doors, each one unlocked and then locked as we passed through it. 'Wait here, please,' Brian said when we entered a waiting room with a row of seats. Other visitors were already waiting—a young woman with a sleeping baby in a stroller, an elderly couple who held on to each other as if fearing for their lives. Others—a hard-chinned woman, who sat alone and didn't make eye contact, and a man wearing a raincoat—gave me the impression that they'd been coming here regularly for some time.

After a few minutes' wait, Brian returned and called out from a list of names. Carol was on the list, as well as Stewie.

Tetley gave his mum a hug before she filed out with the rest of the visitors in Brian's wake.

'I can't believe my dad's being forced to stay in this place,' Tetley said.

I already knew the bail application had been turned down on the grounds that Colin could abscond back to Australia if released. This was ridiculous, of course.

'You've got to get him out of here, Scotty,' Tetley added with a tinge of desperation.

'I will, mate. I will,' I said, placing a reassuring hand on his shoulder.

Twenty minutes later, Carol reappeared accompanied by Brian and tagged with Tetley.

'How's he holding up?' I asked as she took the seat next to mine.

'Oh, Scotty, it's horrible. He's putting on a brave face, but I can see he's scared. How did we get into this mess? We should never have come back to England. Should have stayed in Kirra, safe and sound in our little unit.'

The only words of comfort I could find were to reinforce my promise to her that I would find out the truth about what happened that night. It was a half-baked promise, though, because if the truth meant that Colin killed Janita Sharma, it meant I'd be the one proving it. I obviously wouldn't still be seen as the hero around here if that were the case. In past cases, I'd relied on my gut feeling to a certain extent, and although that same feeling was telling me that Colin was innocent, on this occasion I wasn't sure if it was my heart and not my gut. The evidence so far all pointed towards Colin being the only other person inside the property that night. A shudder of desperation passed through my body. Had I achieved anything at all since arriving in the UK less than a week ago?

You know you have, Scotty!

The voice of my mother instilled an instant calm.

Keep digging, and you'll find the answers.

'Come on, Scotty, you're up.' It was Tetley who snapped me out of my reverence. 'He can't wait to see you.'

38

Colin had lost a lot of weight since I'd last seen him, and although the smile that greeted me was genuine and warm, it did little to mask the pain he was suffering. He was sad, which made me sad too. This wasn't the man I'd known all those years. The father figure, always with a dad joke locked and loaded, always with some gem of trivia that he openly shared. Always thinking of others. Never a thought for himself.

'Scotty, it's great to see you.'

I wanted to hug him, but I knew I couldn't; that would be breaking prison rules. 'Col, how are you holding up, mate?' It was a whisper, and all I could manage at that moment. The sight of him, a lovely man forced to stay in this terrible place, suddenly hit me with a wave of emotion.

'Been better, buddy.' He gestured with an outstretched hand for me to take a seat. 'Thanks for coming, Scott. You'll never know what this means to me and Carol.'

'I had to come, Col. As soon as Tetley told me what had happened.'

'How have the police reacted to your being here?'

'Alright, so far. Thanks to Stewie.'

'Stewie.' A wry smile crossed his face. 'What's the odds of an Aussie being in charge of the case?'

I sensed cynicism in his tone. 'How's he been treating you?'

Col shrugged and gazed around the room. 'He seems like a nice enough bloke. He doesn't believe me, though. I get the impression he thinks this is an open and shut case.'

'Tell me about what happened that night.'

The account that he shared over the next few minutes was pretty much what I expected, almost word for word to the statement he'd made to the police. I could imagine he'd gone over and over it in his mind, with very little else to occupy him. So, I needed to dig a little deeper to see if I could prise out any information he may have missed or forgotten. However small a thing it may have seemed, through my experience, I'd learned that these morsels of information could be very helpful.

'Did you see anyone else that night apart from Janita?'

'Only the chap across the street. He came across a couple of times to complain about the noise.'

'When was the first time?'

'Quite early in the evening, not long after I'd got there. This was a genuine complaint because I was making a noise early on. I needed to cut the timber struts to size before hanging the frame, and then the steel sheets. I was aware this would make some racket, so I purposely cut everything in one go earlier to minimise the noise later.'

'Was he angry? Aggressive?'

'Not really, but I got the impression he was used to confrontation.'

'What did he say?'

'"I hope you don't think you're going to be doing that all night. This is a very quiet neighbourhood" or words to that effect. I don't remember exactly. It was a long time ago, Scotty, and insignificant until recently.'

'How did you react to him?' I already knew the answer to this, not because it was in the police report, but because I was familiar with Col's personality.

'I apologised for the noise. I understood because I agreed with him. It was too late for this kind of work, but I explained how I had no choice and that I wouldn't be too much longer making the cuts.'

'What did he say to that?'

'Just huffed, made some remark about inconsideration for others, then marched away.'

'But he came back?'

'He did. When I was using the nail gun to assemble the frame. I was trying to be as considerate as possible. I'd closed all the doors and windows, even though it was bloody hot that night. And I was working as fast as I could to get it finished quickly.'

'What did he say this time?'

'He was definitely more upset this time, banging on the door. I think what made it worse was that I didn't hear him at first. I think he'd been out there for some time.'

'More aggressive this time?'

'No. More upset. Said he was going to call the police if it went on much longer. Apparently, his mother was ill, and … I assured him I'd almost finished with the hammering. I even asked him in and showed him the frame that was almost built. Then I explained I'd be screwing on the sheets while laying the insulation. I doubted he'd hear the battery drill once I got to that stage.'

'Was he understanding at all?'

Col shook his head. 'No. He was a bloody whinger.'

'What time did Janita appear?'

'About 9.30 pm. I was almost finished, probably had two more sheets to hang.'

My use of silence, prompting him to continue, wasn't on purpose; it was more of a habit from years of interviewing suspects.

'She was dressed to the nines. Glamourous. A real looker. It was a bit of a shock; she scared the bejesus out of me. I was working away, turned to get more insulation and there she was, just standing there in the doorway watching me.'

'In the front doorway?'

Colin nodded. 'I asked her if she was okay. She seemed upset, scared even.'

'What do you mean?'

'She was just staring at me, as if …? I don't know, as if I were an unexpected problem.'

'Did she say anything?'

'Not at first, no. I asked her why she was there. I knew nothing about the owners. I'd just received my instructions from Bill.'

'Bill Patterson?'

'Yep. I'd got the job through him.'

'Why do you think he got you to do it? Why didn't he just do it himself?'

Col shrugged and shook his head. 'It was Friday night. A prick of a job. Him and his lad had been working on the house for a few weeks. Probably didn't want to work the extra hours.'

'What was Bill like?'

'I didn't know him that well. I'd done a bit of work for him here and there. Seemed like a nice enough bloke.'

'And what about his lad?'

The smirk seemed out of place for the situation. 'He was an arrogant little shit. I don't mean little in the physical sense, cause he was quite a big bugger—muscly, tattooed. He was just cocky, you know, and bloody lazy.'

'Did you see him at the site?'

'He was there with his dad packing up when I arrived.'

'You didn't see him again later?'

'No.'

'So, you were telling me about Janita.'

'Yeah, ignored my question and asked me how much longer I'd be. I told her not long, and she went upstairs.'

'And that was it. The last time you saw her?'

'Yep. I'd had a bit of a look around the property when I first got there. The bedroom upstairs was just about finished. There was a king-size bed and furniture covered in plastic sheets. I assumed she'd gone to bed.'

I was dreading my next line of questioning, because as I said, I loved this bloke like he was my own father. But it had to be done. I was here to find out the truth, no matter how much it hurt. 'How were things between you and Carol?'

He shuffled in his seat. 'How do you mean?'

'Was everything okay between you? Were you getting on?'

This time, a defensive frown accompanied his shrug. 'Yeah, we were okay. Why do you ask?'

'You took the job on even though you knew it was your wife's birthday. That's not like you, Col.'

'Things were a lot different back then, Scotty. It was a good-paying job, and we needed the money. Bill Patterson also said there'd be more work for me in the future if I helped him out.'

'So how come you finally gave in and agreed to emigrate to Australia? Because it was Carol who was pushing that, wasn't it?'

'Yes, I wasn't sure I wanted to move halfway around the world, but once I agreed and we did it, it was the best thing we ever did.'

'Even though you had the promise of steady work here?'

'For the sake of my marriage and my family, I made the right choice in the end.'

'But why then?' I was pushing on, and it was killing me to see my best mate's dad sinking into a state of distress. 'I'm just trying to create a picture of what was happening around that time, Col.'

'I know you are, mate. It's just …' He lifted a hand to his face and cupped his mouth. 'None of this is looking very good, is it?'

I leaned over the table and placed a hand over his. 'We're going to sort this out. Keep your chin up. I know you're innocent. Okay?'

He nodded. 'I knew Carol desperately wanted to come to Australia, and I knew it was the right thing to do for the family and all that, but something had been holding me back. Then, when I learned how upset Carol was that I was working on her birthday, I realised that my stubbornness was causing a split. I was also getting disheartened with the way things were going in the UK, the lack of prospects and all that. So, I finally agreed.'

The next question was the hardest, so I launched straight into it.

'Did Janita come on to you?'

'Eh?'

'Did she, you know, proposition you?'

'Don't be daft.'

'You know what she did for a living?'

'I didn't then. I didn't even know who she was then.'

'I've been told a lot of those girls would sleep with men for money, then blackmail them, threatening to tell their wives. Is that what happened, Col?'

He pulled his hand away from mine. 'No, it bloody well is not. I can't believe you're asking me that, Scott.'

'Did you kill Janita Sharma?'

'No, I did not!'

39

The drive back to Lincoln City to pick up Elvis was sombre. The mood didn't change when we rendezvoused with our mate as arranged in the Magna Charta pub close to the Cathedral. The reason for Carol and Tetley's disposition was obvious. But what was up with Elvis? Because I'd known him for so long, I knew something was happening in his head. *Was he slipping back into his depression?* He didn't even ask us how Colin was. I'd need to have a quiet word with him and find out what was going on.

A simple pub lunch was on the cards: chicken salad rolls—sorry, cobs—and a pint of shandy each. Except for Carol and Stewie, who both had an orange juice.

'I can't bear this,' Carol suddenly said, staring down at her cob. 'Here we are free to do what we please, and my Col's locked up in that place. It's not fair. It's horrible.'

Tetley put an arm around her shoulder. 'I know, Mam. Scotty's going to get him out of there, aren't you, mate?'

With a mouth full of salad roll, I nodded.

'It not be long now. He's getting close, in't that right, Scotty?'

I swallowed my food, took a swig of shandy and said, 'That's right.' Of course I was lying, and although it was a white lie, I hated doing it just the same.

'So, what's next, Scotty?' Stewie asked.

'I'm hoping to have a word with Tony Patterson later this afternoon.'

'*Phff*, good luck with that.'

'What do you mean?'

'He's an arrogant shit.'

It was the second time I'd heard that in a day.

'Who's Tony Patterson?' Carol asked.

'He's the son of the builder who hired Colin to do the work,' Stewie said.

'What about his dad?'

'Passed away a few years ago.'

'Well, what if *he* did it? How would anyone know if he's dead?' Carol's logic, although filled with emotion, was palpable.

'That's why I want to talk with his son,' I said. 'He was working for his dad at the time, and he was even on site when Col arrived at the job.'

The drive back to Nottingham was pretty much the same as when we'd left the prison. In the back seat anyway. Carol stared out of her passenger window, Elvis out of his. Tetley catnapped, head wobbling, and was woken every time the car went over a bump.

Stewie and I chatted casually. He was filling me in on the differences between police procedure in the UK and Australia, and then he quizzed me more about the *X* case and the following cases—working with Ben Fisher, the famous murder mystery author; and then Freckles, the child superstar who went missing, feared dead; and then, of course, the last case when I solved the murder of Bobby Sexton, the lead singer of Aussie rock super band, INSEXT.

'I wish it were that glamorous over here,' Stewie remarked. 'It's mainly break-ins, domestic violence, gangs, car theft. The odd killing. It's all nasty stuff.'

'Do you miss Australia?'

'My bloody oath.'

'So, why don't you go back?'

'I'm working on it. Just got to get the missus to see reason.'

We arrived back at Bobbersmill around mid-afternoon. Stewie dropped us off but didn't come in. It was still too early to pay Tony Patterson a visit by my reasoning that he would still be out somewhere working. If he was busy, who knew what time he'd be home, but I was banking on around teatime. According to Doris, and confirmed by Tetley, Gedling was around a 20-minute drive depending on the traffic.

We spent the rest of the afternoon sitting in the back garden drinking tea. Tetley suddenly remembered he had to check his lottery numbers, and when Carol retreated to the kitchen, Elvis and I were left alone.

'What's up, mate? You're very quiet.' I asked.

He shrugged, and the memory of him drifting away into depression after his business failed, returned.

'Talk to me, Elv.'

'I'm going home.'

'Eh?'

'I'm homesick.'

'Already?'

'Yes. I should never have come. You don't need me. I should be back in Kirra rebuilding the business and overseeing the house build.'

'Cassie and Jenny have the house under control.'

'I know, but …'

'But?'

'But I just feel I should be there. I've been busy coaxing back my old clients and finding new ones, and then I suddenly just turn my back on it all, jump on a plane and travel halfway across the world. It's irresponsible on my part, don't you think?'

And selfish on my part, I thought. One reason I'd asked Elvis to accompany me was because I didn't fancy the idea of travelling all this way on my own. But I also thought it would be fun, and good for him to get away. Now I realised I was wrong. It was okay for me; I was keeping myself busy, but for Elvis, basically all he was doing was following Tetley around like a puppy.

'I've made up my mind. I'm gonna book a flight online tonight. Hopefully fly out as soon as possible, tomorrow or the next day.'

'Are you sure, mate?' I knew there was no way I was going to talk him out of it. Once he'd made up his mind about something, he was a stubborn bugger. But I just wanted to be sure he was okay.

'Yeah. I'm missing Cassie like hell too. As much as I'm enjoying being here in Nottingham and all that, I just gotta get back, you know?'

'I understand.'

Carol appeared at the back door. 'Shepherd's pie for dinner, boys. Is that okay?'

'That will be great, Carol. Thank you,' Elvis said. And I could already see a change in his demeanour. He'd made up his mind, and I respected him for that.

'I'll have to have mine later though, Carol, if that's okay?' I said, checking my watch. 'I've got an errand to run.'

'No worries, I'll warm it up for you when you get back.'

While strolling up the street to pick up the Jag from the garage, Elvis was on my mind. I could have argued the merits of his staying, begged him even, but that would have been purely selfish on my part. Although I was convinced that Cassie was the best thing that had happened in his life, I knew he was still fragile, and not the old Elvis I'd grown up with. If he needed to go home, I wouldn't be standing in his way.

<h1 style="text-align:center">40</h1>

Gedling was an ex-mining town—or a pit estate as Tetley called it—to the north-east of the city. It was only a short drive from Bobbersmill, according to Doris, but it actually took around half an hour due to it being rush hour traffic.

Shelford Road was a steep, winding hill that I entered from the top. Tony Patterson's house was at the bottom on the left, facing the Phoenix pub.

The houses on the street were identical, except for the windows and doors, the colours and renders, which had been replaced over the years. One big difference about Tony's house though was a half-finished extension on the right side of the building. On my approach, I noticed a black Chevrolet Ram at the top of the steep driveway. A man, who I assumed was Tony Patterson, was locking a large toolbox on the side of the truck. Wearing a singlet beneath an open, short-sleeve shirt, plaster-splattered shorts, and work boots, he was muscular, with a full sleeve tattoo on one arm and sporadic designs on the other. With receding hair, his most striking aspect was the bling—the gold watch, rings and a thick gold chain around his neck. When I cheekily steered the Jag into his driveway, he looked up, puffed out his chest and marched towards me.

'Tony Patterson?' I asked, climbing out of the car.

'Who wants to know?'

'Hi, I'm Scotty. Scotty Stephens,' I said, approaching him with my hand out.

He didn't shake my hand. 'What do you want?'

'Uhm … you're a builder, right?'

He glanced at the sign along the side of his truck that said, *Tony Patterson Builder,* and with an air of sarcasm, said, 'What gives you that idea?'

The smile I offered was as genuine as the unfinished extension on the builder's house, the house that would never be finished.

'I've got too much work on, Pal. I'm not looking for anymore, so if you can get off my driveway, I'd appreciate it.' Stewie had been right when he said Patterson was a cocky sod.

Plan A was my usual approach of interacting with a potential witness with warmth and honesty. If that didn't work, there was always Plan B. Realising right away that the latter was required on this occasion, I went straight into the plan I'd derived during the drive from Bobbersmill. It basically comprised of flattery, familiarity and a big fat lie. 'Yeah, I understand a successful guy like you would be in high demand. You've got quite a reputation in the building industry.' Ambiguous, yes, but I doubted his ego would notice the cynicism.

He raised his chin and nodded slightly as if to say, 'Yeah, that's right. So what?'

Steering the conversation into familiar territory, I said, 'I hear you're familiar with The Coach House in The Park.'

This caught his attention. 'What of it?'

'I'm uhm …' Time for the big fat lie. 'I'm considering buying it.'

'It's not for sale … is it?' The lowering of the voice and chin told me I had him.

'It's not on the market, but the current owner has approached me. I'm not sure if you are aware or not, but there was a nasty discovery on the property recently.' Of course, I already knew he was aware. The police had questioned him about it, but I wasn't going to let on I knew that. He didn't need to know I was a detective. 'He can't come to terms with what happened, well more his wife, so he wants to sell it as soon as possible.'

'What's this got to do wi' me?' His chin rose once more in defence.

'All work has come to a halt, so if I take it on, I'll need a builder to finish it.'

'There's already a builder working on it, surely.'

'There was, but apparently he's a bit superstitious, says he'll never go near the place again.'

He frowned and narrowed his eyes as if digesting the information.

'I learned that you and your old man did the original work. I think it would be great if you could carry it on, finish it off. You'd be working to new plans.'

'What kind of work ya looking at?'

'A full reno. Rip everything out. I want a fresh start, top quality and to my architect's design.'

'You realise that's gonna be expensive.'

'I do,' I said with an I-don't-care-what-it-costs, shrug. 'But I'd need the work doing right away.'

'There'd be a premium if I have to stop what I'm doing. I've got about six months' work before I should be tekin owt else on.'

'I appreciate that. Name your price, Tony.' Negotiation was easy with fake currency.

His chin lowered again, and with it, the defensive drawbridge. 'I'd need to come and have a look at it. Price it up properly.'

'I can arrange that, but, uhm … I haven't actually decided whether I'm going to take it on yet. I was hoping you might be able to fill me in on some of the history of the place. The owner seems a bit cagey, if you know what I mean.'

'Ah, I can tell you everything you want to know about that property. Come on in, have a beer.' He turned and I followed him up the driveway and around the back of the house. Before entering the building through a glass sliding door, he pushed off his work boots with his feet.

It was a decent-sized house, but definitely a work in progress. The internal doors were unpainted, and the walls were a collage of stripped wallpaper and patches of plaster. We entered the kitchen from the back of the house, which seemed to be the only area that was finished, and I imagined this was down to the insistence of Mrs P. I was also glad to see that there was a large double fridge, unlike the small under bench ones that most English houses I'd visited so far had, which meant the beer should be nice and cold at least. Imagine my shock though when instead of opening the fridge, he reached up into one of the overhead cupboards, pulled out a six pack of Heineken lager, ripped one off and handed it to me. Bloody hell. Beer served at room temperature. I'd heard about the phenomenon. In fact, Elvis and I had it loaded in our arsenal of banter bullets, which we regularly fired at Tetley, but in truth I always thought it was just a myth. When the warm can was placed in my hand, I was struggling to restrain the panic.

The weather was quite pleasant, so Tony led me back out to a patio at the back of the house where a variety of building equipment was stored—a cement mixer, ladders, wheelbarrows. 'Excuse the mess; we're in the middle of a renovation.'

'Right, how long have you lived here?'

'Six years. I should pull me finger out, really. You know what they say.' When he grinned, I couldn't help but notice the discoloured and uneven teeth. 'A builder's house is never finished. Anyway, cheers.' He peeled back the ring of his beer and lifted the can.

Reluctantly, I did the same, and we touched the cans together.

Tony threw back a mouthful of warm beer, and I inadvertently paused, watching him and waiting for the inevitable cringe. I'd only tasted warm beer once before in my life, and that's when the three of us—Elvis, Tetley and I—found a can of Powers Bitter in the back of Colin's ute when we were about fifteen. On that day, without knowing it, we broke the cardinal rule of the Australian lifestyle. Never, ever should a bloke or a sheila drink warm beer. And here I was, about to take my first sip. Bloody hell, talk about a first-world problem.

<h1 style="text-align:center">41</h1>

It was hard to speak with a mouthful of warm beer. I didn't know whether to swallow it or spit it out, and I couldn't help feeling violated, like I'd committed a cardinal sin or been forced to commit a crime.

'I don't actually know that much about the house,' I said after swallowing with a gulp and continuing with my little tale.

'Well, you've come to the right place, pal.' Although the arrogance was still present, the hostility was not. 'What do you need to know?'

'You and your dad renovated it back in the 90s?'

'Yeah. It was pretty much derelict when we took it on. It was a big job.'

'I bet it was a shock when you heard they found a body.'

'It was.' Unlike me, he drank his beer in casual sips.

'You see, this is why I'm hesitant to buy the place. I need to know as much about what happened there before I can decide.'

'It's history now, innit?'

'Did you ever meet the deceased? Before … I mean, you know?'

'Saw her a couple of times.'

'On the day she was killed?' I was using an eager method of questioning to give Tony the impression it was genuine concern, and not that of a detective or a reporter.

'No. I didn't see her that day.'

His eyes told me something different, a sudden blink before looking away.

'What was she like?'

He shrugged. 'A tart, I guess.'

'Were you there that night or the next morning?'

'Why do you need to know all this? It was thirty years ago.'

'I know, I know. I'm sorry. I'm just intrigued. I'm not sure I could live in a house knowing there'd been a murder there.'

'Fair point.'

'Did you know the owner?'

'O'Donnell? Not really, but me dad did.'

'A bit of a gangster, I hear.'

'Yeah. A flash git.'

'So, you were telling me you were there that night?'

'Was I?'

'Sorry, was you?'

'I left around 6.00 pm just as the plasterer was getting there. Dad had asked me to wait for him to arrive.'

'The plasterer?' I asked, being careful not to let on that I knew Colin.

'The killer!'

'Wow! Do you think he did it?'

'Course he did.' He finished his beer and rose from his seat. 'Want another?'

'No thanks; I'm driving.'

He disappeared into the house only to return moments later, opening another can.

'Did you know the guy? The killer, I mean.'

'No, never met him before that night. Dad hired him to do the job.'

'What was he like?'

The nonchalant shrug again. 'I don't know. It was Friday night. I wasn't gonna stick around.'

'Hitting the town?'

'Yep.'

'Did you ever go to Madisons?'

'Nah, we couldn't get in there back then. It was 21s and over, and a bit posh. It was the club where all the footballers and celebs went.'

I wasn't getting anywhere, so I needed to shift gears. 'I heard that the woman who was killed was a prostitute.'

I wasn't sure why, but this ignited a grin on Tony's face.

'Did you know that?'

'Ex-prostitute.' Was that a defensive tone in his reply?

'Right, so she wasn't in the game anymore?'

'No. It was common knowledge that O'Donnell had bought the place to keep his totty in.'

'Totty?'

'He was her sugar daddy.'

'Did you go to the house later that night or the next morning, you know, after the …'

'No. When will you have the new plans?' He stood and it was obvious our meeting was over.

I exhaled thoughtfully. 'Well, if I decide to buy it, hopefully in a few weeks. But to be honest, I'm not sure I want it.'

'You should get it. It'll be a good buy.'

'I'll let you know,' I said, also standing. Before we shook hands, I asked, 'Do you think this bloke … what's his name? Colin … really did it?'

'Who else could have? It was him who sealed the wall off, and the body was inside.'

'Could anyone have opened it up again after he'd left?'

'No, it was sealed shut, plastered.'

That wasn't true. According to the police report, the steel sheets were just screwed on, and there was no need for them to be sealed because the stone would cover it. Once again, I couldn't let on that I had this inside knowledge, so I pushed a little further to see if Tony was actually lying or if he was just mistaken. 'Oh right. The wall was plastered, so there was no way anyone could have opened it back up without making a bloody mess.'

'That's right, and it was a warm night. The plaster would have gone off pretty quickly.'

42

I was glad for an early night. We watched *Coronation Street* and *Britain's Got Talent*. Before retiring to bed, we ate tea and toast for supper.

The next morning, being the typical surfer, I was awake early. Also, being a surfer meant I was reasonably fit for my age, and being aware that this was something I needed to maintain, I decided to go for a run.

The streets were quiet, and there was little traffic on the roads as the day slowly materialised through a cloudy sky. Running was the next best thing to surfing in that it gave me time to think.

After heading down Bobbersmill Road and turning right at the bottom, I soon passed The Wheatsheaf, where we'd had drinks on Sunday afternoon. There, I crossed at the pedestrian crossing and headed up Aspley Lane.

I also had to remember my promise to Tommy Stokes to look into the death of Declan O'Donnell. If his death was the product of a professional hit, whoever financed it had covered their tracks very well. I wasn't planning on devoting too much time to this and saw it more as a distraction. If fresh evidence came to light during the current investigation, however, I wouldn't be ignoring it.

When I reached a roundabout at a wide, tree-lined intersection, I turned left, and something occurred to me. What if O'Donnell's killing was related in some way to the death of Janita? *Hmm.* I'd be keeping an open mind and open ears. The obvious players who were closest to O'Donnell at that time were his wife

Sheila, Tommy Stokes, his son Rodney, and Donna Simpson. But what about Bill Patterson, the builder? How well did he know him? I knew very little about Mr Patterson Sr. Was his son just like his dad? Arrogant and flash? The 80s and 90s were quite a lucrative time for most builders. Bill Patterson was from that era. Was his success at a level that would have put him in contact with the city's underbelly? Could he have been a regular punter at O'Donnell's escort agency? If so, would he have known Janita? This opened up a new train of thought. Although Tony was only a young bloke at that time—19 or 20—he could also have known her, used her services perhaps? Tommy definitely knew her. What if she was playing him too, like she was O'Donnell? He'd already told me he'd visited the property that night, but what if it was later than he'd said? After Colin had left, perhaps? So much later that the witness across the road had gone to bed? Tommy was a thug; there was no doubt about that, and I guessed he'd undertaken some dastardly deeds while working for Declan. Would this include killing people? And if so, would Declan have instructed him to go to the property to take care of business?

Then there was Sheila O'Donnell, and although I was pretty certain that she didn't go to the property and physically kill Janita herself, she had an entourage of young men working for her. If she'd found out about the affair and the little love nest that was being set up, she could have easily arranged for one of her boys to carry out the deed. I also didn't have a problem with the notion that she could have been behind Declan's death. Another chat with her wouldn't go amiss.

Knowing very little about Rodney, I was forced to hold judgement until I'd spoken with him. He'd worked for the family business during that time, so would he have been in contact with the girls? I couldn't rule out the possibility that Rodney could fill in some gaps. Plus, if there was an aversion towards his dad, he might be only too happy to open up.

Donna Simpson was Janita's associate. *How was their relationship? Was there any rivalry? And how well did she know Declan and Tommy?* Although she'd been out of the escort industry for a few years at the time of Declan's death, she could still be a link between both cases.

I'd spoken briefly with William Henley, the witness from across the street, but that didn't count. Being the only witness, he was possibly the most important aspect of the case. But I knew that just talking with him would be hard, never mind winning him over. I'd need a way of approaching him on his terms.

The answer to my dilemma soon came. When I reached another roundabout, I turned left again, hoping I was heading back towards Bobbersmill. It was full daylight now. A sign across the other side of the road caught my eye, and the cogs in my brain immediately turned. 'Neville's Nursery.' Behind a six-foot, chain wire fence were a variety of plants and small trees. William Henley was an avid gardener. Perhaps a nice plant would act as a peace offering? It was still too early; nowhere was open yet, so during the rest of the run home, which was a lot bloody farther than I'd anticipated, I planned out my day ahead. The first thing I'd do when I got back was call Jenny, check on the progress of the new house and catch up with what was happening back in Kirra. Then, after a shower and breakfast, I'd head back to Neville's Nursery, pick up something nice for Mr Henley's garden, and hopefully have a chat with him. Then I'd try calling Rodney O'Donnell in London again. And lastly, I'd call Donna Simpson to arrange another chat with her.

It would be a busy day, and although it already seemed like I'd been in the UK for ages, it was only Tuesday. I hadn't even been there a week yet.

43

At Neville's Nursery, the closest thing I could find to anything exotic was a yucca plant, which looked a bit like a palm tree. Driving out to The Park with the three-foot high plant wedged between the driver's seat and the back seat of the Jag, I was careful on the corners. The last thing I needed now was to soil Uncle John's immaculate cream carpets.

It was around 9.30 am when I turned into Cavendish Avenue, and the estate was quiet. The mums (or dads), after dropping off their kids at school, were likely out having lattes with the other parents or attending their Pilates classes. The office workers had all left for work, so there were a few parking spots on the street. Luckily, I managed to get one right outside William Henley's house.

The six-foot high fence extended all the way around the property with a matching gate across the driveway. The doorbell on the gatepost had a slight delay when I pressed it until I heard the familiar *ding-dong-Avon-calling* chime resonate in the house beyond. Almost instantly, I heard a lock slide across, and the gate opened slightly, just enough for William Henley to poke out his head.

'Yes. What do you want?'

'Hi, Mister Henley. I'm Scott. We met the other day.'

'What do you want?' he repeated. His tone was rushed, impatient and slightly flustered.

'I just wanted to apologise for the other day. We got off on the wrong foot, and I noticed you have a beautiful garden back there, so I …' I held out the yucca as a peace offering. 'I bought you this.'

'You bought that for me?' His expression gave way to a mixture of curiosity and suspicion.

'I did, yeah. It's the closest I could find to anything like the trees we have in Australia.'

The gate opened wider, and Henley stepped out. Taking the plant from me, he said admiringly, 'A yucca gigantea, also known as Y. guatemalensis and Y. elephantipes, originally from the Americas. One of the few succulents that can withstand an English winter.'

'I hope you like it.'

'I do. Thank you!'

'You're welcome. Is there any chance of having a look at your garden? I'm a bit of a keen gardener myself.' He didn't need to know my gardening experience comprised of pushing a Victor mower over a bindii-infested lawn and picking up dog shit.

As he reluctantly pondered my request, I wondered what was going through his mind. *Did he have anything to hide on the other side of that fence? Did the house have a dungeon in the cellar where victims were imprisoned and tortured? Was the healthy greenery of the garden due to all the decomposing bodies buried beneath it?* This was my overactive imagination kicking in, of course. With those beady eyes behind horn-rimmed glasses, and the imposition of a man with a secret, it wasn't hard to imagine him as a serial killer who struck every now and again, choosing his victims carefully. *What the hell, Scotty? You're getting a bit carried away, mate.* As far as I knew, this bloke was a typical law-abiding citizen who chose to live alone and was happy with his lot. And so, what if he was a bit of a nosy parker? He obviously loved living in The Park and wanted to protect it and its traditions.

'Okay, but I'm not answering any questions about …' He pointed to the house across the street.

'Yeah sure. No worries.'

Warily, he turned and allowed me to follow him through the gate. Once inside, he locked it behind us. 'Come on through.'

William led me around the side of the house, where the outdoor area expanded into what could only be described as a mini botanical garden. I hoped the yucca would be very happy there. He placed the plant down by the wall at the side of the back door and then showed me to a shaded lean-to, which was covered with thick vines. With an outstretched hand, he invited me to take a seat at a small circular wrought-iron table. When I pulled out one of the two heavy matching chairs, the cobwebs and dust told me it had been a while since anyone had sat there. But as impressive as the garden was with the well-maintained period house and the delightful, shaded area where we now sat, it was none of those things that captured my attention. It was the animals that were dotted around the small undercover area and even looking out at me from the windows of the house. A fully grown fox frozen in time while creeping across a window ledge. A bluebird resting on a branch seemingly engaged in silent song. A squirrel scurrying up one of the posts of the outbuilding, no doubt on its way to retrieve some of the juicy grapes that hung from the overhead vine.

'Taxidermy?' I asked, looking around and discovering more animals placed in strategic positions. A magpie seemingly in flight but hanging from the roof by an almost invisible wire, a piece of stolen silver in its beak. A mouse poking his head out from between two plant pots as if waiting for the right moment to dash back to his hidey-hole.

'Yes,' William said. 'It's a little hobby of mine, well a bit more than a hobby now since I retired from teaching. When word got out, people started bringing me roadkill they might have come across or carcasses they stumbled upon while out walking their dogs. That kind of thing.'

'Is it difficult?' I asked, leaning closer to the bluebird that sat on the branch of a large potted plant just to my right.

'Yes. It takes a lot of practise.'

'They're amazing!' I said, examining the lifelike perfection of his work.

'Thank you.'

'Do you sell them?'

'Sometimes. Sometimes the people who drop them off might buy them back. And I do a few family pets, mainly cats and dogs, and parrots. The odd goldfish.'

'Do you do it here? At home?'

'Yes. In the basement. Perhaps I'll show you later. Would you like tea?'

'That would be great, thanks.'

'You have a bit of a look around. I'll put the kettle on.' He trundled off back into the house.

My hunch had proved correct. The way to this man's heart was through his garden. I'd learned from experience that to get a person of interest to share information was to meet them on *their* territory on *their* terms.

The sun had come out, and it was quite pleasant as I strolled around the garden. When I reached the other side of the fence at the front of the house, I noticed there was a raised platform about a foot off the ground. Checking first that Henley wasn't watching, I stepped onto the platform and realised that this was the vantage point that gave the nosey bugger a view of the street. And although the house was two storeys, it was set back from the road and the view from the upstairs windows would have been obscured somewhat by the established trees not only in the garden, but along the pavement out front.

After a quick glance down the street in either direction, I stepped off the platform and continued my survey of the grounds. The last thing I wanted was to make Henley suspicious or piss him off, so when he returned carrying a tray of tea and biscuits, I decided not to quiz him about it.

'How do you like your tea?' he asked, placing the tray on the table.

'Milk, no sugar, thanks.'

Henley gestured for me to take a seat as he poured the tea from a teapot into china cups with saucers. 'So why are you really here, Mister Stephens?' He slid one of the cups across the table.

I didn't remember giving him my second name. I'd introduced myself as Scott. Or did I introduce myself when we met briefly over the fence the other day? I wasn't sure.

'I'm interested in purchasing the house across the street.' It was all I could think of. It had worked with Tony Patterson, so I was hoping I'd get the same result.

'The Coach House?'

'Yes, thinking about it.'

'But whatever for? You have a thriving detective agency in Australia. Why would you want to move to Nottingham?'

Bugger! Bloody internet. I wasn't being big headed, but a quick search of my name would bring up my history.

'You have quite the social media following. Why don't you just come clean and tell me why you're really here?'

'Why do you think I'm here?'

'You want to know who killed that girl across the street.'

I was busted. 'Do you know who killed her?'

'Of course I do. They have him locked up in Lincoln Prison.' He took a sip of his tea.

'Do you really believe that?'

'Yes, I do, and I've told the police everything I know. I'm sure DI Weston has allowed you exclusive access to the police report. I'm afraid I can't really tell you anymore than what was recorded.'

His statement had indeed been lengthy and detailed. The questions I had, such as 'Are you sure you didn't see anyone else entering the property that night?' were deflected with definite shakes of the head. And I realised I needed another approach, so I guided the conversation back to the garden and the taxidermy, which he was happy to share his knowledge of.

'I'd love to take a look in your basement,' I said after he'd explained the taxidermy process in great detail.

'Ah, the theatre.'

'Is that what you call it?'

'Yes, you'll see why.' He stood up and pushed the heavy chair backwards with his legs. I tried to do the same, but one of the legs got stuck between a paver and wouldn't budge, so I stepped away from it and followed William towards the back door.

'Shoes off, please,' William said over his shoulder before kicking off his shoes.

'No worries.' I was wearing my runners, which easily slipped off.

As we passed through the back door, I immediately understood the need to remove our shoes to protect the highly polished wooden floorboards. We were standing in a kitchen, quite small for the size of the house, and dark, but I realised that when this house was built, a kitchen wasn't the centre of the home as it is nowadays, strictly utilitarian and out of the way. William led me into a hallway. There was a staircase with cream-painted balustrades topped with the same polished wood banister and matching treads. Beyond that, I could see the front door with the sunlight streaming in through two stained-glass panels at the top half of the door. But we didn't get that far because beneath the stairs there was a door, which William opened. He then flicked on a light inside. We were now at the top of a flight of stone steps. William smiled back at me reassuringly before ascending the stairs. Warily, I followed with visions of Hannibal Lecter and John Christie.

'You're very fortunate, Scott,' Wiliam said as the stairs turned to the right at a small landing. 'Few people get to see this part of the house.'

When we reached the bottom of the stairs, the area was dark and cool, and there was a strong smell of disinfectant. William flicked a light switch on the wall, and when a series of fluorescent lights flickered into life, I realised right away why he had referred to it as a theatre. The white-tiled room with no windows reminded me of a mid-twentieth century operating theatre like the kind you'd expect to see on the *American Horror Story* TV show. *Shit, this guy had to be a serial killer, and here I was being led into his secret lair to be murdered and stuffed.*

On one wall was a stainless-steel bench, and behind it was a matching splashback from which hung various tools and implements, knives of varied sizes, and a hammer that was never designed to drive nails into wood. In the middle of the room was a stainless-steel island where I imagined the animals would be placed before they were skinned.

Scanning the entire room as quickly as possible, as my detective eyes did, I also spotted a large chest freezer across another wall.

'And here you have it,' Wiliam said, holding out his arms and grinning. 'My little theatre of horrors.'

'What have you got in the freezer?' I asked.

'Future projects.' He strolled over to the far wall and lifted the freezer lid.

Looking down through a swirling mist, I could see plastic bags containing bodies of various-sized animals waiting to be immortalised through Williams's art. It was hard to tell what they were, but I was guessing birds and mainly rodents. 'What's the biggest thing you've ever stuffed?' I asked.

William smiled patiently and said, 'We don't use that term—stuffed. We say preserved.'

'Oh right, sorry. What's the biggest thing you've ever preserved?'

'A pony. The Park is full of wealthy families, and when the pony of a little girl died, her parents thought it would be a good idea to have it preserved.'

'Wow. Big job?'

'Absolutely.' He closed the freezer lid.

'Ever thought about stuffi—I mean, preserving a human?'

'Uh, that would be illegal, Scott.'

'Yeah, but you must have thought about it.'

'Of course. I'd love to preserve a full human cadaver.'

I'm sure by now you know exactly what was going through my mind. I thought of Janita Sharma's body, carefully wrapped up in insulation foam, and *preserved*. Could it be this simple?

Case closed.

William did it.

Boy, I had a lot to think about, but right at that moment, the only thing on my mind was getting out of that dungeon alive.

44

We returned to the garden. William Henley wasn't as old as I'd originally thought. Mid-fifties perhaps. It was his old-school manner and the way he dressed that gave the impression he was older. M&S trousers, a woollen cardigan, dark vintage colours. I'd been analysing the man since I'd arrived. The decision to approach him from the angle of familiarity had been the right one; he talked endlessly about his garden, letting his guard down somewhat. There was nowhere else I needed to be, so at that point I was more than happy to let him talk. His horticultural knowledge was quite impressive, and although I had little interest in the subject, I listened patiently, adding the odd faux-attentive nod here and there as he reeled off the Latin names of just about every plant in his garden. By the time he'd finished, we were friends. Not mates of course, but I got the impression he didn't get the chance to talk to people very often.

'Would you like more tea, Scott?'

'That would be lovely, thank you, William.' *Was I losing my Australian accent already?* Bugger me, I'd only been in the UK for a few days.

William returned to the house carrying the tray. The sun was still out; the air was warm and fresh, and the delightful sound of a warbling garden bird recalled my impression of a perfect English setting. While waiting, I pondered over what I'd learned so far: he lived alone, a lifelong bachelor who had spent most of his life living with his mother and caring for her in her latter years. As far as I knew, he didn't have many friends, if any at all. He was a taxidermist and an avid gardener, as well as a nosy parker who cared about what happened on the street he lived on. It didn't sound like I had much, but after breaking through his protective exterior, I was feeling confident now that if there was that tiny bit of information that he hadn't shared with the police, I'd be able to prise it out of him. But I would need to tread carefully. If I were to spook him, I was pretty sure he'd curl up like a hedgehog or pull his head in like a tortoise. Briefly, I contemplated the ploy I'd used on Tony Patterson. Would pretending to be an interested buyer for the house across the street endear him to me more? Now that we were best buddies? Perhaps. But it would be a fragile, short-lived ruse. I was pretty sure William knew just about everything that happened on his street, and if The Coach House was back on the market, he'd know about it, or if I hinted it was, he'd make it his business to find out the details, even quizzing the current owner, perhaps. No, I needed another approach, dare I say a more honest one.

William returned with not only a fresh pot of tea, but clean cups and saucers too. 'I hope you don't mind sitting out here,' he said as he went about pouring the tea.

'No, not at all.'

'Although the weather is still unpredictable, this is my favourite time of the year. Spring.'

'Yeah, mine too.'

'The seasons would be very different from where you're from though.'

'They are. The winters aren't as harsh in Queensland. Summers can be a bit humid on the Gold Coast, but the temperature can remain quite pleasant.'

'Humidity, uh. I couldn't stand that. This is as hot as I like it.' He slid one of the cups over to my side of the table. 'So, tell me about your life in Australia. I'm sure it's very different from the lives we live over here.'

William Henley would have made a good psychiatrist, or even a detective. His gentle questioning, as well as the beautiful setting, made me feel relaxed and somehow safe. For possibly as long as it took him to tell me all about his garden, I spent the same time telling him about my life. The budding future AFL star, who lived in Melbourne until he was 14, the arrogant teenager who, through his selfishness, was responsible for his mother's death. I never spoke to anyone about that time, not even Jenny, so how come I was spilling my guts to a total stranger? He showed some interest in my time as a police officer, and more so when I told him about my recent brush with fame, and the cases I'd worked on so far as a private detective.

'It sounds like you've had an interesting life, Scott.'

'I guess you could say that. What about you, William? Travelled much? Are you retired or …?'

'No, and no. I've actually never been out of Nottingham.'

'Really?' I was careful not to display my surprise as patronising. I'd heard it wasn't uncommon for some English people not to travel too far.

'I was a schoolteacher for a short time until my mother fell sick.' He lifted his chin as he spoke. 'My parents were quite wealthy, well my father was, but he died when I was young, so it was just me and Mum. She never liked me working; said she'd look after me as long as I never went away.'

'Sounds like she loved you very much,' I said, but meant, *Sounds like she controlled your life. The perfect breeding ground for a psychopath.*

'I'm very happy, Scott.' This came across as slightly defensive.

'That's good to hear.' As I lifted my cup and drained the last of the tea, I was contemplating in which direction I needed to steer the interview. Softly, softly was the best approach. Like a sparrow from a stalking cat, he could fly away at any moment.

'I bet what happened at the house across the road was a bit of a shock for everyone on the street.'

'Oh yes. It certainly was.'

'To think that poor girl's body was behind that wall for all those years.'

'I know. It hardly bears thinking about.'

'And it happened so close to you.' Rather than conducting a typical interview, I was displaying a friendly concern.

He nodded passively and finished his tea.

'Terrible. Do you remember anything about that night?'

'Oh yes. I remember everything.'

'Even after all these years?'

He dismissed this with a nonchalant shrug. 'I actually went over there to complain about the noise. It was early evening, and that builder chap was cutting steel in the driveway. What a racket!'

'So, you got to meet the man who's been charged with the girl's murder?' My surprise was fake, of course. I already knew this.

'Oh yes, and he wasn't a very nice person. He told me to fuck off!'

Whoa ... wait a minute. A crack? A lie, perhaps? I'd known Colin Webster for most of my life. Not only had I never heard him use an expletive, not even on Johnno's stag night when we got him absolutely bladdered and we ended up at a nightclub in Surfers Paradise. Even when intoxicated, he was still the nicest bloke you could ever meet. I just couldn't imagine him telling anyone to F-off. Plus, there was no mention of this in the police report. 'Right, so he was quite aggressive?'

'Oh yes. I didn't stick around too long.'

I almost said, "But you went back over later?" but couldn't let on that I knew the details of the case.

'Did the noise continue?'

'A bit longer, yes.'

'So how does the young woman come into all of this? Was she already at the house or ...?'

'No, she arrived later.'

'Did you see her enter the property?'

'Oh yes. She went in while the builder was still there.'

'So, you think Col, I mean the builder, killed her?'

'Of course he did. Pardon the expression, but it went deathly quiet not long after she entered the building.'

'Did you see anyone else enter the property?'

'No. Not a soul!'

'But what about Tommy?'

'Tommy?' The name didn't appear to elicit fear, only curiosity.

'Tommy Stokes. He said he came around earlier while the builder was still there.'

William shrugged as if to reiterate what he'd already said.

'You know Tommy, surely? He lives just around the corner. A big guy. Bit of a thug. Did he come over and have a word with you?'

'I can assure you, Scott. I do not know anyone called Tommy Stokes. No one else came to the house that night that I saw, and they certainly didn't come to my home.'

45

I had a lot to think about while driving back from The Park. One of my strong points as a detective was the ability to identify the telltale signs when someone was lying. A lack of eye contact. A slight twitch. The odd stammer. Shuffling awkwardly in their seats. Not knowing what to do with their hands. William Henley displayed just about all of these attributes when our discussion turned to *that* evening. And even if Henley was the world's best liar, practised in the art of deceit, I knew for a fact that Colin Webster, the kindest, gentlest man you could ever meet, would never speak to anyone the way Henley described. So why did he lie? What was he hiding?

I'd spoken to almost all the players now; the only one left on my list was Rodney O'Donnell. The plan was to go back to Bobbersmill, retreat to the incident/dining room and try calling Rodney again from there. I didn't know what Tetley and Elvis were doing. It was around noon. The sun was still shining, and it was quite hot.

As I drove down Ilkeston Road, guided by the ever-present Doris, my phone rang.

I didn't recognise the number.

'Hello, Scott?'

'Speaking.'

From the gravelly voice, I realised it was Tommy Stokes. 'It's Tommy.'

'Hey mate, how's it going?'

'Not bad. Listen, I hear you paid a visit to the witness across the street.'

How the hell did he know that? Once again, the only person who knew of my movements other than Tetley, Elvis and Carol, was Stewie. 'I did, yeah. How did you know that?'

Ignoring my question, he said, 'What did the snivelling little bastard say about me?'

'Uhm, nothing. In fact, your name never came up.' I wasn't about to encourage him.

'Really?'

'Yeah. Should it have?'

'Well … no. I suppose not.'

'Is there something you're not telling me, Tommy?' I almost called him Tommo. It was an Aussie habit, shortening names and adding an 'o' to the end (Johnno, Davo, Daimo, Stevo, Robbo), but I didn't think that would sit right with Tommy Stokes.

'No. What makes you ask that?'

'It's almost as if you're purposely trying to attract attention to yourself.'

'Does it?'

'Do you think Henley saw you when you went to the property that night?'

'Is that what he said?' His question was a cocktail of sudden anger and panic.

'No, he said nothing, remember?'

'You wouldn't be withholding information from me, would you, Scott? Don't forget I have a vested interest in this case.'

'Do you?'

'Yes, I'm paying you to find Declan's killer, remember?'

I remembered, but I didn't know what *that* had to do with this case. 'Do you think the two deaths are linked?'

His tone suddenly changed to defensive. 'How would I know that?'

'Bloody hell, Tommy. You're doin' me head in, mate.' Shit, I was beginning to sound like Tetley.

'Have you spoken to Rodney yet?' I wasn't sure if this was an attempt to change the subject or if it was related to the conversation.

'No, I'm just about to call him. Is there anything specifically I should ask him?'

'Rodney would never be the man his father was, he didn't have it in him. But he was smart, and because he was quiet, we may have said a few things in front of him he wasn't meant to hear.'

'Such as …'

'Oh, you know, business.'

'Incriminating?'

'Absolutely.'

I was struggling to keep up with Tommy. What was his agenda? Why did he ring me in the first place last weekend? Was he trying to help me as he claimed, or was he purposely trying to put me off the scent? 'So, are you suggesting he may have had something to do with his father's death?'

'Put it this way. One minute he's just a low-level employee with no prospects, and no money as far as I know. His dad had made it clear to me he wouldn't be getting a penny of the inheritance.'

'Did Rodney know that?'

'Yes, he did. Declan wasn't shy in sharing his feelings about the boy he didn't believe was his son. But here's the thing: not long after his father's death, he goes to London and buys a pub. Where would he have got that kind of money from?'

'His mum, Sheila.'

'No, Sheila's money is in a trust. Everything she spends is accounted for.'

'So, what are you saying?'

'I'm saying that Rodney seemed to somehow benefit greatly from the death of his dad.'

'Okay, thanks, Tommy. I'll bear that in mind when I speak with him.'

'You have my number. Call me if there are any new developments, yeah?'

'No worries.'

Trudging through the house, I noticed the back door through to the kitchen was open, and I could hear the boys chatting out the back.

'Here he is!' Tetley exclaimed when I appeared at the back door.

'What the bloody hell's that?'

Elvis was sitting at the outdoor table in just a pair of shorts, but Tetley was lying back in a child's inflatable paddling pool.

'It's the pool, mate. Go an' get ya bathers on. Ya can have a dip.'

'Uhm … I'll be right.'

'Hey, Scotty!' It was Carol calling from the bottom of the garden. She was trimming the privet with a pair of shears. There's some iced tea in the fridge if you want some.'

'Thanks, Carol.'

'How'd ya go this morning?' Elvis Asked.

'Good.' I joined him at the table.

'Any closer to finding the real killer?' Tetley asked.

'It's slow, but I'm getting there.'

'Good to hear.'

'I've got some work to do and an important call to make. What are you guys up to?'

'I've booked a flight,' Elvis said casually.

'Really? So, you're definitely going home?'

'Yep. Day after tomorrow. I got an early-morning flight.'

When Elvis last fell into a depression almost a year ago and flew down to Melbourne to be with his parents, I thought I'd lost him. At that time, there was a distant emptiness in his eyes. I was seeing fragments of that again, and from experience I knew it was impossible to discuss his feelings with him. And there was no way I was going to try to talk him out of his decision. The good news is that when he met Cassie, she seemed to lift him out of his stupor and motivate him to get his life back together. So, if he was missing her, if he needed her to get his mojo back, then so be it. What was best for my mate was the most important thing at that time.

Tetley sat up in the paddling pool, sending water sloshing over the sides. 'So, we were thinking maybe we should all go down to London tomorrow. Have the night down there, then see him off the next morning.'

'That sounds good.' And it did. Not only could we spend some time in London, see a few of the sights, but it meant that if I could arrange it, I'd be able to duck away briefly and pay Rodney O'Donnell a visit.

'Cool,' Tetley said. 'I'll book us a hotel. We'll go down in the Jag.'

'Perfect,' I said, rising from the table. 'I've got to make an important call.' Placing a hand on Elvis' shoulder, I asked. 'Are you sure you're alright, mate?'

His sporadic nod was the thoughtful kind. 'Yeah, mate. I'm good. Sorry I'm leaving you in the lurch.'

'No, that's okay. I'm gonna be busy once we get back from dropping you off, so … you go home. Be with Cassie.'

On my way to the incident/dining room, I poured myself a glass of iced tea from a jug in the fridge, while contemplating the call I was about to make.

46

'Hello, is that Rodney O'Donnell?' After failed attempts over the last few days, the phone had finally picked up.

'Speaking.' The background noise was pub chatter and the *ding ding ding* of a pokie machine paying out.

'Hi, my name's Scott Stephens. I'm a private detective, and I'm investigating the death of Janita Sharma.'

'Who?'

'Scott—'

'No, I mean who has died?'

'Janita. I'm sorry, Anita Madison.'

'What would there be to investigate?' His accent was Nottingham with a Cockney twang. 'They've already caught the killer.'

'The man they have in custody is innocent.'

'That's ridiculous. Don't be ringing here again, eh.' He hung up.

Bugger. Should I have called him back? Maybe, but then wasn't the time. As I had with William Henley, I'd need to work out a different approach.

The next half an hour or so was spent updating the whiteboard. There wasn't a great deal to add—no new facts, only my suspicions that William Henley was hiding something. I was also mindful that Tommy Stokes had reminded me earlier that I'd agreed to look into the death of Declan O'Donnell. So far, I'd been concentrating on Janita. Could the two deaths be linked? I still wasn't sure about Tommy's motivation, whether he was genuinely trying to help, or covering his own arse. I suspected the latter. Like Henley, I was pretty sure he knew a lot more than he was letting on. He had a way of suggesting things without going into detail. The hints this morning regarding Declan's son, Rodney, for example. Was he attempting to control my thoughts? The thing that worried me the most, though, was how he knew about my visit with Henley. He had to have heard that from Stewie. Along with Henley, Tommy Stokes moved up a place on the list of suspects. Yes, *suspects*, not just players. This was a separate list I'd started on one side of the board. So far, the suspects, not including Colin Webster, and not in any particular order, were Javed Sharma, Sheila O'Donnell, Tommy Stokes, and William Henley. Depending on how the investigation went from there, I was hoping the list would shorten, but it could just as easily grow.

For some reason, Donna Simpson, Janita's associate, came to mind. If I were to move forward with both cases, I needed to define the potential links between the two. To do this, perhaps another list of players who were involved with both, was pending (yes, I'm sure you've realised by now, I'm one of those annoying list people). Donna was a friend of Janita's and an employee of O'Donnell. What if she'd also had a relationship with her boss? And what if it came to fruition once Janita was out of the way? If so, she would have known O'Donnell more than she had let on during our previous conversation. I had her number in my phone, so I called her.

'Hello Scott. It's nice to hear from you again.'

'Hi Donna. I was wondering if we could meet up for another chat.'

'Sure. When were you thinking?'

'Uhm, this afternoon?'

'Okay, but don't come to the house this time. I've got to pick up Emily from nursery at three o'clock. I usually take her to Wollaton Park to burn off some energy. How about we meet there, say 3.15?'

'That sounds great. I'll see you there.'

After my previous visit, I vaguely had a recollection of how to get to Wollaton, and I assumed that Wollaton Park was close to Donna's house. Not that it mattered; Doris would show me the way.

It was just after lunch when Carol, God bless her, poked her head around the door. 'I've got a nice bit of ham, Scotty. Would you like a sandwich?'

'That would be great, thanks.'

She moved farther into the room and lowered her voice. 'How are you getting on?'

'Good.' Then something dawned on me. Possibly due to my concern for her wellbeing, and her fragile state, I realised I hadn't asked her about her recollections of that time. There would be a need for gentleness. 'Carol, would you mind if I asked you some questions?'

'No, love, I don't mind at all.'

She closed the door behind her, and I gestured for her to take a seat at the dining table. Outside the back window, we could hear the muffled sound of a friendly banter exchange between Tetley and Elvis.

'Them lads. It's great to see you all together again. Is Elvis okay?'

'Yeah. I think he's just missing Cassie.' I hoped he was just missing Cassie.

'Bless him. What would you like to know?'

'In the police report, it mentions that you and Col weren't getting on so well.'

'Oh, that's just silly. We might have had the odd argument, but who doesn't?'

'What were you arguing about?'

'Oh … you know. Family. Life …'

'Is it true that you wanted to go to Australia and Col didn't?'

'He wasn't completely against the idea. He was worried about leaving everything behind and starting again in a strange country.'

'It was a big move.'

'It was, and that's what worried him.'

'So, what made him change his mind?'

'My nagging, probably.' She laughed, but I could see her eyes were welling up. 'No, seriously though. I think he just realised it would be for the better.'

'Just like that?'

'He wasn't happy with the work he was getting. It was the early nineties. I seem to remember there was a recession going on at that time.'

'And was it around the time he'd done the work at The Coach House that he decided or …?'

'Oh gosh, it was a long time ago, Scotty. I can't be a hundred per cent sure.'

'The application was submitted on June 24th, three days after he'd done the job in The Park.'

'Is that right?' She narrowed her eyes slightly as if trying to look back into the past.

'You must have discussed it that weekend, because the 24th was a Monday.'

'Yeah, I suppose we must have. The emigration forms were already filled out, though. I'd taken care of them months before. They just needed signatures and dating.'

'Do you remember what sort of mindset Col was in that weekend? Did he seem worried about anything?'

She exhaled and looked beyond me as if searching through her memory. 'Like I said, it was a long time ago.'

'But finally getting him to sign those forms must have been a very exciting time. One you'd never forget, I would have thought.'

'You're good at this, aren't ya?' she grinned.

'I'm not bad, eh?'

'I've never seen you at work before. I can see now why they call you Golden Balls on the Coast.'

We laughed, and I loved the fact that she maintained her sense of humour, but I hated the fact that I needed to press her further. 'Did he warm to the idea once the decision was made?'

'Yes … but I don't recall him being excited like me and the kids.'

'Do you think he wanted to go through with it? Or did he just do it for you? Or … or was there another reason he suddenly wanted to leave the country?'

'You're a bogga, and I can see what you're doing.'

I leaned over the table and gave her hand a gentle squeeze. 'I'm just trying to get a complete picture. Also, these are the questions that the prosecution will ask if this goes to court.'

'I know. I know. Colin and I were … *are* very happy. We always have been. Even when we didn't see eye to eye on certain things, we'd always make up.'

The question that I wanted to ask, but didn't, was from another seed that Tommy Stokes had planted in my mind. Could an escort have tempted Col? And if so, could she have threatened to expose him to his wife if he didn't pay her a certain amount of money? I didn't want to believe it. But I couldn't ignore the possibility. How well did I really know Col—the kind, caring and gentle bloke who took us fishing and camping when we were kids? Was that the real man? Or was there a dark persona behind the façade?

Nah!

47

After about a kilometre—or should I say half a mile—past the road I'd turned into when visiting Donna Simpson a couple of days earlier, I came to a long stretch of crumbling red brick wall on my left, about 20-foot tall and covered in moss. It stretched along one side of a wide, tree-lined road until it was broken by a large open gateway. Turning onto the property, I was met by an enormous green space bordered by ancient oak and sycamore trees. In the distance, standing proudly on the top of a grassed hill, stood a magnificent building that ignited a feeling of familiarity. I knew that building from somewhere. *But how could I?* Unlike my normal practice, where I'd conduct a little research before visiting a place or a person, I hadn't had time before leaving Bobbersmill to look up Wollaton Park, opting instead to relax in the garden with Tetley and Elvis enjoying ham sandwiches and pickled onions, with Walkers Crisps, and a fizzy soft drink called Tizer pop. Momentarily, I thought I'd got it. It was Downton Abbey. Of course, it was, with its turrets and its sandstone walls. But then my theory was shot when I noticed a sign with the image of a well-known superhero on it. *Bugger me.* Wollaton Hall was the Bruce Wayne Manor from the Batman movie, *The Dark Knight Rises*. Wow! I wasn't expecting that.

Parking the Jag in the car park just inside the gate, and climbing out into the warm air, the smells of freshly cut grass, the smoke from a far-off bonfire, and the sound of a familiar squeak carried on the wind. Following the direction of the sound, I found myself standing outside a children's playground. Inside, Donna was pushing a little girl on a squeaky swing. When she noticed me, she waved. I waved back and strolled towards her.

'Hiya,' she said, smiling as I approached.

'G'day, Donna. How's it goin?'

'Good. This is Emily. Emily, this is Scott.'

'Hello, Emily.'

'G'day, mate.'

My surprise at the little girl's Australian greeting must have shown because Donna burst into laughter.

'It's *Bluey*! It's her favourite show at the moment.'

'*Bluey*, eh?' I said, squatting down as the swing slowed to a halt. 'I like Bingo.'

'Me too,' Emily said in a pixie voice. Then I realised she was wearing a *Bluey* T-shirt.

'Good to meet you, Emily. I'm Scotty.'

We shook hands.

'Are you from Austria?'

'Australia, yes I am.'

'Do you know *Bluey*?'

'Not personally, but she lives close to me.'

'Cool. Mum, I want to go on the slide.'

Donna lifted the child out of the swing and set her down on the ground. The little girl took off heading for the slide. Her destination, though, was beneath it, in a little play area set out like a shop.

'She'll be in there for ages,' Donna said. With a good view and not too far away from the slide, we sat on one of the park benches. 'So, what did you want to see me about?'

When interviewing a suspect, a witness or a player for the first time, my approach was usually gentle and cautious, but if a second visit/interview was warranted, it meant there needed to be not just a good reason for it, but also an outcome, which usually meant a slightly different approach. By this time, the interviewee was usually questioning why I needed to speak with them again. Most times, they were sick of me poking my nose into their affairs. Also, bearing in mind that I was speaking with them in no official capacity, they could easily tell me, politely or impolitely, to piss off at any time. So, if there was information there that needed prising out, now was the time to do it, one way or another.

'I just wanted to clear a couple of things up. I've harvested more information since we last spoke, and there are a few things that just don't add up.'

'Like what?' She was defensive and guarded, but still friendly.

'Well, you mentioned Janita owed you money.'

'That's right.'

'It was quite a lot of money though, wasn't it?'

She shrugged. 'Not enough to worry about.'

'That's not what I've heard.' I'd heard nothing of the kind, but she didn't know that.

'From whom? That was between Anita and me, so I can't imagine how anyone else would even know about it.'

'You know Tommy though, right? He seems to know an awful lot.'

'Tommy Stokes?' She laughed. 'Are you serious? Tommy?'

'Wasn't he your boss?'

The laugh turned into a giggle. 'No. Tommy wasn't anybody's boss. He was Declan's gofer.'

'He seems to know a lot about you and what you girls got up to.'

'Yeah, that's because he was a pervert. So, you've obviously spoken with him?'

'Oh yeah.' I could feel my credibility slipping away.

'Then you'll already know what he's like. A self-important nobody. Sheila only lets him run the clubs because she feels sorry for him.'

It was tiny, but it was the kind of breakthrough I'd been looking for. At our last meeting, she claimed she hadn't seen Sheila for years or had anything to do with the firm since quitting the business in the mid-nineties. So how did she know Tommy had been running the clubs since Declan's death? *Be careful, Scotty. Don't push too hard, or else you'll lose her. Bring the conversation back to level ground.* 'How well do you know him?'

'Knew him …'

'Sorry. Knew him.'

'He thought he was something he wasn't. Probably still does.' The smile returned, and I was glad of it. 'I bet he told you he's running Nottingham. Am I right?'

My shrug was hardly noncommittal.

She peered over to where her daughter was making cakes with sand. 'I can just imagine what he's told you, but …' She paused as if choosing her next words carefully. 'Don't underestimate him. I used to imagine that if one day he cracked, he could be a very dangerous man.'

'Do you think he killed Declan?'

'What?' She directed her attention back to me with surprised eyes. 'That's a bit random, isn't it?'

'Is it? What about Janita? Could he have killed her?'

'Bloody hell. You're going for it, aren't you?' She sat back and ruffled her shoulders.

'You just said it yourself; he might be a dangerous man.'

'Yeah, but …' She looked at the ground with searching eyes, and I could tell that my accusation had directed her thinking pattern to the possibility.

'I happen to know that he went to The Coach House that night.'

'Really?'

I had her full attention again. 'He told me himself.'

'Why would he tell you that?'

It was the question I'd been asking myself since Tommy first made contact and asked me to meet with him. If the outcome of the police investigation was a foregone conclusion, as everyone seemed to expect it was, why didn't he just keep quiet? And why did he contact me and feel the need to spill his guts? Was he afraid that I would unearth something the police had missed? If so, this would fall in line with my suspicion that he was trying to put me off the scent. It also might confirm my suspicion that William Henley was withholding some vital information.

'I had nothing to do with Anita's death. I can assure you of that.'

I wanted to believe her, but as with the other players, I still sensed there was more she wasn't telling me.

'Did you hate her?'

Once again, she paused cautiously. 'I was angry with her. And although I never got my money back, I was glad when she'd left. Well, you know what I mean. I thought she'd left.'

'Tommy reckons you girls used to blackmail the punters. Threatened to tell their wives what they'd been up to if they didn't pay you more money.'

'I never did. That was Anita's thing.'

'Is that what happened that night with the builder?'

'I don't know; I wasn't there.'

'So, you never went to The Coach House that night?'

'No, of course not.'

'Have you ever been to The Coach House?' You'll know by now that I'm good at reading expressions. Like a reaction to the sound of the dentist's drill, certain questions, usually the unexpected ones, can cause a slight response, a flinch, an involuntary frown, a blush.

'Uh … no. Where is it again?'

'You know exactly where it is.' Scotty-Hercule Poirot was back. 'You moved in not long after Janita disappeared. How long did you live there?'

Her eyes returned to the ground, defeat and some panic present in her demeanour.

'Were you still living there when Declan was killed?'

'How do you know all this?'

Poirot was on a roll. 'It would have been quite an advantage for you, Janita disappearing like that.'

Remaining quiet, eyes still searching the ground, she frowned as confusion seeped into her disposition.

'It wouldn't have taken much to arrange for someone to go around and take care of her. Tommy perhaps?' Like the famous Agatha Christie character, my accusations were totally fictitious.

Donna jumped to her feet. 'I've got to go.' Then she marched over to the slide, picked up her daughter, and carried her to a stroller I hadn't noticed earlier by the gate.

'I'll probably need to speak to you again, Donna ...' I called after her. '... or most likely the police,' I added as she headed towards the car park.

With nothing left to do that afternoon. I certainly wasn't going to leave without a look around the Bruce Wayne Manor and the amazing grounds that surrounded it.

<h1 style="text-align:center">48</h1>

During the drive home, my phone suddenly went crazy. *Ping …
ping … ping … ping.* It was a series of texts, one after another.
They kept coming, so I kept driving until they stopped, which
didn't happen until I was almost at Bobbersmill. Although eager
to see what it was all about, I patiently parked the car in the
garage, then did that annoying thing I hate when other people
do—walked along while checking my phone. Twelve messages,
eleven photographs and one video, all from Jenny. I was about to
enlarge the first image when another text came through. It simply
said: *Call me when you've had a chance to check these out. What an
exciting day! Jen xxx.*

I already knew what the pictures were of. It was D-Day. The
day me, Jenny, Elvis, and Cassie had been waiting for. The day we
finally broke ground on Ruby Street.

The first picture was of Jenny and Cassie holding up their
thumbs, in the middle of the block wearing hard hats, high-vis
vests and smiles as wide as Kirra Beach. The second image showed
a JCB excavator travelling the short distance from the road to
the block. Various shots of the digger followed these in different
positions until it was in place. The last image showed Jenny, Cassie
and Bob (the builder) standing beneath the airborne bucket,
double thumbs this time and those same excited smiles. The
video went on for about three minutes and showed the excavator
breaking the surface of the soil and scraping it back. Wow! The
build was finally underway. Strangely, beneath the obvious feeling

of jubilation, there was also a touch of sadness, and I realised it was for the old house. The home that Elvis and I had shared all those years was gone, and all traces of it wiped from existence. All those happy times—the peeling paint, the bindii-infested back garden, and of course the legendary man shed. By this time, I was leaning on the front gate of the house on Bobbersmill Road. I rang Jenny straightaway.

'Wow!' was my first word when she picked up. 'It's finally happening!'

'Yep. How good is that?'

'Bloody brilliant.'

'So, you got all the pictures, and the video?'

'I did, thank you. They're amazing. God, I'm missing you, mate.'

'Ditto.'

Checking my watch and doing a quick calculation, I realised it was early in the morning back in Queensland, just after 2.00 am. 'What are you doing up this early?'

'Just got home. Did a late shift. I had the morning off to be at the house site but then had to work back late. There's been a string of burglaries over the last few days, and from the CCTV images, it looks like it's the same gang of youths. Last night they upped their anti and threatened an elderly man with a knife. It's getting pretty nasty, the little bastards.'

'You'll catch 'em.'

'Oh yeah, my oath.'

'So, tell me about the building site. What's happening?'

'Ah mate. What a day. Bob's not messing around. The pad's been cleared, and they've started digging out for the slab and the plumbing and whatnot.'

'God, I really wish I were there. I really wanted to be present when they broke ground.'

'I know, but I'll keep you updated. The work you're doing there is more important. How's the case going?'

I filled her in on what I'd learned so far.

'Sounds like this Tommy character is a bit sus.'

'I know. What I can't work out is why he contacted me. If he'd stayed out of it, I wouldn't even have known he existed, never mind have him pegged as one of the main suspects.'

'How's Carol?'

'She's good, bless her. As good as can be expected. She's looking after us, anyway. Hey that reminds me. Uhm … Elvis is flying home tomorrow.'

'What?'

'Yeah, he's not enjoying being away from Cassie.'

'She didn't say anything yesterday.'

'Really?'

'Do you think he's told her?'

'Don't know. I would have thought so.'

'I'll find out. I'm seeing her later today. Alright, I'll let you get off. What else have you got planned for tonight?'

'Nothing. That's what's worrying me. It seems there's only two things to do around here in the evening. Watch the telly, or go to the pub.'

'Hmm. What will it be?'

'Don't know. We'll see what Lord Tetley's got planned.'

'Okay. I'll talk to you tomorrow. Love you!'

'Love you too.' Reluctantly, I hung up.

Tetley and Elvis were still in the back garden when I entered the house. It looked as if they hadn't moved all day. Elvis was still seated at the small outdoor table; Tetley was still in the paddling pool, only this time he was seated upright with his legs crossed. Both of them held cans of Carling Black Label Lager, and by the looks of the small pile of crushed empties by the fence, they'd had a few.

Carol waved from the bottom of the garden. She'd certainly been busy. The entire privet hedge on three sides was now at a neat, uniform level. 'Put the kettle on, Scotty, and I'll make us a brew,' she said as she swept up the last of the cuttings into a wheelie bin.

'Get yourself a beer, lad,' Tetley said.

Retreating into the kitchen, I filled the kettle from the sink tap and placed it on the stove, then grabbed myself a beer from the small fridge. At least it was cold.

'So, what ya been up to today?' Tetley asked.

As I just had with Jenny, I filled them in on what had happened during the day, only not in as much detail. Tetley didn't need to know about the accusations against his dad, that he might have been involved with the escort.

I suddenly remembered the exciting news. 'Hey Elv. Did you get the pictures?'

'Pictures?'

'Yeah, the house. They've broken ground.'

'Oh. I haven't checked my phone. It's charging up in the room.'

I was pretty sure Cassie would have sent him the same pictures I'd received from Jenny. Dragging a chair over, I plonked myself down by his side, pulled out my phone and showed it to him. To my surprise, he didn't seem too excited.

'Are you okay, mate?' I asked.

Tetley remained uncharacteristically quiet.

'Yeah, I'm alright,' Elvis said. 'Just homesick, that's all.'

'You'll soon be back. I wish I could come with you. What have you blokes been doing today?'

Before Tetley could answer, Elvis held out his hands and said, *'This!'* It was more of a spit.

'So, you've been here all day?'

'Got to enjoy the sunshine while you can, Scotty,' Tetley said. 'It might be snowing next week.'

Although I'm sure he was exaggerating, I got the feeling that the fine weather was a delicate luxury that we were lucky to be experiencing at that time of the year.

After another nice evening meal prepared by Carol, it was Tetley who chose from the two choices of entertainment on offer. *EastEnders*, and *Emmerdale*, or the nearest pub. He chose the latter.

49

As much as I hated the idea of Elvis travelling home on his own, the prospect of spending some time in London was exciting. But more importantly, it meant I'd be able to speak face to face with the last player on my list, Rodney O'Donnell.

Although Elvis' flight wasn't until 9.00 am the following day, we left at 6.00 am, which meant we'd have a full day and a night in the capital city before he left. Elvis had packed the night before, and his mood had lifted somewhat as he sat in the comfortable passenger seat of the Jag.

'I'm really sorry about this, Scotty,' he said, opening up for the first time. 'I should never have come. I thought I was over all this anxiety shit, but …'

'It's alright, mate. You don't have to explain anything.'

He turned his head to face Tetley, who was sitting in the back, and addressed us both. 'It's not you guys. I think I'm just missing Cassie, and what with one thing and another.'

'You've always been a sad twat!' Tetley said. Bless him for subtly breaking the tension the only way he knew how. At least it made Elvis laugh.

'So, what's your plan, Scotty?'

'Well, I thought I'd spend today sightseeing with you guys. Then after we drop Elvis off at the airport tomorrow morning, I'll duck out and see a man about a dog.'

Now it was Tetley's turn to laugh. I'd used the phrase that *he* often used to explain whenever he was going somewhere, without letting on where he was actually going. It could be used in all situations—going for a job interview, going to the doctor's, going to the toilet. But then his expression hardened when he realised what I'd meant. 'What am I gonna do if you're off gallivanting?'

'I don't know. You can wait in the car, or I can drop you off somewhere for an hour. It's important. It's about the case.'

'Right. I'll let you off then.' He hunkered down on the spacious back seat and made himself comfortable.

The journey itself was uneventful. After heading towards the Derbyshire border, we turned southbound onto the M1 motorway, where we remained for most of the drive.

Elvis said very little, choosing to gaze out of the passenger window instead. Thankfully for him, I wasn't one of those annoying people who felt they needed to initiate a conversation; I was just as comfortable with silence, pondering my thoughts. It seems Elvis was too, which was still quite a strange sensation. A year ago, he would have been chatting excitedly, pointing out of the window at anything that caught his eye, marvelling at this strange yet familiar land. And then there was Tetley. He must have been tired because it was very unusual for him to be quiet. Then I realised that although he was putting on a brave face, he was worried sick about his dad. He just wasn't showing it.

When we turned off at the motorway at the Wembley exit two hours later, Tetley entered the address of the hotel into the satnav, and the familiar voice of Doris directed us to our destination.

The Don Revie Hotel was a three-star establishment within walking distance of the famous stadium. In fact, when we checked into our room, we could see the top of the steel bow that spanned the sporting structure over the buildings.

'Did you just get the one room?' Elvis asked, looking at the smallish double bed and the one single.

'Yeah. Mam's paying, so I didn't want to go overboard,' Tetley said, throwing his rucksack on the double bed.

'Carol's paying? Mate, why didn't you say? I'll be paying for it, not your mum,' Elvis said.

'Bloody hell, Tetley,' I piped in. 'I would have paid for the accommodation if I'd known.'

'It's okay; it's all taken care of,' Tetley said. 'Anyway, what's wrong with this?'

The glance that Elvis and I shared silently spelled out our thoughts, but before we could protest, Tetley exclaimed with excitement. 'We're in London, boys. Come on, let's get out there.'

He was right, and although Elvis and I allowed him to change the subject and he was ready to hit the city within minutes, I'm sure we were both thinking the same thing—there was no way Carol was paying for all this. I'd sort that out when I got back to Nottingham.

Although the hotel Tetley had booked wouldn't have been my first choice, when we stepped outside to find it was only a short stroll to the underground, I realised the location was good, and the fact that it had parking was a huge bonus. After travelling into the bowels of the earth on an escalator among hundreds of scurrying commuters, we boarded a tube train headed for Leicester Square.

The day was an absolute success. Purchasing tickets on the hop-on-hop-off, open-topped Big Red Bus, meant we got to see and visit all the sites—Buckingham Palace, the Tower of London, the Houses of Parliament. And before we knew it, it was late afternoon. Tetley had taken complete control of the day and did a sterling job as our tour guide. By early evening, we'd returned to our hotel, got changed and headed back into the city to experience the nightlife, the highlight of which was a twilight ride on the London Eye.

'I'm gonna miss you, Elv,' I said, placing a hand on my old mate's shoulder.

'Yeah, me too,' Tetley said, pulling us in for a group hug. We had the spacious glass bullet gondola to ourselves. I didn't realise that the enormous wheel travelled so slowly; a full revolution took around 30 minutes. So, we had plenty of time to chat, but little to chat about.

'I bet you're looking forward to getting back now, mate,' I said to Elvis as the amazing view of the city sprawl revealed itself to us.

'Yeah. I'm missing Kirra, that's for sure.'

I was suddenly struck by an anxious feeling similar to the kind I'd experienced during the highs and lows of the X case, and it was something I hadn't felt since that time. Like Elvis, was I beginning to question my reasons for being halfway around the world? One thing was sure: I realised I too was missing Kirra, but most of all I was missing Jenny.

The evening was capped off with a pub crawl of Covent Garden. Elvis and I took it easy on the booze, Elvis for obvious reasons—he didn't want to board a plane for a long-haul flight with a hangover, and I needed to be fresh in the morning for my unannounced meeting with Rodney O'Donnell. Tetley, on the other hand, having no such commitments, went for it, and we ended up just about carrying him back to the hotel around 11.30 pm.

After a buffet breakfast and an early check out, the drive to Heathrow Airport was a solemn affair. Elvis needed to drop his luggage off and check in two hours before his flight, and he insisted we didn't park the car and come into the airport. So, we said our goodbyes at the drop-off area outside Terminal 4.

'Take care, mate, eh?' I said, embracing him tightly.

'Will do. And you make sure you nail this case. Bring Colin and Carol home safely.'

'You have my word.' While Tetley said his goodbyes, I climbed back into the car. Bloody hell, was I crying?

Effortlessly guiding his suitcase with one hand, Elvis looked back as he made his way into the terminal and gave a final wave. Tetley sat in the car and waved back until an Indian parking attendant moved us on.

50

'That's alright. I'll just have a wander around the East End,' Tetley said as we negotiated the traffic out of Heathrow Airport.

'No, you won't,' I said with a slight grin.

'Eh?'

'Have you checked your phone this morning?'

'No, why?' He scrambled into his pocket to retrieve his phone. When he saw the message from me, sent at 5.00 am, his eyes nearly popped out of their sockets. 'You are kidding me.'

'Nope. We're on the way there now.' The idea of leaving Tetley to his own devices while I hung around hoping to grab a meeting with Rodney O'Donnell, hadn't sat right with me, so I'd been tossing around a few ideas of things I could arrange for him to do—see a show perhaps, attend a guided tour of one of the many historical sites. It was too early in the morning for a Westend show, and to be honest, I doubted he'd be interested in the kind of history I had in mind. But I needn't have bothered, because when we'd left the motorway the previous day and followed the signs to our destination, the perfect venue revealed itself. The night before, after stealing a moment to myself, I'd jumped online and booked a ticket. Earlier that morning, before leaving for the airport, I airdropped it to my little mate. In all the excitement, he must not have noticed the text message.

Amidst all the steel and glass of the enormous modern structure, it was warming to see the remnants of the iconic old building in the form of two stone towers. When I pulled up as close to the Bobby Moore statue as I could get, Tetley couldn't contain his excitement.

'You're a legend, Scotty! I can't believe you've done this.'

'I know. I'm awesome.'

He leaned over from the passenger seat and gave me a hug.

There was no parking that close to Wembley Stadium, only a drop-off zone, so we arranged to meet back there after the tour of the hallowed grounds was over.

'If I'm not here, there's probably a café inside or a coffee shop round about, so text me to let me know where you are, and I'll pick you up when I'm finished with O'Donnell. Yeah?'

He nodded eagerly, desperate to get out of the car, and I realised he hadn't heard a word I'd said.

'Go on, bugger off. I'll see you later.'

Almost skipping towards a small queue outside the entrance, he turned and waved like he was four years old again, going to kindy for the first time.

Rather than attempting to drive into the city, I parked the car in the park-and-ride on the outskirts of the stadium, close to Wembley Park Tube Station. The train was packed with intercity commuters, and I had to stand for the fifteen-minute journey.

Thanks to the guidance of Doris and the walking app, The Horse and Groom was a short stroll from Whitechapel Station. It was mid-morning, and the pub wouldn't be open until 11.00 am, so I was expecting to have to hang around for a bit. During the short stroll, I went over in my mind why I was there and what I was expecting to achieve from an interview with Declan O'Donnell's son. Rodney wasn't a suspect in the death of Janita Sharma, and although he was on my list of players, the reason I wanted to speak with him wasn't because of his relationship (or lack of) with his father, it was mainly because something Tommy Stokes had said. "That boy was always hanging around, listening to things he shouldn't." At that point, I wasn't even sure if he'd be able to offer anything tangible about the night Janita was killed, but maybe he had information about his father's death. And then again, maybe, just maybe, he could shed some much-needed light on both cases. In reality, though (and this was a scenario I was prepared for), he'd probably tell me to bugger off.

When I turned into Brick Lane, the whitewashed walls of The Horse and Groom Public House, with colourful flower boxes beneath quaint French windows, were the centrepiece of one of those little pockets of history that are scattered throughout the city, especially the East End. The narrow street made me think of Arthur Conan Doyle and a time of horse-drawn cabs and street urchins.

The pub was obviously closed, but as I approached the establishment, I couldn't believe my luck. Down one side of the building was an alleyway. A Heineken delivery van was parked next to an open wooden trapdoor in the ground. Rodney O'Donnell stood chatting with the driver.

Although he looked different from the photographs I'd seen of him—older, a little podgier—it was the red hair, although now receding, and the arctic blue eyes that were unmistakable. He wore a linen shirt and shorts; his feet were bare, and he seemed to be checking through the delivery on a clipboard.

Scanning the alleyway, I realised that apart from the trapdoor, there was no other way into the pub on that side of the building, so he would have to pass me when he'd finished with the driver. This proved true when he patted the young fellow on the back and handed him the clipboard.

Heading my way, he acknowledged me with a nod.

'G'day. Rodney, isn't it?'

He stopped, looked me in the eye and cocked his head to one side. 'Who's asking?'

'I'm Scotty Stephens. We spoke on the phone.'

'You came all the way down here from Nottingham?'

'I came all the way from Australia!'

'Well, you've wasted your journey, I'm afraid. I've got nothing to tell you.'

When he attempted to pass me, I stepped in his way. 'I just want a chat, that's all. I'm working on the Janita Sharma case. I know you had nothing to do with that, but I wondered if you could just, I don't know, shed some light on the goings-on around that time.'

'It's not really a time in my life I'm keen to recollect.'

'I know. You didn't get along with your dad. I've heard.'

'It's more than that. A lot more. Now if you'll excuse me, we're just about to open.' He tried to push past me once more, but I stood firm.

'Please, mate, I've come a long way, and there's an innocent bloke sitting in jail for a crime he didn't commit.'

'Do you really believe that?'

'I do.'

'What evidence do you have?' At last, a spark of interest.

'Quite a lot, actually.' I lied.

It's the little things you notice. The Rolex watch that he checked told me he was doing alright for himself. 'We're opening soon, so I haven't got time for this, I'm afraid.' He pushed past me.

'I'm not going anywhere, Rodney, until I get some answers,' I called after him.

<h1 style="text-align:center">51</h1>

The Horse and Groom opened at 11.00 am on the dot. Rodney didn't look so happy when he unbolted the front door to find me at the front of the queue of two—me and an old bloke with a ruddy nose and a newspaper under his arm.

Making my way straight to the bar, a friendlier face, an older man with dyed dark brown hair, tinted glasses and a bright orange Polo shirt, greeted me.

'Good morning. What can I get for you?' he asked with a genuine smile.

'I'll just get a pint of shandy, please, mate.'

'Sure.' While pouring lemonade from a soft drink hose, he eyed me suspiciously then said. 'Where do I know you from?'

By this time Rodney had joined him behind the bar. 'He's a detective from Australia.'

'Oh, my goodness.' He almost dropped the half-filled pint pot. 'That's it. You're Scotty Stephens.'

'You know him?' Rodney said, surprised.

'Of course I know him. He's Scotty-bloody-Stephens.' He put down the glass, leaned over the bar and offered me his hand. When we shook, a thick gold chain on his wrist jingled. 'What an honour it is to have you in our humble abode, Sir.'

'Thanks.'

'I'm Eric. You're a long way from home. On holiday?'

'No, I'm working a case.'

He was about to pour the beer into the glass but instead he cradled his face in his hands. 'Oh, my goodness. A murder?'

'Don't encourage him, babe,' Rodney said as he served the old chap.

'Don't you know who this is?'

'No. And I don't want to.'

'Oh, please excuse my partner,' Eric said. 'He can be such a mardy little sod sometimes.'

The two exchanged a mischievous glance.

Eric finished topping up the pint pot and passed it across the bar. 'That's on the house, Scotty.'

'Eh?' Rodney protested.

'You really don't have any idea who this man is, do you?'

'No. Should I?'

'Thank you.' I was enjoying the exchange between them. I'd said very little so far.

'He's only Australia's most famous detective of all time. Please excuse my other half's ignorance, Scotty. I'm a bit of an amateur sleuth myself. I follow all the big cases, usually in America, but I know all about you. The *X* case, the killings in the Gold Coast hinterland. Creepy. Then there was the case with the ex-child star. What was his name?'

'Freckles.'

'That's it. And then, of course, the murder of Bobby Sexton. Wow, you nailed that one.'

The last comment caught Rodney's attention. 'Bobby Sexton? The lead singer of INSEXT?'

'Yes,' Eric said answering for me. 'This is what I'm trying to tell you. This man is crime-fighting royalty.'

'Did you meet Phil?' Rodney asked after handing over the old boy's change.

He was referring to Phil Sexton, the other half of the famous duo, and older brother of the deceased. 'I did. I got to work closely with him. Now he's a good mate.'

'He gave Scotty a classic Porsche.'

'Really? What's he like?'

'INSEXT is my husband's all-time favourite band,' Eric said, lowering his voice as if his partner couldn't hear.

Since our brief telephone conversation the day before yesterday, I'd been pulling out my hair trying to figure out a way to break through Rodney's tough exterior. The exchange outside the pub earlier hadn't helped, but thanks to Eric, he was opening up to me. *Ah, the benefits of fame—*

Twat! Tetley's voice interrupted.

'He's a really nice guy. Down to earth, you know?'

'Wow!'

'What can we do for you, Scotty?' Eric asked. 'I'm sure you haven't just wandered in here for a shandy.'

I took a sip of my drink then nodded before wiping away the foam from my top lip. 'I'm here to see Rodney.'

Eric gasped, his eyes opening wide and flicking between me and his partner. 'Rodney? Why would you need to speak with Rodney?'

'He's here to ask me about Declan O'Donnell,' Rodney said, staring me in the eye.

'Oh, thank goodness,' Eric said, fanning his face with his hand. 'I thought you were going to say my Roddy was a serial killer there for a minute.'

'Rodney, can I speak with you in private? It won't take long.'

The two men shared another glance and Eric nodded in support.

'I'll get you Phil Sexton's autograph,' I threw in.

Rodney exhaled loudly and came around the bar. 'Follow me.'

As I followed him through a double doorway, I looked back over my shoulder and mouthed, "Thank you!" towards Eric.

'I don't really know how I can help you,' Rodney said, showing me to a seat in what looked like a posher part of the pub. On the door, etched into opaque glass, was the word, 'Lounge'.

'I had nothing to do with the escort side of the business. I didn't even know any of the girls.'

Bugger me. A lie right off the bat. That was if I was to believe Donna Simpson, of course, when she said Rodney got on with all the girls like he was one of them.

'So, you never met Janita Sharma?'

The confused frown prompted me to add, 'Anita Madison.'

'Oh, no. Never.'

'You are familiar with the case, of course.'

'Yes. The police questioned me.'

'What was your relationship like with your dad?'

'We didn't have one. He hated me, and I hated him.'

'Why was that?'

'I didn't live up to his expectations. The son of the great Declan O'Donnell. Declan was a homophobic thug. There was no way I was ever going to please him.'

I noticed he didn't refer to Declan as his father or his dad. 'Did you try?'

He sat back in his seat. 'All the time.'

'Did you ever go to The Coach House in The Park?'

'No. I didn't even know it existed.'

'Does the name William Henley mean anything to you?'

'No. Should it?'

As was my way, I ventured into a little harmless speculative fiction to incite a response. 'I have it on authority that you visited the property on the night of Janita's death.'

'What? That's bullshit.'

'Is it?'

'Yes. Who the hell told you that?'

'A witness has come forward.' I lowered my voice for effect. 'The police are looking into it.'

'That's crazy. I had nothing to do with that poor girl's death. Have you spoken with Tommy?'

'Tommy? What's he got to do with it?'

'He was Declan's henchman. If anyone needed sorting out, he was the bloke to do it.'

'And is that what Janita needed? Sorting out?'

He looked away and gazed towards the window without seeing it. 'I overheard them talking.'

'Tommy and your dad?'

He nodded. 'Declan said the girl was a problem that needed to go away.'

'How do you know which girl he meant?'

There was a brief smile. 'Tommy, not being the sharpest tool in the shed, asked the same question. Declan replied, "Anita".'

'What happened next?'

'Declan told him to go to the house and fix the problem.'

'And did he?'

Rodney lifted his shoulders and shook his head.

'How come you didn't tell any of this to the police?'

'I just didn't want to be involved.'

'But you're telling me now.'

'If there really is a witness claiming that I was at the property that night, that's a lie. Look around you, Scott. I've got a good life down here. I'll defend that to the death.'

'So, you'd be willing to throw Tommy under the bus.'

'If self-preservation is required, then so be it.'

'What do you think happened that night?'

Slam, slam, slam … The shutters went down one by one. Rodney's expression cooled and his eyes hardened. 'I've said enough. They've got the killer. As far as I know, the case is just about closed.'

Nodding, I lifted my glass and took a mouthful of shandy.

'Is there anything else?' Rodney asked.

'If you don't mind, I wanted to ask you a few questions about your dad.'

He exhaled impatiently again, but I was glad that he remained at the table.

'Who do you think killed him?'

'*Ha* …' It was a nervous laugh. 'Take your pick. They were lining up.'

'Who was?'

'The other families. The other gangs vying to take over. That's the law of the jungle. When the alpha male becomes weak, a new buck takes over.'

'And there wasn't anyone in Declan's firm to fill the role?'

'Certainly not me if that's what you're getting at. I wanted out.'

'Tommy? Sheila?'

The laugh again, a little more prolonged this time. 'No. The O'Donnell dynasty was all but over.'

'But if Declan's grasp was so weak, surely the opposing gang could have just taken over without the need for violence.'

'Obviously not.'

It was apparent by the nervous twitches and the impatient glances over his shoulder, that the interview was coming to an end, so I decided to skip lunch and go straight to dinner. 'How much did you hate your dad?'

'What's that supposed to mean?'

'Did something happen between you?'

'No.'

Fuck it, Scotty, get to the point. 'Did you kill Declan O'Donnell, Rodney?'

I was expecting him to blow up, but that wasn't what I got. There was a hesitation, and once again, as with all the players I'd interviewed so far, I was left feeling that there was something he wasn't telling me.

Rodney pushed back on his chair and stood.

In the interests of keeping all channels of communication open, I also stood, offered him my hand and apologised for the invasive questioning. Reluctantly, he allowed me to follow him back into the bar, where I perched myself down on a bar stool, and engaged in a friendly chit chat with Eric. Thankfully, after a few minutes, Rodney seemed to calm down, and when I steered the conversation back to my INSEXT anecdotes, we were soon mates again.

During the drive back to Nottingham, Tetley talked nonstop about his tour of Wembley Stadium. The conversation being one-sided meant, with little input from yours truly, apart from the odd "Ooh" and "Wow," that I was able to think about the events of the last few days. In my mind, I was rearranging the whiteboard, shuffling the players, promoting some of them to suspects, demoting suspects to players. When we reached a large service station at a place called Toddington, we pulled off the motorway for a late lunch. As I was parking the car, my phone rang. It was Stewie.

'G'day, mate.'

'Hey Scotty, how's it going?'

'Good.'

Tetley pointed to a McDonald's sign and raised a thumb as if to say, "You alright with that?"

Raising my thumb too, I nodded.

'What have you been up to, Scotty?' Stewie asked.

I filled him in on my findings so far.

He listened without interruption. Then, once he was up to speed, he said, 'The reason I'm calling … well, there are two reasons really, but first, Sheila O'Donnell. She's had a stroke.'

'Oh no. Is she okay?'

'I'm not sure yet. It's only just happened. They rushed her to the Queen's Med.'

'That's not good.' I couldn't help wondering how Stewie knew about this if it had only just happened. It's not like it would have been broadcast on the news. 'You said there were two reasons.'

'Yeah. I don't know if this means anything or not, but I thought it might interest you. Javad Sharma, Anita's brother, has just come into a nice windfall.'

'How come?'

'Anita left a will. She left everything to her brother. A substantial amount of money.'

'What sort of money?'

'Over a million pounds.'

'Wow!'

'She'd been stashing money away into a savings account since the mid-eighties. Leading up to her death, the deposits got bigger, a lot bigger. The last transfer she made only a week before she went missing was for two hundred and fifty thousand pounds. The money has sat there maturing in a high-interest account for the last thirty years.'

'Making Javed Sharma a wealthy man.'

'Yeah. Interesting, eh?'

'Will you be speaking with him?' I asked.

'What for? The case is closed, remember.'

'Not until Col Webster is proven guilty.'

'I know. That's why I'm calling. My caseload is pretty hectic at the moment, and I won't be wasting any more police time and resources on the Anita Madison case. As I said, my superiors are happy with Colin's arrest. It's a done deal as far as they're concerned.'

'But you don't feel that way?' There had to be a reason why Detective Inspector Stewart Weston was taking the time to keep me informed. Or was it the other way around? Was it me who was keeping him informed? *Hmm.* He seemed like a good bloke, but I needed to keep my mind open to the possibility that he had an ulterior motive for keeping me close.

Tetley had a Happy Meal. I had a Big Mac combo, and I have to say, the burgers weren't as good as they are in Australia. A bit greasier perhaps, less flavoursome.

It was late afternoon when we reached Bobbersmill. As we pulled up outside the house, I had an idea. 'You go in, mate …' I said to Tetley. '… I've just got an errand to run.'

'Yeah, no worries. What do you wanna do tonight?'

'A quiet one, I think. I've got some catching up to do.'

'Okay, see you later.' He climbed out of the car, and I watched him amble merrily across the wide pavement. He was hurting inside; I knew he was. Worried about his dad, but from the outside you'd never know it. Tetley was the life and soul of any party, the wise cracking clown, the king of banter, it was only because I'd known him for so long—thirty years and counting—that I could pick up on those subtle little differences in his behaviour. The wit was still there, but not as sharp as it had been, and the speed of his playful putdowns and clever comebacks had slowed somewhat. I was glad that the tour of Wembley I'd organised proved a hit. At least it took his mind off what was happening in the real world for an hour or so. No doubt he'd be bending Carol's ear as soon as he entered the house.

Doris had become more than just an AI assistant to an Australian traveller. Her familiar Aussie accent gave me some comfort while I was driving to destinations that I would never have found without her. Like most places around Nottingham, the Queen's Medical Centre University Hospital wasn't far from Bobbersmill.

The big Jag wasn't at home in public car parks. The narrow spaces made it difficult to park. After driving around and around the multi-storey complex, I eventually found a spot on the top floor. While riding the elevator back down to the ground, an idea surfaced.

The hospital foyer was large and very busy. I had absolutely no idea where in the enormous building Sheila would be, so I joined the queue at the information desk. When I reached the front of the line, the director in my head called, "Action!"

'Hi,' I said to the young receptionist behind the counter and, trying to hide my Aussie accent, I followed up with, 'I'm here to see Sheila O'Donnell.'

The girl lowered her eyes to the computer screen on the top of the desk and tapped at the keyboard. 'She's in the West Block, C Floor, Ward C4. She's only been here since this afternoon. There are no visitors allowed except for next of kin.' She looked up at me expectantly.

'That's fine. I'm her son. Rodney O'Donnell.'

'Okay.' She pointed back over my shoulder. 'Follow the blue line on the floor until you come to the elevators. Go up three levels to Floor C, then take a left until you come to Ward C4.'

'Thanks, you've been very helpful.'

My plan to hopefully speak with Sheila all hinged on the chance that if Rodney had been notified, which I was sure he would have been, that he'd still be on his way up from London. However, if he was already here, my plans were shot.

It was all to do with the smells, the subtle lighting and the rushed atmosphere that prompted the memories whenever I visited a hospital—memories of that terrible night when my mother died. It wasn't just the nausea; it was anxiety, tightening of the chest, sudden dehydration, an overwhelming sadness, and guilt. No amount of therapy could remove these triggers. Being the cause of your mother's death wasn't a burden to be held by a fourteen-year-old boy. She didn't want to drive that night. She was scared of driving in the dark. But I made her do it. Me, the up-and-coming AFL superstar, the arrogant little shit who missed the team bus home because he was losing his virginity to one of the older cheerleaders in the female toilets.

Stepping into the crowded lift, I took a deep breath and closed my eyes.

It was a fair old stroll to Ward C4; the building was huge. From a small foyer, I noticed a couple of Sheila's, let's say fellas, seated in a waiting room drinking coffee from paper cups. Keeping my head down, I headed towards the counter.

'Hi, I'm here to see Sheila O'Donnell.'

'Right, and you are?' an Indian nurse with the name tag 'Jasmin' asked.

'I'm Rodney O'Donnell,' I said almost in a whisper. 'I'm her son.'

'Oh, right. She's a bit poorly …' The nurse rose from the desk. '… and a bit vague, but she's responsive.' Then, leading me through to a private room at the end of the ward, she added, 'She needs her rest, so if you can keep it short, that will be good.'

'No worries.'

Sheila was lying in a hospital bed hooked up to a heart monitor. There was a pipe from her nose and a series of tubes from one of her arms. I wasn't taking too much notice of my surroundings. The nausea was definitely kicking in. Thankfully, the nurse left us alone. As I approached the bed, Sheila's eyes opened, and she frowned.

'Who are you?' Her words were slurred, and her mouth drooped heavily to the left.

'I'm Scotty. We met the other day.'

'Did we?' She closed her eyes.

It was time for another chapter from the Scotty Stephens' book of fiction. 'I'm Rodney's friend.'

'Rodney? Where's Rodney?'

'He's coming. He'll be here soon.'

'Good. I need to see him. Need to tell him. Say I'm sorry.'

'Tell him what, Sheila?' After checking over my shoulder that no one was watching from outside the door, I leaned in and lowered my voice. 'What do you need to apologise to Rodney for, Sheila?'

'For not being honest with him … for not telling him who his real father is …'

It was hard, but I needed to keep pushing. 'Who was his real dad? Was it Tommy?'

'We did it for him. We did it to protect him.'

'Did what, Sheila?' I was trying to keep calm, but I could tell that I was about to uncover a revelation that could change the whole direction of the case. 'Who is—'

The door behind me flew open. 'What the fucking hell are you doing here?'

Turning, the inflamed faces of Rodney O'Donnell and nurse Jasmin confronted me.

<h1 style="text-align:center">53</h1>

That evening, after a welcomed healthy dinner of quiche and salad, I stood before the whiteboard, pondering. As far as I knew, I'd now spoken to everyone with relevance to the case. Now it was time to dig deeper. Stir things up a little. First, I needed to establish the roles that each of the players filled.

Putting aside my biased opinion, Col was still at the top of the list. Purely because he was there that night, the same night Janita was killed.

Under motive, I wrote words I didn't believe: possible marital problems, may have paid for sex with Anita Madison, flew into a rage when confronted with the threat of blackmail, killed the girl and hid her in the wall. Of course, because I knew Col so well, this scenario was ludicrous, but to a jury, who didn't know him, the facts all pointed to this being the most likely scenario.

Next Declan O'Donnell. A powerful thug, by all accounts. The patriarch of Nottingham's leading firm. Did he go to the property himself that night, or did he send someone to take care of Janita on his behalf? Motive? Declan found out that Janita had stolen a substantial amount of money from him and that she was about to do a runner. Did he also know she was pregnant?

Next was Sheila O'Donnell. Sheila was another powerful figure around that time. Did she know about her husband's affair? She certainly had the resources to organise a hit. Did she send a member of her entourage to put an end to the affair once and for all? Motive? If she'd got wind that Janita was pregnant, would that have threatened her standing in the family? Would Declan have left her for the younger woman?

Next was Tommy Stokes. There was something that bothered me about Tommy; his willingness to open up to me was hard to understand. In fact, it was more than a willingness; it was as if there was a need for him to share his involvement. This, however, didn't mean that what he was telling me was the truth. Maybe he was steering me off in a different direction. Was he protecting someone? Motive? Perhaps there wasn't a motive; perhaps he was just doing his job, carrying out Declan's instructions. He openly admitted to me, but not to the police, that he had gone to The Coach House that night on his way home. Did he stay longer than he'd stated, or did he go back later that night after Col had gone home? This was a feasible scenario. Or was he trying to protect someone?

Next was Javad Sharma, Janita's brother. He had told the police Janita had approached him for a loan, and he'd refused, and that was the last time. Motive? He already knew she was leaving town, perhaps even the country. He would have had to have acted quickly to get his money back. Did he find out about The Coach House and confront her that night? The fact that he'd recently inherited Janita's fortune didn't really play a factor in my mind. The murder took place thirty years ago, so he obviously didn't get his money back at that time. Was the killing from pure rage?

The next name on the list was a bit of a wild card, and the only reason it was there was because all the evidence surrounding the case hinged on his single testimony—it was William Henley. And although his statement confirmed that Janita arrived at the property with Col's recollection, what if everything after that was pure fantasy? If so, what reason would he have to lie? Did he witness something he's not told the police? Did someone threaten him to keep his mouth shut? Or did he have a personal reason to lie to the police? Motive? What if he'd returned to the property after Col had left? He was a single man, and there was an attractive escort in the house across the road. Could he have approached her for sex? How would he have reacted if he'd been turned down? Or if Janita had threatened to tell his mother? Would he be capable of murder? *Hmm?* Possibly.

Next was Donna Simpson, Janita's associate and one-time friend. She'd worked for Declan O'Donnell as an escort at the same time as Janita. Recently, I'd learned that after Janita went missing, she became Declan's girl and moved into The Coach House. Not having Janita around certainly worked to her advantage. Did she encourage Janita to leave by loaning her money to assist with her plans for a new life elsewhere? Or was there something more sinister? Motive? What if Donna was jealous of Janita's relationship with Declan? Did she want him for herself? If so, surely Janita's plans to leave would have worked in her favour? But what if the pregnancy changed all that? Would Donna have been capable of hiding the body, though? Doubtful. Unless she had help.

Next was Tony Patterson, the builder's son. I have to admit that the reason he was next on the list was mostly because of his evasive, cocky attitude, but apart from that he was also present when Col arrived at the property. Did he lie about the plaster? Or was he merely mistaken? It was a wild guess, but could he have returned to the property either in the evening or early in the morning, found Janita sleeping upstairs, engaged her services and then refused to pay. Or did she threaten to expose him? This was very unlikely. Tony would have been a young single buck. If he was arrogant in later life, I could only have imagined what he'd have been like as a teenager. This would likely be something he'd boast about, so the threat of being blackmailed would have been a joke. But what if there were other factors involved? Could he have raped and killed her?

Next was Dave Anderson, the stonemason's apprentice. He was the first on the scene the next morning, but not as early. And this was the only reason he was on the list. Motive? None that I could see, unless there was also a sexual interaction with the victim, which I doubted.

As I stood back from the whiteboard, my phone suddenly dinged; it was a message from Jenny, with an image. The message said, *"Hey boofhead, take a look at this. Will call you shortly."* Ignoring the banter, I opened the image and gasped. It showed the block of land on Ruby Street, but with a major difference: the footprint of the new build was now clearly visible. Timber formwork bordered the outline of the ground floor, and there were pipes and wires sticking out among sheets of reo laid in readiness for the impending concrete pour. Wow! Unable to wait for Jenny's call, I was about to call her when my phone rang. It was Donna Simpson.

'Hey Donna, how's it going?'

'Hi Scott, good thanks, well …'

'Well?'

'I just got a call from Tommy Stokes.'

'Tommy? What did he want?'

'He wanted to know what I'd spoken to you about.'

How the bloody hell did Tommy know I'd spoken with Donna?

As if reading my mind, Donna said, 'He still seems to know everything that's going on around here.'

'What did he say?'

'He just asked me outright what we'd discussed. I said nothing of any importance, and certainly nothing to do with him.'

'Did he become angry?'

'No, on the contrary, he almost seemed disappointed.'

Hmm. I knew exactly what she meant.

'Did he say anything else?'

'Just that I needed to be honest and open with the police.'

'And are you, Donna?'

There was a heavy pause on the other end of the line before she answered, 'Of course. I've told you everything.'

54

'The slab will be poured by the end of the week, weather permitting,' Jenny said.

'Wow. It's certainly moving quickly. I wish I were there to see it,' I said, seated at the dining room table.

'Me too. Did Elvis get away okay?'

'Yeah. He should be in Dubai by now,' I said, checking my watch. I told her about our sightseeing tour of London and then where I was up to with the case.

'Any standout suspects so far?'

'Two or three, but there's just no evidence.'

'Keep digging. You'll find what you need.'

'Yeah, I know.'

After a weather and surf report, and bringing me up to speed with the new caseloads she was working on, we finally said goodnight, and I have to say, the longer I was away from her, the harder it was getting to end our calls.

The top five names on the list, after Col, were no longer just players; they had been promoted to suspects, and that's how they would be addressed from then on. The next morning, the plan was to speak with as many of them as possible. Unfortunately, due to Declan being dead and his wife Sheila now in the hospital, they were unavailable. So next was Tommy Stokes.

'Tommy. It's Scotty Stephens.'

'Hello, Scott.' His deep voice sounded groggy, and I guessed early mornings weren't his favourite part of the day.

'You asked me to call you should anything important come to light.'

'That's right, I did.' His attention piqued. 'What have you found?'

'Can we meet up? There's a lot to discuss.'

'Of course. How about you come out to the house?'

'Sure.' This would be perfect because Tommy still lived in The Park not far from The Coach House, but more importantly, not far from my next planned port of call—another visit to William Henley. Having no phone number for William, a cold call after meeting with Tommy would have to suffice. I wasn't wearing my watch, but out of habit, I checked my wrist. 'Shall we say, 10.00 am?'

'That's fine.' He gave me the address. 'I'll see you at ten.' He hung up.

The house was quiet. Tetley was still in bed. Carol was out working in the garden, squatted over one of the flower beds, pulling out weeds. To say the house didn't belong to her, she was certainly working hard keeping it spotless, and I guessed this was because she needed to keep herself busy.

Breakfast that morning was Weetabix and toast. After showering and getting ready in the bedroom that I no longer had to share, I spent a solid hour just staring at the whiteboard. Thinking, contemplating, throwing around ideas, exploring likely scenarios, of which there were a few forming. A technique I'd used often in past cases, once certain information came to light, was to pick a scenario and run with it as if it had happened. This meant approaching a suspect as if sharing the knowledge they were hiding. It was dangerous, of course. If I was getting close to the truth, there were four possible outcomes: the first was that the suspect would clam up and refuse to speak with me further, the second was that they would simply laugh in my face, the third would see them becoming aggressive and violent, and the forth and most unlikely was that they would break down and confess their sins.

During the drive up to The Park, I wondered how Tommy would react after hearing the theory I was about to unleash on him. I have to admit, it was a very weak notion; in fact, I didn't even believe it, but it was the reaction I would be gauging. A chance, hopefully, to see the real Tommy Stokes. Until now, he'd been strangely cooperative; no, it was more than that, he'd been suggestive, as if he were trying to put ideas into my head.

As the Jag crawled along another tree-lined street that was typical of The Park, Doris informed me that the destination was on the left. A tall, wrought-iron gate stood across the entrance to a double driveway. As I turned off the road and was just about to reach out and press the intercom, the gate slid open. When I pulled inside, I saw Tommy standing on the stoop of a mock-Tudor-style mansion. He wore a white, Terry towelling robe, green and white striped board shorts, and a pair of white slides. The enormous beer belly that poked out of the open robe didn't seem to be something he was ashamed of. As he approached the car, I realised he was dripping wet.

'Scott.' He held out his hand as I stepped onto the gravelled driveway. 'It's good to see you again.'

We shook hands.

'A Jag, eh?' he said, admiring the car. 'God, that takes me back. I had one just like this back in the day.' We went around the house and into the back garden where there was a swimming pool and a nice, shaded gazebo.

'I've just had a swim and was about to have some breakfast. Would you care to join me?'

'Oh, that's very kind, Tommy, but I've eaten, thank you.'

'No worries.'

I followed him to the gazebo, and we took seats opposite each other at a stone-slabbed, outdoor table. And as if on cue, a small Asian woman appeared, carrying a tray.

'This is my wife, Gloria,' Tommy said as she placed the tray on the table. On it was a bowl of muesli, a jug of what looked like off-white milk—possibly soy—and a tall glass of orange juice.

Gloria bowed her head slightly in my direction.

'She's got me on a healthy diet, Scott.' He patted his chest with one hand. 'The old ticker's been playing up a bit just lately. Can we get you a drink?'

'That orange juice looks quite nice.'

Gloria bowed once more, then returned to the house.

With a lack of enthusiasm, Tommy poured the soy milk onto the bowl of muesli and kneaded the cereal with his spoon. While he did so, I glanced around the expansive garden. Like William Henley's, it was a well-kept plot to an untrained layman like me. The two-storey house with dormer windows in the roof was quite large, and I couldn't help noticing the difference with Declan O'Donnell's house in Broxtowe, where Sheila now lived, which was two basic council houses knocked into one. Looking at Tommy as he spooned a mouthful of soggy cereal into his mouth while trying to breathe through a restricted boxer's nose and reminding me of a pug, it wasn't hard to question the difference between his lifestyle choices and the ones that his boss had made. Sure, Declan owned The Coach House, but he didn't live there.

Gloria returned with a glass of orange juice, placed it down in front of me and returned to the house once more.

'So, you said you had some fresh evidence, Scott?' Tommy said, after swilling down a mouthful of juice.

'Yeah, there are a few things I'm looking at, Tommy. But uhm …' I lowered my voice for effect. 'At the moment, all the evidence seems to point to one person.'

'Really? Who?' His eyes were wide open now.

'You!'

'Me?'

'Yep!'

'You think I killed Anita Madison?' His patronising tone was accompanied by a slight grin.

'I'm pretty sure you did, mate. Yeah.'

He grew excited. 'I can't wait to hear this. Tell me what you've got,' he said before shovelling in another spoonful of muesli.

'Does Rodney know you're his father?'

55

Tommy suddenly stopped chewing and fixed me with an unnerving stare.

'Did Declan know?'

'What the hell are you talking about?'

'Well, you see, there's something that's been subconsciously puzzling me all this time, something I didn't even realise until this morning. If Declan hated his only son, Rodney, so much, would he have killed the woman who was carrying his child?'

'Perhaps he didn't know she was pregnant. She stole from him. Nobody crossed Declan O'Donnell.'

'But let's suppose he did know. And let's also suppose that Sheila found out too. It was an enormous inheritance that Declan left her, which will inevitably go to Rodney once Sheila passes away. But what if Declan produced another heir? How would that change the dynamics?'

'It sounds like you should be speaking with Sheila.' He raised a hand and flicked his fingers.

As if waiting for the command, Gloria instantly appeared with the tray carrying a teapot and two mugs. After placing it down, she poured two cups of black tea, then returned to the house.

I finished my juice, and set the glass down on the table. 'I already have,' I said. 'She opened up to me in the hospital yesterday—'

'Hospital?' He sat upright in his chair.

'Yeah. Didn't you know?' So much for the bloke who knew everything that went on in this town. 'She had a stroke yesterday.'

'What? Is she alright?'

'It was minor, apparently. She just needs some rest.'

He relaxed a little and narrowed his eyes. 'What did she say?'

All right, Mr DeMille, I'm ready for my close-up. There was no script, but I was working with pure fiction now. 'Oh, she told me everything … all about you, and Rodney, and uhm …' I nodded in the way a person does to prompt a response.

'You're talking rubbish, man. She must have been delirious.'

'The thing is, Tommy, I have mentioned none of this to the police yet. I thought I'd give you the opportunity to put the record straight first.'

Tommy poured soy milk into his tea and stirred the cup. 'You think you're a clever little bastard, don't ya?'

'I do all right.' I was purposely being cocky now, while analysing Tommy's every twitch and gesture.

'Is this all you've got? You realise that a simple DNA test will show just how fucking useless your detective skills really are. Fuck me, I thought you were better than this, Scott.'

'Would you be willing to take a DNA test?'

'Of course.' He laughed. 'I'm not Rodney's father, and I can disprove anything that Sheila told you.'

'I have it on good authority that you returned to The Coach House that night.' I had no such information; it was all still part of the impromptu performance.

'Bullshit. You have nothing of the kind. If you do, perhaps the person giving you that information is trying to lead you astray.'

'Like *you* did, you mean? Inviting me over to your club, feeding me false accusations.'

'I was trying to help you, you idiot.' He didn't appear to be angry, which was strange because I was accusing him of murder. 'Would I have really told you I'd been to The Coach House if I'd had anything to hide?'

'Well, that's what I couldn't work out at first. Why were you openly sharing those details with me and not the police?'

'I think it's time you left, don't you?'

'I haven't finished my tea yet, Tommy.'

'Don't let me have to throw you out, Scott.'

'Okay, look …' It was time to come clean. There was useful information Tommy still had, I was sure of it, so I couldn't afford to burn my bridges. 'You're right. I've got nothing. This was just a stupid technique to provoke a reaction.'

'Well, you certainly did that. I was just about to throttle ya.'

'I apologise. Forgive me?'

He eyed me warily.

'Sheila did say something, though, Tommy, that got me fired up.'

'Oh, yeah?' There was caution in his tone.

'She said, "We should never have done it," or words to that effect.'

'And you assumed she was talking about me.'

'Well yeah. Who else do you think she could have meant?'

'There was a lot going on in my life back then, Scott. I didn't have time to worry about what Sheila was getting up to.'

'When Declan told you to go to The Coach House that night, what were his instructions?'

'Not to kill her, if that's what you're thinking. He just wanted to know where she was.'

'And he asked you to find her?'

'No.' He straightened up and leaned forward. 'Regardless of what you may have heard, I wasn't his bloody gofer. It was actually my suggestion to call in on the way home just in case she was there.'

'What would you have done if you'd found her?'

'Give Declan a call. Let him know.'

'Did you call him to say she wasn't there?'

'No … I never gave it another thought. Perhaps I should have.'

'Could Declan have gone over there later that night?'

'I don't enjoy talking about my late friend this way.'

'But he was your—'

'He was the boss. He could have gone over there.'

'Would he have killed her, do you think?'

'Not if he knew she was pregnant.'

'And what if he didn't know? What if he'd caught up with the woman who had been lying to him for the last few months, still working as an escort behind his back, and then stealing a large amount of money from him?'

'Then yeah. He would have wrung her neck, or more likely got someone else to do it.'

Someone like you. I thought it, but didn't say it.

'Listen, uhm … what I said before about finding Declan's killer. Forget about that, eh?'

'Why?'

'It was a stupid request. Better to let sleeping dogs lie, I think.'

'I'm suspecting that when I find out who killed Janita, it might also shed some light on Declan's death.'

'How so?'

'Call it a detective's intuition, but I've got a nagging feeling that the two deaths are linked in some way.'

'Nah, it was the McCanns or the Patels who took Declan out. Between them, they run Nottingham now.'

'Maybe. But what if it was someone within the inner circle?'

'There was no one close who wanted Declan dead. He was a hard man, but he looked after his own.'

I was about to tread on thin ice again, but I couldn't help myself. 'He certainly looked after you, Tommy,' I said, glancing around the property.

'You cheeky bastard. You're doing it again.'

It was difficult to suppress a mischievous grin.

Once again, he leaned forward, but this time he lowered his voice. 'I've worked hard for every penny I have, you little shit.'

Uh … I'd finally hit a nerve.

'You think Declan is responsible for all of this?' He waved an arm around. 'Have you seen where he lived? I've always been a man of my own resources. Declan never gave me nothing!'

56

William Henley's house was literally just around the corner from Tommy Stokes' place. He appeared almost instantly after I rang the doorbell, as if he already knew I was there.

'Scott, it's good to see you again.'

'G'day, William. I hope you don't mind my just showing up. You did say whenever I was in the area.'

'That's right, I did. Come on in. I've just put the kettle on.'

I was getting used to the ritual of drinking tea wherever I went. It seemed like the kettle was always on.

'How have you been?' He led me around to the side garden and to the patio in the shade.

'Good.'

William disappeared through the side door of the house. This time I followed him, but instead of entering the building, I stood in the doorway that opened into the kitchen. Remaining silent, I watched him as he turned up the heat on the gas stove. He was mumbling, kind of arguing with himself as he worked.

The kettle boiled with a whistle, and William poured hot water over tea bags in the mugs. There was no sign of the teapot and bone china on this visit.

We returned to the garden and took seats in the shade. Once again, I needed to be careful. There was important information that only William could supply, I was sure of it, but if I pissed him off, I'd be thrown out of there for sure. The relationship we'd established at our previous meeting was still fragile.

'So, I already told you everything I know about what happened that night. I'm sure you haven't come back to admire the garden.'

It was time for another acting masterclass. This one would need to be more subtle. I had to remember that everything surrounding the case of Janita Sharma's death hinged around the testimony of the man sitting across from me. He was the reason Col was sitting in Lincoln Prison; he was the reason the police had just about closed the case before it had even started. I needed to keep him on side. If there was anything he wasn't telling us, or if what he'd already told us was untrue, I needed to find a way of gently prising it out of him. 'Look, I have to be honest with you. The case is going nowhere. It looks like everyone was right; I've wasted my time coming all this way.'

'It sounds like you were only doing what was right by your friend.'

'I hope so. Talking of friends, the reason I was able to pop in while passing was because I was visiting a friend not far from here.'

'Oh, that's nice.' He took another sip of his tea.

'His name's Tommy. Tommy Stokes.'

When William flinched and almost spilled his tea, it was the exact reaction I'd been hoping for.

'Do you know Tommy? He lives just around the corner.'

'Uhm, no. I can't say I do.' He was lying.

'Probably a good thing. He's a bit of an unsavoury character. In fact, you might have seen him that night … you know?' I flicked my head back toward the street.

William frowned.

'He came around on his way home—in a Jaguar like the one I'm driving.'

'No. I can't say I saw him.'

'Maybe it was later, after you'd gone to bed.'

'No. I don't sleep too well. I tend to hear any noise from down there.'

'Hmm, that's odd, isn't it?' Tommy said he came around while the builder was still there, but I suspect he may have returned, possibly on foot.'

'Well, that's possible. If he was quiet, he might have slipped in while I was busy doing something else.'

Busy doing something else? You mean you'd left your post as the neighbourhood sentinel? 'Strange you didn't see him if he came around earlier though.'

'There was quite a bit of noise earlier that evening. I'm not a nosey parker, Scott. I don't spend all my time watching what's going on in the street.'

Yes, you do, I thought but didn't say. 'No, of course not. I know that. So, Tommy could have come around without you knowing?'

If William's shrug was meant to confirm my theory, it actually did the opposite; it said, "Nothing happens on this street without me knowing about it." And if this were the case, he would have known if Tommy had called in at The Coach House, or if not *Tommy*, someone else.

'Did he see you watching him?'

'Who?'

'Tommy.'

'We've already established that I don't know anyone called Tommy.'

'A big bloke, thick-set, face like a burst sausage. Sorry, that's an Aussieism, A face like a boxer.'

'No, I don't know anyone like that.' He sipped his tea again and looked away.

'I could imagine it would be very intimidating, scary in fact, if someone like that threatened you.'

He shook his head and continued to drink his tea.

'If not Tommy, then who?'

'I'm sorry?'

'Someone came to The Coach House after Colin Webster, the builder, left. And I reckon you know who it was.'

'I've told the police everything I know.'

'Did he threaten you?'

'N, no, I … I don't know what—' He was getting flustered. 'I don't know what you mean. I only saw the builder there that night.'

'Or was it the owner, Declan O'Donnell, who arrived after the builder had left?'

'No, I've already told you, I—'

Reaching over the table, I placed a hand on his. 'It's okay, William. It's okay. Nobody's going to hurt you now. O'Donnell's dead, but if it wasn't him, all you've got to do is tell me who it was and I'll have them arrested.'

His chest heaved as he inhaled and exhaled loudly. Then, searching in his pocket, he produced an inhaler and thrust it into his mouth.

'Who was it, William? Who came to the house later that night and killed Janita Sharma?'

57

He hadn't thrown me out, but William asked me to leave in no uncertain terms. I'd definitely hit a nerve when I asked him what really happened that night, and I was now convinced that someone else had come to The Coach House after Col had left. I just needed to find out who.

While sitting at the lights waiting to turn out of The Park and onto Derby Road, my phone rang. There was a number displayed, but I didn't recognise it. When I answered and switched to speaker, a familiar voice said, 'Hello Scott.' It was William Henley. 'Can you come back? I've had second thoughts.'

'Of course, I'll see you shortly.' I wasn't about to ask the reason for the change of heart at that point. After hanging up, I put the car in reverse and travelled backwards a short way, until I was able to conduct a three-point turn—which in reality was a six-point turn with the Jag's short turning circle—then headed back in the direction I'd come.

William was waiting for me at the front gate, gesturing for me to pull into his driveway.

When I climbed from the car, he led me around the house once more, to the shaded spot. We resumed our seats, and he sat quietly for a moment, eyes down, wringing his hands as if he were choosing the words he was about to deliver.

'Have you remembered something else, William?' I asked, offering him a gentle prompt.

'Uhm, yes … yes, I have.' He shot a cautious glance my way.

'It's okay. Take your time.' There was no hurry; all I had to do was be patient and listen.

'There was someone else that night. I remember now. Someone did come to The Coach House later.'

He looked at me and I nodded slightly as if to say, "I thought so, but it's okay, mate. Carry on."

'I'd completely forgotten. It was a long time ago; you must understand. My only real recollections of the night were of the contractor, and I think that was because I was angry about all the noise he was creating.'

'This other person. He? She?'

'He.'

'When did he arrive?'

'Around 2.00 am.'

'Did you recognise him?'

'I did, although he was dressed a lot differently to his normal attire. I'm guessing he'd been out on the town. He was drunk; I could tell by the way he weaved and staggered as he walked.'

'Who was it, William?'

'It was the builder's son.' He didn't make eye contact; instead, he continued to stare down at the table like a naughty schoolboy who had been caught telling fibs.

'Tony?'

'Yes. The cocky one.'

'Did he go into the house?'

'I think so. He turned into the driveway.'

'And how long did he stay for?'

'About an hour.'

Was this guy literally up all night watching the street? He certainly wasn't exaggerating when he said nothing happened in The Park Estate without him knowing about it.

'Did you see or hear anything from the property?'

'Not a thing. He didn't put on the lights.'

'Didn't you think that was odd at the time?'

'Not really, but in hindsight, I realise now how important this information is.'

'Well, it means that Colin Webster may not have been the last person to see Janita Sharma alive. Is there anything else you can remember, William?'

'No, that's it, I'm afraid.'

'You've been very helpful; I really appreciate your time,' I said, standing and offering him my hand.

Sitting at the same lights at the Derby Road junction, I had a moment to call DI Weston.

He picked up just as the lights turned green. 'Hey Scotty.'

'Stewie, how's it goin?'

'Good. What's up?'

'I've just had an interesting chat with William Henley.'

'Oh, yeah.'

'Yeah, he's remembered something very important.'

'Really? What?'

'That someone else visited the property after Col had left.'

'No way.'

'Yep.'

'Who?'

'Tony Patterson.'

'The builder's son?'

'The same.'

'Wow. Interesting.'

'Where are you?'

'I'm in Chesterfield following up on a lead for another case.'

'Will you be bringing Tony in for questioning?'

There was a long pause, and for a moment, I wondered if I'd lost connection. 'I doubt it.'

'But surely this is a solid lead?'

'Did anyone else see him?'

'Not that I know of.'

'So, all you have is the evidence of the dodgy old bloke who lives across the street.'

'Well, that was enough to charge Col.'

'No, it wasn't. All it did was merely reinforce that Colin was the person who sealed the wall where the body was found.'

'But Tony could have undone all that and resealed it.'

'Could he have, though? Listen, I understand, mate,' Stewie continued. 'You're doing the job that Carol brought you over here to do; you might be biased, though.'

Hmm? Was I? 'Would you mind if I questioned him?'

'No, not at all. Go for it, but just be careful, eh?'

'Thanks. I will.'

'And keep me informed if you find anything important.'

'Will do.'

Once again, I waited until late afternoon to pay Tony Patterson a visit, choosing the same time as the previous call, assuming it was the time he usually got home from work. As I was driving down Shelford Road, I looked into my rearview mirror and realised his truck was following me, so at his driveway I drove on a little farther, waited as he turned into the property, then reversed and parked in front of him.

'Ay up, Scotty, lad. How's it goin?'

'I'm good, mate. Yourself?'

'Fair to middlin, fair to middlin.'

I had no idea what that meant but acknowledged his friendly demeanour as we shook hands.

'Did you get it?'

'I'm sorry?'

'The Coach House? Did you buy it?'

'Can we talk, Tony?' I wasn't about to reveal my true identity out there on the driveway and tell him I'd lied about purchasing

The Coach House, and that I suspected he might have killed someone over thirty years ago. He was a big bloke, cocky, and he was likely to go off when I confronted him. As before, he led me into the house and through to the kitchen. Without asking, he reached up into the overhead cupboard and pulled out two warm cans of beer.

'Not for me, thanks, mate,'

Ignoring me, he tore off the ring pulls on both and handed me one. 'You're not gonna let a bloke drink alone, are you? Besides, I'm sensing a bit of bad news here. Did the sale fall through?'

'There was no sale.'

'Eh?'

'I lied about that.'

'What do you mean?'

'I was never going to buy The Coach House. I just used that as a way of getting close to you.'

He slammed down his can of beer onto the kitchen countertop. 'You're a bleedin' reporter.'

'No, I'm a detective. I'm working on behalf of Colin Webster, the man accused of Janita Sharma's death.'

'Why didn't you just say that in the first place?'

'I didn't think you'd—'

'Get the fuck out of my house.' He stepped forward menacingly.

My self-defence skill level was that of basic Queensland Police training, but my experience during my years as a uniformed constable dealing with late-night drunks on the streets of Surfers Paradise meant I understood how best to handle a potentially dangerous situation. Talk it down first. If that didn't work, take down the aggressor. Benny Carrigan, an old mate and a retired Rugby League front rower for the West Sydney Tigers, once told me, that even years into retirement, his trained mind still weighed people up who he met for the first time. He would work out the best way to take them down—a skill that had been drummed into him since turning pro in his teens. In the same manner, I'd already worked out the best way to take down Tony Patterson should the need arise. 'Listen, mate, I apologise for misleading you, but I thought I'd better come and have another chat before the police do.'

His body was tensed and trembling, but he fell short of grabbing hold of me. 'The police? Why would they need to speak with me?'

There was a need to be creative; the old I-know-what-you-know scenario was always a good fallback. 'I think we both know the answer to that, Tony.'

'What the hell are you on about?' He was still angry, but at least his advance towards me halted.

'We have a witness who will swear under oath that you arrived at the property in the early hours of the morning and stayed for around an hour.'

'What?'

'If you've got nothing to hide, mate. Don't lie. But if you are hiding something, now's the time to come clean about it.'

He turned away from me and gazed out into the back garden.

'It's true, isn't it? You were there that night.'

58

We went out the back of the house and sat on a low retaining wall with our backs to the unkempt garden. I hadn't touched my beer—too warm for me. Tony, however, had skulled half of his in one mouthful.

'Do you want to tell me what happened, mate? Why were you there that night?'

He stared up at the house as if inspecting the guttering.

Patiently, I waited for him to speak.

'It was a long time ago … I was bladdered. Been out on the town all night with the lads. Dad had asked me to go to The Coach House early the next morning to make sure the site was ready for the stonemason. There was no way I'd be getting up early after a night like that, so in my drunken state I decided I'd go after parting with the lads.' With his focus remaining on the upper level of his house, he grinned as if recalling the times of a carefree youth. Then his expression suddenly hardened. 'But there was no one there. The place was dark and quiet.'

'Did you go inside?'

'Yeah. I needed a piss. We had keys hidden under a rock in the courtyard. All the trades knew they were there.'

'So, Colin wasn't there? What time was that?'

'No, he'd gone. It was him who returned the keys to their hiding place. Not sure of the time. Must have been late—early hours.'

'Did you know Janita Sharma was upstairs?'

'No. I didn't go up there. There was a bog downstairs; it wasn't finished, but the plumbing was working.'

'Then what?'

'I had a piss. Checked the new wall. It all looked good, so I left.'

'Are you sure that's what happened, Tony? Is there anything else you need to tell me?'

'No, that's it.'

'Okay … are you familiar with the cross-examination techniques that are used in a court of law?'

He lowered his gaze until our eyes met. 'Only what I've seen on the telly and that.'

'Good, well, it's like that, only a lot worse.'

'Are you saying I'll have to go to court?'

'Oh yeah, and not just that. Have you been incarcerated before?'

'Jail? Now hang on a minute—'

'Well, you've already lied to the police, and now we have a witness who can place you at the crime scene around the same time as the killing took place.'

'Will I need a solicitor?'

'My bloody oath, you will. You'll need the best, and they aren't cheap.'

'This is bullshit.'

'It *is*, mate, but if you tell me what really happened, I'll be able to speak with the police, perhaps make this whole thing a lot easier.'

'No, I'll get a solicitor.'

'Oh, come on, Tony. The truth will come out in the end. You don't want to prolong it and drag your family through this.'

'Well, that's just it. I'm telling you the truth, but you don't believe me.'

'Okay, let me tell you how it's going to go once you take the stand in court. You've seen the shows, so you'll know what I mean. In your drunken state, you went to the property knowing that you could gain entry with the keys that were hidden in the garden.

After using the bathroom and inspecting the work that had been carried out earlier that evening, there are two scenarios: one is that you wandered upstairs, knowing that the upper level was furnished. You went up there to take a nap, sleep off the effects of the alcohol, perhaps. But to your surprise, you found a young woman sleeping there.'

'That's pure bullshit. It never happened.'

'The second scenario is that Janita Sharma, after hearing a noise from downstairs, came down and confronted you. I can only imagine what a shock that would have been. Did she threaten to call the police?'

'Never happened, pal. None of it.'

'The witness claims that you stayed inside the property for about an hour. That was either a very long piss, or you really took your time inspecting the new wall.'

'What is it they say in the shows? No comment.'

'Ahh, well done. That's exactly what I was hoping for.'

'What do you mean?'

I'd already deduced during our first meeting that although Tony Patterson was arrogant and somewhat successful in his chosen trade, he wasn't that smart. He displayed some insecurities, which I was about to uncover. 'Before becoming a private investigator, I was a detective with the Queensland Police, Tony. Which means I've done thousands of interviews with suspects just like you. And in every single case, as soon as they throw out the "No Comment" response, I know they've got something to hide. *We* know—the police, the solicitors, the prosecutors, the judge, and the jury.'

'Really?'

'Yep.' When I looked into his eyes, I saw a scared, confused little boy struggling with the situation that had just been presented to him.

He finished his beer and placed the can thoughtfully down on the top of the low wall.

'Okay … I did go upstairs.' He paused as if expecting me to interrupt. I didn't, so he continued. 'You were right, I needed to sleep. Just thought I'd grab an hour then head back to Derby Road and get a taxi, which is basically what I did. But there was no one there, Scott. You've got to believe me. I do recall that the bed was unmade, but there wasn't anyone in it, or anywhere else in the house, and I'll swear to that on the Holy Bible.'

Doubting that he was a religious man offered a redundancy to the last comment, but whether I believed him was irrelevant, because there was absolutely no proof to argue his account. If he had been on the property for only an hour, would that have given him time to kill Janita, undo Colin's work, hide the body inside the wall and put it back as it was? 'Why didn't you tell the police about this, Tony?'

He shrugged. 'I don't know. Scared, I guess. It looks like they've got the bloke that did it, so why complicate things?'

And that was exactly what was worrying me. If Tony's recollection of that night was true, and The Coach House *was* empty, and if William Henley was to testify that he only remained inside the property for an hour, this was more incriminating evidence against Col. It meant that Janita was killed before 2.00 am, and if Colin didn't do it, she must have been killed between the time when Col left and when Tony arrived at 2.00 am. Bloody hell. I suddenly felt like I was getting nowhere.

<h1 style="text-align:center">59</h1>

Did I believe Tony Patterson? I can't say I did, and I can't say I didn't. Without proof, there were only two options available to me: believe the suspect's account of what happened, or go with my gut feeling. Could the fact that I had a personal vested interest in proving Colin Webster's innocence be compromising my usual instincts? I didn't want to believe Tony's account. I wanted to believe that he found Janita Sharma sleeping in bed, then in his drunken state, he raped and killed her. That was the more feasible scenario.

When I drove back towards Bobbersmill, it was rush hour once more and the traffic was bumper to bumper. Personally, I never got upset when stuck in traffic; I usually used the time to think. While sitting in a queue on Ilkeston Road, I gave Stewie a call and told him what I'd learned about Tony.

'Sounds like I'll need to have a little chat with Mister Patterson,' he said after listening quietly.

'Yeah, it wouldn't be a bad idea. He definitely made a false statement. It might be a good idea to speak with William Henley again, too, see if there's anything else he's forgotten to mention.'

'Will do. The first chance I get. I doubt any of this is going to change the outcome, though, Scotty.'

He was right, and I knew it, but who knows, another visit from the police might dislodge another piece of vital information that was missed or conveniently forgotten.

We ended the call, and while the car crept slowly along, my mind went over the recent events. Then I realised there was something bugging me—something I'd missed, perhaps? It felt like an itch that I couldn't scratch. With no evidence, I could neither prove nor disprove whether Tony was telling the truth. But didn't this also apply to William Henley? His words resonated in my memory—"*Nothing happens on this street without my knowing about it.*" And so far, this had proved true. Did the guy have a 24-hour surveillance system set up in his house? Tony arrived at around 2.00 am and left at 3.00 am. Surely William wasn't awake at that time. And if he was, was he watching the street? "*Nothing happens on this street without my knowing about it.*" Where had I heard that before? That's right, Tommy Stokes, it wasn't the exact same expression, but it meant the same, only on a different scale. "*Nothing happens in this* town *without my knowing about it.*" When my mind shifted to Tommy Stokes, the itching sensation returned. William had denied seeing Tommy that night, even though it was Tommy who'd told me he'd called in briefly while Col was still there. If William really did see everything that happened on the street, he would have seen Tommy, especially in the early evening. So why would he lie? And if he lied about that, could he have lied about Tommy returning later? Of course he could have.

It was a good fifteen minutes by the time I turned back into the exclusive estate. After the mayhem on the busy roads, it was like entering an enchanted village—quiet and peaceful. Once again, the only sound was the beautiful song of a blackbird, heralding the impending dusk of another day. There was nowhere to park outside William's house; I had to travel a couple of streets away before I could find a spot. Then, as I walked back, I realised I was halfway between Tommy's house and William's. I needed to speak with them both, but after consideration, I realised I'd get nothing out of Tommy without proof, so I headed over to speak with William first.

It was unusual to have to wait outside William's gate. On my previous visits, he'd appeared almost instantly on the first ring of the doorbell, as if he'd already known I was there. On this occasion, though, there was silence. After pressing the bell a couple more times, I called out to him. 'William, are you home?' There was no reply. Subconsciously, I'd got the impression that the man suffered from agoraphobia. I hadn't seen him outside the property boundaries, so I assumed that was the case. But if I was wrong—and it looked like I was—it meant he had to go out sometimes, shopping and whatever else. I called out one more time, but there was no reply. Stepping back out onto the street and checking my surroundings to make sure no one was watching, I eyed up the six-foot-high gate. One advantage of being a surfer was that if you surfed regularly, you were automatically guaranteed a certain level of fitness. While lapping up the sensation of riding the perfect waves, you were also getting a full-body workout without even knowing it. This was something I was glad for as I stealthily scaled the gate.

'William, are you here?' For some reason, I had lowered my voice. There was no reply, so I approached the front door. The two opaque glass panels in the top half of the door allowed a skewed vision of the interior, but in the fading light it was impossible to get a clear view. Instinctively, I tried the door handle, but it was locked. On either side of the door was a window, and although the glass was clear, the net curtains hanging inside also obscured the view. Creeping around the side of the house, I remembered there was a back door that led to the kitchen. When I reached it and tried the handle, it too was locked. My phone *dinged*, and without thought or hesitation, I retrieved it from my pocket to find the screen illuminated with a message from Jenny. Tapping the screen, an image opened of Jenny, Elvis and Cassie smiling with their thumbs up. They were standing on a concrete slab, but not any old concrete slab. It was *our* concrete slab; it must have recently been poured. Completely forgetting where I was, I was about to tap out a reply to Jenny's text when I heard a sound behind me, a rustling, but before I could turn to see what it was, there was an almighty *WHACK!* on the back of my head.

And the lights went out.

60

Heck, that must have been one hell of a night. I didn't recall having a hangover like that for a long, long time. I remembered leaving the Kirra Hotel with Elvis and Tetley after a long session. Then the three of us stumbling around Kirra Point and into Coolangatta. Thankfully, my celebrity status meant we didn't have to stand in line outside the Cooly pub. Manu, the bouncer, waved us through, and as per normal since the outcome of the *X* case, our drinks were free. There was a band playing as we weaved through the crowded bar. People were dancing and having a bloody good time. Now here I was the next morning, lying there, automatically listening to the surf across the road, gauging the wave height in my mind, a little afraid to open my eyes in anticipation of the pain that would only increase once I allowed the sunlight into my brain.

The only problem was, I wasn't lying down. I was sitting up, and there was no sound of the surf, only silence. And as the brain fog gradually lifted, I realised there had been no night out at the Kirra Hotel or Cooly pub, no alcohol, no music, and no dancing. Bound with my hands behind my back, I slowly opened my eyes. Adjustment from dark to light was still required, but it wasn't from the warm Gold Coast sunshine streaming in through the bedroom window; it was from a series of strip lights in the ceiling.

'Good. You're awake.'

The most ridiculous part of this scenario was that I'd actually pictured this scene playfully when William first gave me the tour of his theatre, as he called it.

'I'm going to remove the gag. It's okay if you want to yell out. No one will hear you down here.'

Then why the hell did you gag me, dickhead? I thought as he untied the rag that was around my mouth.

'Sorry about the whack on the head, but you broke into my property.'

'Call the police then. Report me.' My mouth was dry and tasted of paraffin.

William laughed. 'I don't think that's a good idea, Scott.' His phone rang. He glanced at the screen before answering it, then stood quietly listening to the voice on the other end.

Cocking my head to one side, I was trying to hear the other side of the conversation, without success.

'Yes, I've got him here,' William said.

Silence.

'Yes, yes, okay. I'll see you soon.' He hung up.

Of course, my mind was perusing the different scenarios that had inevitably led to this moment.

If William Henley had returned to The Coach House that night thirty years ago, after Col had left, killed Janita Sharma, and hid her body in the wall, this would account for him being awake when Tony Patterson arrived later, and his extra vigilance in those early hours of the next morning. But if that was the case, then who the hell had just called him on the phone? My mind automatically clicked onto the next possible, and more likely, scenario. Tommy bloody Stokes. Of course. It was Tommy who had returned to the property that night and committed the murder, either on instructions from his boss, Declan O'Donnell, or Sheila, perhaps? It all made sense. After committing the crime and covering up all traces, did he realise he was being watched by the nosy neighbour across the street? Of course he did. And how would he have reacted?

It was time to put my theory into practice. 'Did he threaten you, William?'

William's frown prompted me to continue.

'Did he see you watching him?'

The frown deepened into an inquisitive glare.

'Did he hurt you?'

The silence remained.

'Okay, let me tell you what I think happened. You heard someone arrive at The Coach House not long after Colin the builder had left. Did you know who he was before that night?'

Instead of answering, William continued to stare at me like a schoolteacher prompting his student to find the answer without help.

'What happened before he left? Did he approach you?'

Still no reply.

'It's okay, William. You haven't broken the law. You were threatened, and you were afraid. I can imagine Tommy Stokes would have been an imposing character thirty years ago.'

There was a flinch and a grin that I couldn't read. 'You think you've worked it out.'

'Am I close? Did Tommy Stokes kill that girl?'

William checked his watch. 'Our guest should be here any moment now.'

Of course he would. It was perhaps a five-minute walk from Tommy's house.

'It's not too late. I can help you. Untie me and call the police. We'll apprehend him together before they get here.'

William chuckled. 'Scotty, Scotty, Scotty.' It was the first time he hadn't called me Scott. 'If only it were that easy.'

'It *is* that easy. He won't be able to hurt you. He'll be going down for the rest of his life. And as for the firm. I don't think it even exists anymore.'

The doorbell rang through the house.

'Ah, our guest has arrived. I won't be a minute.' He walked around me and I heard him climb the stone stairs. Unable to crane my neck that far, due to the egg-shaped lump that throbbed like buggery on the back of my head, I waited, listening. I heard the front door open and pictured William heading down the driveway towards the front gate, then opening it and letting Tommy in. After a brief discussion, which I couldn't hear but imagined was the reason for the brief pause that followed, I heard the front door close, followed by footsteps coming back down into the cellar.

Willian appeared by my side, and I could sense there was somebody else standing behind me. 'I think you two already know each other.'

Still, I couldn't crane my neck far enough to see who it was behind me, so William tipped the chair backwards with me on it, and turned it to face the other way.

Fuck me! The face that scowled back at me with hatred and anger wasn't what I'd expected to see.

Fuck me again! I didn't see that coming.

<h1 style="text-align:center">61</h1>

'Rodney?'

'Not such a smart-arse detective after all, eh?'

'You? But why?'

'Never mind all that.' He leaned in close. 'Do you realise what you fucking did?'

'Me? No. What?'

'You killed my mother, you cunt!'

'What? Sheila's dead?'

William gasped and lifted a fist to his mouth.

'She was supposed to be resting,' Rodney continued, 'but you pushed your way into her room, demanding answers to your questions.'

'Ah, look, mate, I truly am sorry to hear about your mum. But is that what this is all about? Is that why I'm here trussed up like a Woolie's chook?'

Rodney and William exchanged glances. William seemed deeply upset by the news of Sheila's passing.

Then Rodney said, 'Partly. And I'm going to make you pay for what you've done, but—'

'You were getting too close, Scott,' William interrupted, wiping a tear from his eye. 'There was one flaw to my testimony, and one that I was hoping the Nottingham Police wouldn't pick up on which, until now, had proved correct. But then you came around asking your questions. "If you know everything that happens on this street, how come you didn't see Tommy Stokes arrive earlier that night? And if you did, why didn't you mention it to the police?" You weren't going to let that go. Am I right?'

'Spot on.'

The glances again.

'Especially after you'd also forgotten about Tony Patterson arriving in the early hours of the morning,' I added.

'So, you thought Tommy came back later to finish the job?' Rodney said.

This time the glances were more than just glances; they were prolonged as if the two were communicating telepathically.

'Wouldn't it be lovely if we could just leave it at that?' William said.

'I guess we could have,' Rodney said. 'If you were convinced that Tommy was the real culprit, you would have gone after him.'

'I guess you're just not that smart, are you, Rodney?'

Rodney lunged forward and bitch-slapped me across the face. Although it stung like hell, I couldn't help but grin.

'Is that all you've got?' I wasn't sure why I felt the need to taunt him.

He was about to hit me again when William stopped him. 'He's winding you up, son. Can't you see?'

Rodney stepped back. 'But he's got to pay for what he did, Dad.'

Whoa, whoa, whoa. Back the fuck up ... Dad? Did he just call William, Dad?

'And he will,' William said, fixing me with a stare. 'It's gone too far now. It's time to end this.'

'You're Rodney's father?' I asked.

'Yes. Yes, I am.'

'You and Sheila?' It was hard to imagine the powerful blonde bombshell of yesteryear even associating with a man like William Henley.

'She was the love of my life,' William said, his eyes glazing. 'But then she got seduced by that monster, Declan O'Donnell. You see, Sheila and I were at school together, and we were in love until O'Donnell showed up on the scene. Unbeknown to me, she was seeing him as well as me. And then she got pregnant, but of course she couldn't tell O'Donnell that the baby belonged to someone else, so she pinned it on him. Having been raised in a Catholic family, he had no choice but to do the right thing and marry her.'

Looking at the two men standing side by side, it all made sense: the red hair, the fair skin, the reason Rodney shared none of the attributes of O'Donnell.

'Wow!' Even though the pieces were falling into place, I still needed to think, because there was one thing still puzzling me. 'Where does Janita Sharma fit into all of this?'

'Ah … Anita Madison,' William said, averting his eyes towards Rodney.

'She was going to take it all!' Rodney said, taking up the narrative. 'Declan knew I wasn't his son. If he'd found out that Anita was pregnant with his child, life for me would have been a lot different now.'

'He would have cut you off. But didn't he, anyway?' I asked.

'He did, kind of, but Mum still held the purse strings, so as long as they were together, I'd be alright because Mum vowed to look after me.'

'So, Janita was a threat.' I still refused to call her Anita.

'Imagine if the baby was a boy, a clone of Declan. Where would that leave me?'

'But how did you know she was pregnant?' I asked. 'That information only came to light after the autopsy, thirty years later.'

'Donna told me. Those two were quite close, but Donna was my friend.'

'Why are we even telling him all this, Rodney?' William piped in.

Rodney took a deep breath and exhaled before answering. 'Because it's good to finally get this off my chest.'

William nodded as if he understood.

'So, it's not too late to hand yourselves in,' I said rather casually. 'You don't want to make matters worse by killing again.'

'Ha,' Rodney's laugh was without humour. 'If only that were true. No, I'm afraid we've come too far for that, Scott. And besides, you killed my mother.'

'And what do you think you're going to do, eh? Kill me now and hide the evidence?'

The mutual shrug by both men said something like, "Well, we've done it before. What's to say we can't do it again?"

Rodney said, 'The murder case is closed, the builder will be convicted, and life can resume as it was.'

'But they're gonna come looking for me, you idiot.'

'I'm sure nobody knows you were coming here,' William said.

'Of course they do. I've been under strict instruction from DI Stewart Weston to let him know of my whereabouts at all times and check with him first before approaching a suspect or a witness.' If only this were true. Seemed like a bloody good idea at that moment.

Rodney flicked a worried glance towards William.

'It's okay,' William said in a reassuring tone. 'I'll just tell them I haven't seen him since our earlier meeting. They'll believe me.'

'So, what are we going to do with him?' Rodney asked, diverting his attention back to me.

62

William returned to the workbench. Still unable to turn my neck, I instead matched Rodney's intense stare while my ears followed William's movements behind me. Hearing him lift something down from the wall behind the bench, I knew straight away what it was. I'd seen it earlier when I was facing the other way. The ten-inch-long knife had hung prominently on the wall among other tools and implements that William no doubt used for his taxidermy. It was the first thing I saw when William returned to my line of vision, held in front of him like a sword.

Rodney giggled, and I realised for the first time how unstable he was.

William moved around until he stood directly in front of me. The knife was only a couple of feet from my face.

'You really don't want to do this, guys,' I said, trying to remain calm.

'You're right,' William said, 'but we must.'

I had nothing to bargain with.

'Just do it,' Rodney said, 'or I will.'

A sudden movement on the stairs behind my two attackers caught my eye. A shadow. *Was there someone at the top of the stairs?* If so, I needed to buy some time.

'Listen … okay … but before you do this, let me tell you what the police already know.'

The resemblance between the two men was apparent when they both cocked their heads to one side and frowned in the same manner.

'I spoke with DI Weston before coming here.' Speaking slowly and just above a whisper, I had their attention. 'You see, you were right, William. It was bugging me that you hadn't mentioned to the police about Tommy visiting the property.'

The shadow on the stairs slowly grew, and I realised someone was creeping down into the basement.

'Once the realisation hit, my detective mind put two and two together and it all made sense. I have to admit I didn't suspect it was Rodney who carried out the killing; I thought it was Tommy.'

The shadow on the stairs suddenly stopped moving, and when a head slowly poked around the corner at the midway landing, I understood why. Staring back at me through the dim light was Tommy Stokes. He must have been listening as he was descending the stairs.

Without flinching, I carried on with my false recollection of the phone call I never made—*should* have made—to DI Weston before entering William's property.

'He's lying,' Rodney spat. 'If it were true, the cops would be here by now.'

'Oh, they're on their way,' I assured him.

Willian hesitated, and I could see the hand holding the knife was shaking.

'Come on, old man,' Rodney yelled. 'Do it!'

Tommy had reached the bottom of the stairs now, and with a silent stealth that I would have dismissed for a man of his size, he remained undetected.

William lifted his chin and looked down his nose at me. He was sweating profusely.

'William,' Rodney said, lowering his voice to a sympathetic level. 'He killed Sheila.'

As if pushed into a dare, William stepped forward, but as he raised the knife, Tommy Stokes lunged out of the shadows, twisted at the hips, and threw an elbow across with all his might, making contact with William's temple.

William dropped the knife, and the sideways momentum sent him flying into Rodney. Tommy, quick as a flash, and once again exhibiting a level of fitness that I never would have thought possible, scrambled for the knife as it bounced off the tiled floor. Unfortunately, the bounce wasn't in his favour—it too followed the momentum of William's fall, and landed at Rodney's feet. Now it was Rodney's turn to show agility as he scooped up the knife. Like a gladiator, he skipped to one side and held out the weapon.

'What the hell are you doing here, Tommy?' he growled while William lay on the floor, dazed and groaning.

'Never mind about that, Rodney. What the hell are *you* doing?' Tommy said, his stance like a heavyweight wrestler weighing up his opponent.

'If you leave now, Tommy, and forget about this, I'll take care of you. I'm running the firm now.'

Tommy laughed. 'You? Running the firm? *Ha*, you couldn't run a fuckin' bath, youth!'

Rodney jabbed the knife in the air and matched Tommy's bobbing and weaving. 'If you don't leave now, I'll fuck you up, old man.'

'Come on, then.' Tommy gestured with a hand for Rodney to step forward. 'Let's see what you're made of.'

While the two men jostled, I switched my attention to William. 'William,' I whispered. 'It's okay, untie me. This has nothing to do with you. You've done nothing wrong.' Being an accessory to murder and helping to cover it up were serious charges, but he didn't need to know that at that moment. 'You don't want this to go any further, William. I can help you.'

He sat up, rubbing the side of his head with one hand, and righting his skewed glasses with the other.

I wasn't sure if he was listening to my words, or if he even knew where he was. 'It's over, William. Time to do the right thing.'

Just then, Rodney lunged forward and drove the knife towards Tommy's chest. At the last possible moment, Tommy turned his torso, and the knife embedded deep into the top of his left arm. But before Rodney could pull out the blade and continue with the attack, Tommy swung back around to face him, and punched Rodney in the face with his right fist. There was a sound that reminded me of a breaking egg when Tommy's enormous fist smashed into Rodney's nose, sending him flying into the wall behind him.

As if in full control of the situation, Tommy turned to check on William, seemingly oblivious that the knife was still sticking out of his arm. 'You okay, Scott?' He asked after realising that William was no longer a threat.

'I am now, mate,' I said. 'I'm bloody glad to see you.'

Tommy noticed the knife in his arm, so he slowly pulled it out, glanced down at Rodney, who was out for the count, and then returned his attention to me. 'You've got yourself into a bit of a scrape, lad.' He leant down and cut through the gaffer tape that bound my legs to the chair, then went around the back of me and did the same with the tape around my wrists.

'Thank you,' I said, standing from the chair and loosening my wrists.

Blood was seeping through the hole in Tommy's sports jacket where the knife had been.

'We need to get you to hospital, mate.'

'Don't worry about that, just do what you've gotta do here. Make your phone calls. I'll keep an eye on these two.'

He was right; I needed to call Stewie right away. I figured that would get things moving quicker than making a cold call to the police. But before I did, my curiosity got the better of me. 'Tommy, how come you're here?'

He took off his jacket, then grabbed a large cotton ball from a bag on William's bench and dabbed at the wound on his arm.

'I wa' driving past earlier when I saw yo jump over the gate, and I realised sommat' must'a bin' goin' on.' He winced as he continued to dab his arm. 'So, when I got home, I parked the car in the garage and come back on foot. The house wa' dark and quiet, and I wa' about to ring the doorbell when a car approached. Ducking behind one of them big conifers, I watched as the car swung into the driveway and Rodney climbed out. He wa' in a hurry, almost running to the gate. Then I heard the doorbell ring, and a few moments later I saw William let him in.'

'So, you followed him?'

'I waited a few minutes, then come over the gate like yo did. The front door wa' open, so I crept inside.'

'I owe you my life, mate!'

'Think nowt on it. You'd best make them calls, eh?' He knelt down and assisted William to his feet.

Retrieving my phone from my pocket, I called Stewie's number.

63

We sat in the Jag waiting outside the gates of HM Lincoln Prison, me in the driver's seat, Carol in the passenger seat, and Tetley in the back.

'I can't believe this is happening, Scott,' Carol said. 'He's coming home. He's really coming home.'

I'd lost count of how many times Carol had said this during the journey from Nottingham to Lincoln, but I didn't mind. It was so good to see her happy again, and that also went for 'the excited little kid' in the back seat who had chatted nonstop for the entire journey.

'And it's all down to you, Scotty,' Carol continued. 'If it wasn't for you, my Colin would have been behind bars for the rest of his life.'

'We owe everything to Tommy Stokes.' This same conversation had also taken place umpteen times since Rodney and William were arrested, and all the charges against Col were dropped after William's confession to assisting to hide Janita's body in the wall after Rodney had killed her.

'I know, but if you hadn't come over from Australia, none of this would have happened,'

'Too right,' Tetley agreed. 'I always knew Scotty was a superhero. I mean, don't get me wrong, he's still a twat. But he's a super twat.'

Carol giggled as she shot a playful glance over her shoulder. 'Uh, how much longer do you think they'll be?' she said, returning her attention to the large arched gate.

'Any minute now, I'm sure,' I said, checking my watch. And bugger me, as soon as I said it, a doorway in the gate opened, and out stepped Stewie. He waved to us after spotting the Jag, then stepped to one side. Behind him was a smaller figure—a thin man, slightly stooped, carrying a paper bag with his belongings in it.

'Ah, there he is,' Carol cried, jumping out of the car and dashing across the road. When she reached her husband, she threw her arms around him and covered him in kisses. Tetley wasn't far behind. I held back a little, taking my time to lock the car and give them some time together as a family.

Stewie approached. 'Well done again, Scotty,' he said, shaking my hand. 'I thought he was a gonner.'

'That's understandable, Stewie. The evidence wasn't exactly in his favour.'

'But your determination exposed the truth.'

'Kind of.' I wasn't about to take the credit for this. Yes, I'd exposed the real killer, but it wasn't who I'd thought it was, and if Tommy hadn't have shown up that night, I'd probably be at the bottom of the River Trent now cut up into pieces, or however William and Rodney would have disposed of my body.

'I've learned an important lesson from this, Scott.'

'Yeah?'

'My oath. From now on, I'll be looking at each case from a different point of view.'

'Well, that's good. It pays to keep an open mind where possible.'

Stewie held out his hand, and I shook it. It was a firm handshake, the kind that reflected mutual admiration. 'I'll see you on the Gold Coast, mate,' Stewie said, smiling.

'Awesome. I'll send you a wedding invitation.'

'I'll be there.' He squeezed my hand one more time, then headed towards his car.

At first, I couldn't help feeling a little awkward as I approached the three family members who were still hugging, but when Carol saw me, she wiped a tear from her eye and stepped to one side.

When the smiling face of the little man that I loved so much greeted me, I was suddenly overcome with the need to cry. Tears streamed down my face. As we embraced, Col whispered two words in my ear: 'Thank you!'

The journey back to Nottingham seemed to take only half as long. I think that was because happiness fuelled the car. When we reached home, the first thing Col did was take a shower (luckily, Carol had put on the immersion heater before leaving that morning). The plan was to have a night at home, a barbecue and a few beers in the backyard. Being the Aussie, I was drafted as chef, but I didn't mind one bit.

When I was about to put the snags on the hotplate, my phone rang. It was Jenny. 'Hey gorgeous, hang on a minute.' Looking over my shoulder, I caught Col's eye. Without me having to ask, he read the situation and took over at the barby. Heading into the incident room that would soon be a dining room once more, I closed the door behind me.

'How's it goin?' Jenny asked.

'Good.'

'Have you arranged your flight home yet?'

'I have. I'll be home for the weekend.' I'd already filled her in on the outcome of the case—that was a few days ago. It was Tuesday evening now, so I'd be heading home on Thursday night. It was hard to believe I'd only been in the UK for two weeks.

'Listen … uhm,' Jenny said, lowering her voice as if there were a need to whisper. 'There's something I need to tell you.'

'What's up? Is there a problem with the house?'

'No, the house is fine. Well, it's a pain in the arse, but there's nothing there I can't handle.'

'What is it then?'

'Look, it's too big to tell you over the phone, so I'll wait until you get home.'

'Jennifer Daisy Radford, you better bloody tell me right now.' My voice rose in anticipation.

There was a pause on the other end of the phone, and I heard her take a deep breath before she said, 'I'm pregnant!'

How would you rate this book?

I hope you enjoyed reading *Good Riddance*. If so, I would be truly grateful if you would consider writing a review.

Reviews are a very important way of enabling me to reach a wider audience and bringing my stories to more readers just like you.

If you purchased your book from one of the online stores, you can login to your account and leave a review there.

Or if you have a Goodreads account you can post your review at:

Thanks in advance, I really appreciate your support!
Andrew

ACKNOWLEDGEMENTS

As a proud Queenslander, I'd like to begin by acknowledging the traditional custodians of this land which we inhabit, and pay my respects to the Elders past and present.

Thank you to my editor, Julie Guthrie, for your concise edits that force me to work a little harder, of which I am grateful. And a big thank you to the best beta readers ever, Carole Phillips, and Jane McDermott.

ABOUT THE AUTHOR

Andrew McDermott was born in Nottingham, England. A naturalised Aussie he has lived on the Gold Coast Australia since 1989 with his wife, Jane. He is a patron of the Gold Coast Writers Association, and currently resides at Kirra Beach.

Other books by this author...

Scotty Stephens Gold Coast Detective - Book 1

X

The eyes of the world are on Australia's Gold Coast, but for all the wrong reasons. Seven young women have been killed over a two-week period. The cause of death on each occasion was a slash to the throat in the shape of an X.

Detective Constable Scott Stephens is inexplicably plucked from obscurity, promoted to Detective Inspector, and placed in charge of the investigation.

Gold Coast Mayor, ex-AFL star, and billionaire property developer, Julian Monroe, has a lot to lose. Along with his involvement in various multi-million-dollar projects, his long-anticipated cruise ship terminal and casino resort is at a sensitive stage with potential investors.

Scott unearths withheld CCTV footage of the killer fleeing the scene of the last murder. The face of the offender is unmistakable - it's the mayor's son. The only problem is, he has an identical twin.

Scott not only needs to determine which twin is the killer - the brash, up-and-coming AFL star of the Gold Coast Suns, Dillon Monroe, or his brother, Troy - but he also faces a backlash from his employees when he suspects there's been a cover-up.

An explosive climax ensues, around the vibrant streets of the Gold Coast, when the killer's attention shifts, catapulting Scott's plight in a new direction - a fight for his life.

Purchase your copy from all good online book stores or at:
<u>www.andrewmcdermott.com.au</u>

Download the prequel, X'posé, for free at:
<u>www.andrewmcdermott.com.au</u>

MARY'S MANSION

After a costly divorce and twelve months in rehab, murder mystery author B.A. Fisher is under pressure to write his next bestseller.

He rents a property in the Gold Coast hinterland—Mary's Mansion—a loggers' cottage in Tallebudgera Valley. Steeped in history, the tiny cabin was built in the 1800s by one of the first settlers, Callum Murphy, where he lived with his wife, Mary.

The energy of the valley inspires Fisher and he quickly sets to work, completing a new book in record time. *The Valley of Kate* races to the top of the bestseller lists worldwide.

When appearing at the Byron Writers Festival, Fisher is confronted by James Fenton, the owner of the horse stud adjacent to Mary's Mansion. Fenton accuses the author of plagiarising the story from an unsolved murder that took place in the cottage five years previously—while naming Fenton as the killer.

With the prospect of being sued, Fisher seeks the help of Gold Coast Private Detective Scotty Stephens to clear his name. But Scotty has his doubts when Fisher reveals it was the ghost of Mary Murphy who helped him write the book.

Delving into the case, Scotty realises the author's plot is undeniably close to the actual unsolved murder. While changing the names only slightly, Fisher not only indicts Fenton but also denunciates the characters of the respectable Tallebudgera community.

Scotty moves into the cottage and sets to work, gaining the trust of the valley folk. While doing so, he unearths a mystery far greater than the throwaway plot in Fisher's book—one that spans over a century of Tallebudgera history.

Will the ghosts of the valley be with him or against him?

Purchase your copy from all good online book stores or at:
www.andrewmcdermott.com.au

Also by ANREW McDERMOTT

FLIRTING WITH THE MOON

High-profile LAPD detective, Joe Dean, loses his career, his family, and his sanity when the twelfth victim of the serial killer – The Moon – is taken from right under his nose.

Twenty-five years later and Joe is a reformed character operating as a private detective. While working on a case, he comes across a book called *Flirting with The Moon*. Each of the twelve entries is a precise description of The Moon murders, which could only have been written by the killer.

The publisher is tracked down to Sydney, Australia but the only details they have of the author is a pseudonym and a post box number in a Far North Queensland town called, Candle Stick Bay.

Obsessed with the possibility of finally bringing The Moon to justice, Joe flies out to Australia and travels to the remote tropical North to find a tiny picturesque town overlooking the Coral Sea.

While posing as an American tourist, he secretly digs for clues and unearths some surprising secrets about the town and its inhabitants. But as his investigation twists and turns, the murders begin once more, and Joe is forced to confront the demons of his past.

Purchase your copy from all good online book stores or at:
www.andrewmcdermott.com.au

Download the prequel, Hidden Moon, for free at:
www.andrewmcdermott.com.au

Also by ANDREW M^cDERMOTT

THE TIGER CHASE

Dr Elizabeth Smith brings a rare Chinese tiger to the La Zoo, but the tiger is stolen on its arrival. Detective John Dean of the LAPD hates two things in life, strong willed woman, and cats. His worst nightmare is realised when he is ordered to retrieve the tiger with Dr Smith and travel back 2000 miles across America in a station wagon, with the tiger in the back, and a gang of crooks in hot pursuit.

The Tiger Chase is an action-packed story that incorporates drama and humour with a wealth of information about one of the most precious, yet most endangered, species on earth the South China tiger.

———————————

An entertaining story about the fight for survival which is sure to raise awareness about the very real threat of extinction facing the mystical and majestic South China Tiger.

Nick Rhodes, Duran Duran

For the first time in history, this most ancient tiger – the South China Tiger, is brought to the consciousness of the western public through story telling. The Tiger Chase has captured the spirit of the Chinese tiger, ancestral to all other subspecies, as well as the culture associated with it. I hope that the awareness it raises would encourage the reader to join us in our fight to save this cultural symbol and protector of nature from the fate of extinction.

Li Quan, Save China's Tigers (Charity)
www.savechinastigers.org

Purchase your copy from all good online book stores or at:
www.andrewmcdermott.com.au

Sign up at the link below to join Andrew's mailing list and receive your free ebooks, his bi-annual newsletter, be the first to know about up and coming titles, and have direct contact with the author.

"I would love for you to be part of my writing community. Your opinion is dear to me and I hope you will enjoy the books in my catalogue and all future releases."

Andrew

X'posé (X prequel)
Hidden Moon (Flirting with The Moon prequel)
Download your free ebooks here:
www.andrewmcdermott.com.au

You can also follow Andrew at:
Facebook: https://www.facebook.com/andrewmcdermottauthor/
Instagram: https://www.instagram.com/andrewmcdermottauthor/
X (Twitter): https://x.com/andymcdauthor